THE KUIPER ROGUE
C. P. SCHAEFER

THE
KUIPER
ROGUE

C.P. SCHAEFER

This is a work of fiction. Names, characters, places and incidents are imagined and fictitious. Any resemblance to persons living or dead is entirely coincidental.

Copyright © 2023 by Charles Schaefer
All rights reserved.

Library of Congress Catalog number: TXu 2-393-209

ISBN 979-8-9890608-0-1
eBook ISBN 979-8-9890608-1-8

Printed in the United States of America

Edited by Claire Ashgrove
Cover Design by Jeff Brown
Interior design by Sabrina Milazzo, www.sabrinamilazzo.net

First Paperback Edition

For Jenn

For more information and to stay up-to-date with tour dates, new releases, and book signings, please visit www.cpschaefer.com and sign up for the mailing list.

PROLOGUE

The World Space Council had great expectations for outward colonization in the late twenty-first century. Living biodomes on the moon and Mars set the standard for sustainable habitats that produced food and breathable air. These prototypes had proven a system ready for the challenges of the outer solar system.

Saturn's moon Titan proved equal to that challenge. At twice the size of Earth's moon, Titan had a substantial atmosphere, a rocky surface with mountain ranges of solid ice, and oceans of liquid methane at temperatures near absolute zero.

The Titan base was a statement project with advanced systems and high-tech add-ons that stretched the imagination. Even the designers were impressed when they realized what they'd created.

This crowning achievement among the gas giants was hailed as a milestone in space exploration. But no one anticipated an ominous threat lurking in the icy cold regions beyond the planets, or the ancient prophecy of its destructive effects on our solar system.

PART I

Chapter 1
GAIA 3 – Titan Moon base

"All right, Sys," Will Vandolah said. "What exactly am I looking at here? A pinwheel in outer space?"

"Processing," Sys replied. "No similar configuration in file catalogues."

"Curved blue streaks but emanating from what?" he mumbled.

"Was that a question, sir?" Sys asked. "You seem frustrated."

"No, it wasn't," he replied. "*I was just processing.*"

A long silence.

"It's four AM." Will rubbed his eyes and refocused on the artificial sky, but the throbbing stridulation of chirping insects was too distracting. "Fuck!"

No response from the System Operator.

"Okay, Sys, this makes no sense." He sighed. "My brain is fried, and I'm sorry I raised my voice. Save down and let's regroup tomorrow evening."

***

It was sunset in the Living Hemisphere with a faint orange glow on the horizon and a few stars twinkling into view. Will sat in a foldout chair on the desert plateau and ran his fingers through his sandy brown hair. He didn't care much for fashion, sporting a modest wardrobe and utility boots.

He considered the chance circumstances that got him here on Titan. His life and career were on a launch pad to the stars, as he had always dreamed. He was assigned to the new Gaia 3 station; with its high-tech planetarium and orbiting telescope, he could do research like no other astronomer in history. And it was his mother, of all people, who got him assigned.

Margaret had spent most of her adult life in space, leaving young Will behind with relatives. At first, Will watched each of her launches with pride and awe, but as he grew up without her, that pride turned into resentment and troubled him still.

But other, more complicated, events from his past lay waiting to play out on a stage he had not yet imagined.

The humming of pumps sent wave after wave of water on a slow run through streams and ponds. Then it dawned on him that light sparkling off the water was moonlight, not sunlight. He quickly reached for a remote audio device and laser pointer.

"Okay, Sys, the daytime simulation has run its course. It's time to overlay this western sky with some local stars," he said. "Please end standard star simulation and playback local sequence of the northern celestial hemisphere saved since the previous session."

"Processing…." Sys said.

Will set the Shoemaker Observatory that orbited Titan on a wide-angle search of the visible spectrum for routine sky-watching.

His interests were short-range searches in the visible spectrum. He wrote a filtering routine to screen out superfluous information and for playback in a twelve-hour cycle.

Despite the technology, the way to track new incoming objects was to sit and watch—the same system used for centuries. The more familiar one was with a given area of the sky, the fewer distractions from the known starfield. Whether a detective on a case, a doctor studying an x-ray, or a traveler reading a road map, the mind filtered out the non-essentials until it found what it wanted.

"Complete," Sys said.

The sky suddenly came to life with pre-sequenced subroutines flashing one after another, numerical coordinate systems, graphical latitude, longitude line work, reverse image infrared, and finally, the view of the northern celestial hemisphere over Titan. The only unnatural piece was a data display box on the horizon with the time of day—time lapsed for the current display—tracked objects, and standard enhancement options.

"Titan skies are totally different, but I'll find it," Will muttered, his blue eyes studying the stars. "Oh, there it is."

He aimed his laser pointer at the North Star and picked the *Enhanced Playback* option from the display box. A smaller box then appeared with more options: Playback Speed, Reverse Imaging, Numerical Coordinates, and Graphical Coordinates.

"Forty-eight to one, all previous and fifteen degrees longitude, fifteen degrees latitude," he said.

The illustrated longitude and latitude lines appeared, and the sky moved at a highly accelerated rate. Forty-eight times faster than usual—at that speed, the milky way crossed the night sky in fifteen minutes.

Will's gaze was upward, searching for out-of-plane objects, long-period comets approaching from random angles. Objects not listed in the Guide Star Catalog or part of a modified database were automatically targeted by the System Operator and highlighted.

The motion stopped, and the northeast quadrant grid was flashing. One box in that area was highlighted, from longitude forty-five to sixty degrees and latitude sixty to seventy-five degrees.

"Identify," he said, with a face of recognition.

"Processing... Item number 2092211. Diameter 0.2-kilometer, Mass 3.14 E 10 KG, Inclination to the ecliptic 67 degrees."

"Stop," he interrupted. "We cataloged this one last week. Save for future reference and continue with sequence."

"Processing... Complete."

The playback continued at high speed. The motion stopped again; this time, the northwest quadrant was flashing, about thirty degrees above the horizon, but the giant desert rock obstructed its view.

"Damn that rock," he whispered. He aimed the laser pointer at the display box and picked the zoom option. "Sys, raise the image twenty degrees latitude and magnify two hundred percent."

The block was empty, but this was not surprising; the system often picked up local ice and dust particles from the rings.

"Back up sixty seconds and replay," Will said, never leaving a stone unturned.

The zoomed box went black before stars appeared again in motion. Then suddenly, a small streak appeared.

"There it is again," he said. "Let's start over with fresh eyes. Sys, please confirm this is the object we studied last night."

"Processing... Correct, coordinates seem to agree, accounting for movement since last observation."

He released a sigh of relief; he had not dreamed it. Although he had cataloged hundreds to date, none were officially recognized as new comets. Since he was the only one this far out with an observatory, no one could confirm the data.

"Again, back up sixty seconds but magnify ten to the third," he said.

The zoomed box went black, and the stars appeared again in motion. The slight streak appeared again, a bluish-green color covering a width equal to fifteen degrees of the screen. Another peculiar quality of the flash was that it did not appear in a straight line; it appeared curved.

"Sys, let's begin the standard tracking routine with orbital elements and spectral analysis," he said, staring at the eyebrow-shaped streak. "Save this event sequence to file 2092312 and continue with playback."

"Processing… Complete," Sys said as the sky went black while the System Operator prepared the next display sequence.

***

The dome is a computer-enhanced planetarium that simulates both daytime and nighttime skies and promotes photosynthesis. Images in screen-saver fashion replicate the movement of clouds, the sun, the moon, and stars.

THE KUIPER ROGUE

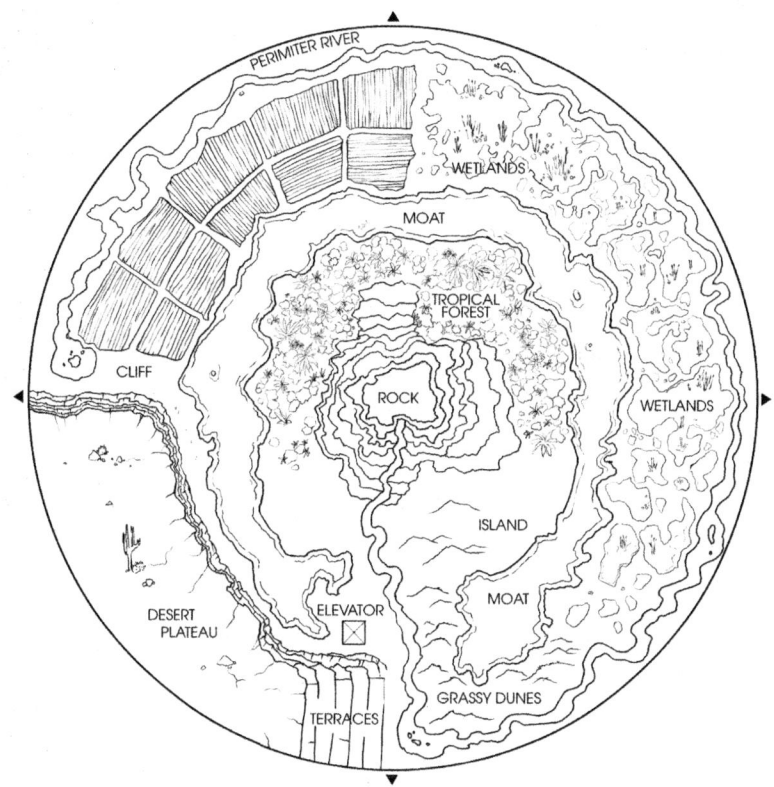

THE LIVING HEMISPHERE

Gaia 3 was a hollowed-out globe separated at its equator by an upper Living Hemisphere and the lower Dead Hemisphere. The Living Hemisphere was stadium-sized and had acres of natural earth biomes under an interactive Earth-type sky. The Cerametallic domed surface was supported on curved, steel truss framing. Forests, wetlands, deserts, and agriculture combined with rock formations and streams to make a living habitat. Countless insects, animals, and fish inhabited the living world, sharing recycled food, air, and water.

***

A fluttering sound near the edge of the rocky cliff caught Will's attention as a night owl dropped onto an unsuspecting rodent.

"Nice catch," he said quietly. The owl lifted into the air toward a cave with the rodent in its talons. He relaxed and took in the sounds of nature.

"Well, guys, it's just you, me, and another starry night," he said.

A hundred thousand insects pulsated their calls through cooling air. Crickets and tree frogs blasted in rhythm as waves gently washed onto the beach while Saturn's image sat low on the horizon just above the desert rock.

An evening of sky-watching on top of a long workday was exhausting. Time passed, his eyelids drooped, his head nodded, and he soon fell asleep under a warm blanket.

***

"The stone is missing from the king's eye!" the lead man shouted. "You stole it. Where is it?"

Will stood motionless; he'd been here before. Was he dreaming? The lead man hit him across the face, knocking him to his knees. A big man pulled him back to his feet. He was terrified. Were they going to shoot him? Why was this happening?

"I don't know where it is," Will growled back. "The stone fell off in the cave. We went back to look for it but couldn't find it."

The crowd of men exchanged curious stares, then turned back to Will.

"The guardian's eye must be found," one man said.

"Well, it's down in the cave," Will said matter-of-factly. "All you have to do is go look for it."

"We have," the lead man said, raising a gun to Will's brow. "Your ex-friend Murphy told us the same story. We've extracted all the sand in the cave and found nothing!"

Will pushed the gun aside. "Then someone else must have gone down there and found it. Was the cave guarded every minute of every day since the discovery?"

No response, just straight faces.

"That's what I thought," Will said. "Then why is it so important that you threaten a man's life for it?"

The lead man moved face to face with Will. "Because, my wise little friend, it represents the end of things as well as the beginning of things. It is prophecy."

***

Singing crickets gave way to chirping birds, and soon it was morning. Will awoke in his chair with a spiny lizard perched on his chest.

"Jesus!" He jumped, brushed it away, and watched it scurry through the sand to the foot of a cactus.

"What a dream," he whispered, brushing his fingers through his hair with an eye on the lizard. "And it's nearly sunrise. I wonder if *you* saw anything interesting last night?"

Will grumbled and cursed himself as he packed his gear. "I hope Markham covers for me."

He hurried off, slipped, and nearly kicked a rock over the edge of the beachhead.

"Sys! Save star simulation twenty-two hundred to zero-five hundred hours," he shouted, stumbling through the sand. "Do it now, before sunrise, or we'll lose it."

"Processing… Complete," Sys replied.

C.P. SCHAEFER

He ran over to the pressurized elevator shaft, pressed *Clear/Seal*, on the display panel, then entered. "Level sixteen, please," Will said and stepped into the elevator. It proceeded down.

Chapter 2
ANOTHER STARRY NIGHT

Margaret Vandolah stood barefoot and knee-deep in the moat. She dipped a meter stick in the blue-green water; the gauge registered six point three.

"Near neutral but low," she murmured. "Water is slightly acidic, but everything else is fine." Her people were probably aware of the situation already and making appropriate adjustments to the buffering equipment, but she wrote it down anyway.

Margaret was a striking woman. Eyes in the crowd turned when she entered a room, a compliment since she didn't dress the part. She was forty-eight years old, wore no make-up, and had nothing but science and biology on her mind.

The World Space Council really wanted her for administrator of the new Titan base. During planning and developmental stages, she'd overseen everything from personnel and work schedules to flight control and life support.

Decades of hard work and commitment had finally panned out when she took command of Gaia 3. Having served lesser roles on Gaia 1 (the moon) and Gaia 2 (Mars), she was now prepared to fulfill her lifelong dream of heading up a high-tech base in the outer reaches of the solar system.

She looked around for any sign of Libby Owens, the field biologist responsible for daily maintenance and monitoring the life cycles. The dense forest and mountain in front of her made it impossible to see much past the dunes.

"Kirby! Miller! Have either of you seen Libby?" Margaret shouted. She couldn't tell them apart with the sun glaring down in the background. They hung from ropes alongside the forty-meter-tall artificial rock structure, carefully inspecting caves for snake habitation.

"Not up here!" Miller shouted.

A controlled kill was underway to contain the number of snakes in the ecosphere. Rodent populations were nearly extinct in the desert, and now small reptiles in the jungle were disappearing.

The low-gravity environment enhanced the physical abilities of all species in the ecosphere. The snake's ability to move and strike was astonishing, almost leaping onto its prey.

"Over here!" a voice shouted from the other direction.

Margaret turned quickly, water splashing at her feet. At first, she didn't see anything, but a purple outfit stood out from the green flora.

A short, dark-haired woman in her late twenties was on her hands and knees, busily tilling a patch of soil. Libby was an attractive young woman but didn't dress the part, she kept things simple and to the point. Whether planting, harvesting, or pulling samples for research, the work continued. But sadly, she was tired of this short-handed startup phase and couldn't wait for the second phase crew to arrive.

Margaret loved her passion for all living things. She was a nurturer and protecter of anything that could not defend itself.

Libby came to Titan to make a name for herself in Ecotechnics. When the call had come from Margaret, she'd jumped at the opportunity. It was also good timing for her to get away from the chaos on Earth. Actually, to get away from a bad relationship that was dragging her down.

"Hey, Margaret!" Jim Miller shouted. "Libby's over there in the garden."

"Thanks, couldn't have found her without you." She grinned.

She hiked the shore of the moat with her pH gauge and waded through the perimeter river near the farm area.

"How's it going over here?" she asked.

"All good," Libby replied. "We processed the last harvest yesterday. I thought we'd try planting wheat here this time."

"Wouldn't that upset the nitrogen balance?"

"No, this should work nicely," Libby replied, then stood and walked over to the rice paddies. "I'd like to get Will out here today," she said, washing mud off her hands. "To help with planting. Have you seen him?"

"No, I haven't," Margaret replied. "He didn't come down for breakfast, but I'll have him report to you later this morning.

I checked the pH of the waters. The moat is in the low sixes; are you aware of that?"

"I haven't checked for a couple of days, but that wouldn't surprise me," Libby replied.

"Why not?" Margaret asked. "It could be a problem."

"The waters always get out of balance after harvest." Libby followed. "An unusual number of organics float around, but the system adjusts itself to accommodate. It should correct itself within a few days."

"I'll go along with that," Margaret nodded. "I'm finished with my morning chores. Could you use some help?"

"Sure, that would be nice," Libby replied with a crooked smile. "Besides, it might make him feel guilty to see his mother turning soil. Maybe I could get him to help round up rodents later today."

"You don't need to do that; I can use the exercise," Margaret said. "Hiking over here made me think I need to work these muscles."

The two worked for a few minutes without saying a word. The smell of rich organic soil was refreshing for a person living more than a billion kilometers from Earth, especially since Margaret hadn't been up top in the Living for a few days.

"You know, Margaret," Libby said, "it's not the pH situation that bothers me. It's the oxygen level that I can't figure out."

"Oxygen level?" Margaret wiped her brow with a forearm. "We don't have an oxygen problem."

"Not a problem really, just a situation," she said. "For the past few weeks, the natural recycling process has yielded only about seventeen percent oxygen into the air. We've been mixing stored oxygen into the supply air system to bring it up to twenty percent."

"Why wasn't I made aware of this?" Margaret asked.

"Balance problems are ongoing," Libby replied. "Markham did a status check of the mechanical and structural systems and found no leaks. I assumed the problem was caused by the recent harvests. There is just less biomass to keep up with the oxygen demands from animal life. When the problem was pinpointed, we were going to make you aware."

"Have you discussed this with Avery?" Margaret asked. "He needs to be made aware of anything that's out of balance in the biosphere."

John Avery was the head of biophysics. All problems with the microcity of the ecosystem, from animal diseases to water problems, usually ended up on his desk.

Libby should have kept this to herself until the proper time. She felt Margaret was questioning her abilities. The next logical step in the solution process was to get Avery involved, but she preferred to avoid dealing with Avery.

"I want to do a few more status checks first," Libby replied. "I'm hoping we don't have to get John involved."

"Why don't you see what happens today," Margaret said. "If you can't come up with anything, then get with Avery in the morning. I want to see an answer by the end of the week."

Margaret tried not to appear concerned. "I think I'll go find my son. He should help you plant. You have more important things to do."

"Okay, thanks."

As she walked away, Libby's head dropped. *Why did you bring that up?*

Margaret made her way through the muddy field and up on the mountainside where Kirby and Miller still hung from ropes, scratching, squealing, and wreaking havoc with the primates.

"Keeping busy, guys?" she mused.

Kirby turned to her as if nothing unusual was going on. "Hey, Margaret! Did you find Libby?"

"Yes, I did. Thank you." She sighed.

"Good, just checking. If there's anything else we can do, let us know."

***

Margaret walked down the beach toward a pressurized elevator shaft. She pressed *Clear/Seal* on the display panel, and the airlock whisked open. The scent in the air went from organic to dusty mechanical.

"Pressurizing, please wait," Sys said.

The mood changed on the elevator ride down to the Dead Hemisphere. The sounds of nature gave way to a constant rumble of generators and air handlers. The Earthly environment changed to sheet metal so quickly it became claustrophobic.

The Dead Hemisphere was the lower half of the one-hundred-and-fifty-meter diameter sphere. It was a structural steel space frame intertwined with mechanical ducts and miles of process piping. The view from any of its sixteen levels of catwalks was a maze of structural steel, glass partitions, piping, and open-grate metal stairs.

Margaret's thoughts drifted to Will. *Where is he? I need him up there helping Libby. At least he's here with me, and that's something. I'm so grateful they let him go on the mission.*

Based on Margaret's passionate request, the board had granted Will an internship on Gaia 3. They assumed she and Will were inseparable, but in reality, they hardly knew each other.

"Pressurization complete," Sys said. "You may proceed."

Margaret gasped. "Oh, Sys, you scared me to death. Living quarters, please."

She stepped into the elevator and watched the towering rock structure disappear behind closing metal doors. The elevator started downward.

System Operator's AI protocol coordinated system-wide functions, interfacing with the Living and Dead Hemispheres. Sys utilized a vast memory/storage capacity to accommodate systems command and ongoing scientific research programs.

"Level sixteen," Sys said. The elevator slowed to a stop. She stepped out and walked toward command, where Will was supposed to be working with Richard Markham.

Heavy metallic footsteps rang through the corridor as she approached command. Margaret had a distinctive walk, and Markham knew she'd be looking for Will. Markham was on level fourteen, his ears burning in anticipation of her approach.

"Margaret!" a voice came from below. She turned but didn't see anyone.

"Down here!"

She spotted an outstretched arm waving a couple of levels below. Richard Markham was middle-aged, slightly overweight, and wore glasses. He sported his standard purple one-piece outfit with pride as part of his no-nonsense demeanor. As Operations Engineer for the facility, he specialized in mechanical, electrical systems, and knew the base inside and out.

"Have you seen Will this morning?" she asked.

"About two hours ago," Markham replied. "I had him working on an air circulation problem, but he kept nodding off, so I sent him up to get some rest."

"Libby just mentioned the air problem. Have you found anything?" she asked, leaning on a steel guardrail.

"Not yet. We haven't noticed anything unusual," Markham said. "Will started Sys on a diagnostics routine. I'm not too concerned, but I'll let you know if something comes up."

"All right, keep me posted. I want to see the results as soon as they're available." She started toward the living quarters.

She passed the cryonics lab and turned down the corridor to the living quarters. She reached Will's room and found his door ajar, so she quietly stepped inside. It was dark except for a kitchen counter light. He was asleep on the couch, fully dressed, with an open book lying on his chest. His mouth hung open as he breathed heavily in a deep, exhausted sleep.

"Wake up, wake up," Margaret said, shaking him.

"Mom, what are you doing here?" he asked, rubbing his eyes. "What time is it?"

"After ten," she said. "Up all night with the stars again?"

"Yes, and no." Will sat up. "I was there but slept through most of it."

"I know how important your cometary research is," she said. "You're doing a fine job bringing the new telescope online, but it's not your only priority."

The Shoemaker Observatory had to be monitored constantly. It needed to interface with the Gaia 3 AI unit, and Will was the intermediary for those procedures.

"You're right," he said and set aside the telescope's tech manual. "The more I read this stuff, the less I know about it."

"Sometimes, you need to put things down for a while to get them out of your head," she said. "Pick it up later, and it becomes crystal clear."

"Sounds more like a warning than good advice."

"Markham has work for you. And Libby needs your help, too."

"Yes, I'll get right up there," he said. "Sys should be finished with oxygen/mechanical diagnostics soon. Would you like to see the results?"

"No thanks, you go ahead," she said. "By the way, we have a few people playing poker tonight, any interest?"

"Normally, I'd say yes," he said. "But I found something interesting last night with the sky simulation, and Sys should have finished the tracking routine by now."

"A new object?" Margaret asked.

"I don't know what it is. Come up and take a look after poker if you like. I mentioned it to Markham, and he's coming up to check it out."

"I'll see if I can make it."

Chapter 3
2092312

"Sys, please playback event sequence 2092312 saved from the last session," Will said, seated on his couch and biting on a sandwich. "Show me the odd-shaped object from the event."

He would be devastated if it were noticed on other objects in the sky simultaneously. It could be a filtering problem or poor alignment of the telescope. But this was so unusual—an object with a curved streak.

"Processing… Complete," Sys said.

The three-dimensional image of the northern celestial hemisphere appeared in a flash with graphical line work and reverse image infrared. One sector in the northwest quadrant flashed.

"Remove all filtering routines, back up sixty seconds, and magnify ten to the third," he said.

"Processing… Complete."

The screen went black for a second, then the stars reappeared in motion. The eyebrow-shaped streak appeared again but was more distinct. There was a definite shape to it, in two directions. Will stared curiously at the object, but he could not waste time on it; he needed to see if other objects were suffering from the same distortion.

"Sys, let's hold at this time frame but look at a few planets, deep sky objects, and constellations with the same magnitude," he said.

"Please specify."

"Let's see," he said. "Earth, Jupiter, any of the Messier Galaxies, Sagittarius, and Polaris."

"Processing... Complete."

The computer randomly picked items and rotated the sky to center them on the view screen. Will saw no other object was affected. The curved shape could have meant that the camera was somehow nudged, but there were no other distortions. So it was the movement of the one object, not the instruments—this thing was spinning! The curved streaks had to be outgassing, shooting away from a comet!

He just saw today's results. Was the object still outgassing? He packed a few things and headed for the Living Hemisphere.

***

Elevator pumps whisked. Will walked out and planted his feet on the beach's white sand. He hiked up the desert terraces toward his usual perch. He took in the concrete mountain as he walked; it was lifeless, as lifeless as the world outside the biosphere. *What a place to call home. Step outside, and you crystallize instantly. Lie on top of that rock, and fry like an egg.*

"Did somebody turn up the sound system?" a voice came from below. Markham crossed the beach and walked toward the desert plateau. He stopped and poised himself to jump the first step in the darkness.

"Bugs get pretty noisy up here, especially at night," Will said as he watched the middle-aged Markham negotiate the terraces. "Even an old guy can jump those steps on this moon."

"I guess so." Markham made it to the top, wiping his hands. "It's hard to believe how real this all looks, and you've picked the best seat in the house."

"Wait 'till the bats come out and screech owls, too," Will said, grinning as he sipped a glass of tea. Markham didn't like things that swooped down out of nowhere. He eyed cactus tops and the rocky cliffs for anything perched and poised for flight.

"They had trouble getting used to the low gravity," Will continued. "Especially landing and catching prey. They really get disoriented at night so stay low."

"Why don't we get this new object of yours on the view screen," Markham grumbled.

"Working on it," Will replied. "Hey, how was poker night?"

"I lost. Avery won, like usual," Markham said. "So what exactly are we going to see?"

"I don't know," Will replied. "I've never seen anything like it."

"What do you mean?"

"I mean, this is unusual," he said. "It shows up as curved streaks, like eyebrows."

"Curved streaks?"

"That's right."

"Has Sys completed the tracking routine?" Markham asked.

"That's what we're going to find out," Will replied. "It doesn't appear to be a mechanical malfunction; no other objects show the same distortion."

The elevator air pumps whisked open below and cast light into the dark ecosphere. Margaret stepped out onto the sandy beach, determined to show an interest in her son's hobby.

"Hello! Will! Richard! Are you up here?" she shouted.

"Over here!" Will shouted and used his flashlight to lead her up the terraces. The unexpected visit lifted Will's spirits.

"Am I too late to see your new find?" she asked, reaching the campsite.

"Not at all," Will replied. "You're just in time. But it's not much of a find; it's just a curiosity. You might be disappointed."

"You have a flashlight?" Markham interrupted.

Will smirked.

"You really do spend a lot of time up here at night," she said, noticing the blankets and other gear sprinkled about the area.

"It can get a bit nippy," he said. "I'd like to build a campfire, but Libby would kill me."

"And I'd help her," Margaret joked.

"I don't have extra chairs." Will smiled. "But the blankets might come in handy."

"That's all right," Markham gestured. "You two go ahead."

"Okay, Richard, you stand, and we'll sit." Will spread the blanket over the sand. "Bats always go for the highest target."

"Let me help you with that." Markham sighed and grabbed one end of the blanket.

"So, this is your observatory," she said, sitting back on the blanket.

Her blue eyes took in the detail of the artificial heavens. "And what exactly will we be observing?"

"Exactly, would be object number 2092312," Will replied. "But just what it is, we're trying to figure out."

He sifted through his book bag and pulled out a remote audio device and laser pointer. "Sys, please playback event sequence 2092312 saved from the last session," he said.

"Processing…"

He turned to Margaret. "First, we'll review the results from last night. "Then we can get Sys' tracking results."

"Complete," Sys said.

The sky went black for a second, then started rearranging itself with a flashing sequence of subroutines.

"You've been busy with this," she said. "What all is it doing?"

"These are standard overlays and mapping sent down from Shoemaker," he replied. "It's sorting through the database, searching for the requested options."

The sky came to a final display showing the northern celestial hemisphere over Titan.

"So, is this what the sky would look like above us if we could see through the clouds?" Margaret asked.

"Well, not exactly," he replied. "The sky is centered above Titan, but the horizon I have chosen is the ecliptic plane. I thought it would be easier to look at the half of the universe directly above the plane of the planets. It's easier to keep track of that way."

"Makes sense," she said.

Will aimed the laser pointer at the data display box and picked *Enhanced Playback, Playback Speed, Reverse Imaging,* and *'Graphical Coordinates.*

"Forty-eight to one, all previous and fifteen degrees longitude, fifteen degrees latitude," he stated. "Sys, let's use constellation lines and names. Also target and name Polaris."

The mapping lines adjusted, fixed objects and Saturn turned bright pink, and the sky moved in a time-lapsed fashion. The zodiacal constellations moved around the horizon like horses on a carousel while Polaris remained fixed.

32

"Sometimes I have the constellations and Polaris marked; it's less confusing that way," he said.

"Don't do it for our benefit," Markham said. "Unless you're giving a pop quiz in the morning."

"That's okay. It removes some confusion," Margaret said. "So, this routine makes things easier?"

"That's right," Will said. "But I don't follow this fast-paced stuff any better than you. I try to spot unusual motion."

"This whole thing is unusual motion," Markham blurted.

Suddenly, the sky stopped moving with the northwest quadrant flashing, the same as the night before near the concrete mountain. Margaret and Markham leaned forward in anticipation as Will aimed the laser pointer at the display box and picked the zoom option.

"There we are," he said, then spoke into the audio device. "Sys, raise the image twenty degrees latitude, back up sixty seconds, and magnify ten to the third."

The zoomed image disappeared, stars moved again, then motion stopped, and a bluish-green streak appeared.

"See the curvature," Will explained. "Most moving objects show as straight lines, but this one has curved lines, and the color is unusual, too."

"It looks like an interstellar dust cloud, a nebula, or something," Margaret said. "What's Sys found out about it?"

"Strange, isn't it? Let's see what it is," he replied. "Sys display results of tracking routine on object 2092312."

"Processing... Complete. Information from the tracking procedure is as follows:" Sys said. The sky went black, then displayed a spectrum chart of emitted gasses.

"Look here." Will aimed his laser pointer. "The prominent spectral features are methane, carbon monoxide, and nitrogen. Exotic ices that aren't found very often in nature."

"Sys," he continued. "Please explain the orbital elements analysis problem."

"Insufficient information available from event one for a complete determination of orbital elements," Sys said.

"Understood." He sighed.

"Will," Markham said. "Sys just said there was insufficient information from event number one. Is there an event number two?"

Will's eyes flashed; that had not occurred to him. "Sys, playback all event sequences associated with object 2092312."

The screen went black, then the magnified quadrant began moving. This time a curved streak appeared in the opposite direction. The screen went black again, and another streak appeared. The sequence continued for two more events, both with arched-shaped linework. The display flashed again and again.

"This has to be outgassing," Will speculated. An excitement perked up inside him. "These must be surface explosions; it's the only possible explanation."

"Surface explosions?" Margaret inquired.

"Yes, that's why they're curved," he replied with a twisting hand motion. "But this would have to be something big."

"I don't understand," Markham said as the screen finally came to a stop.

"Let's start from the beginning," Will said. "Sys, playback 2092312 event number one at the same magnitude but reduce speed to 1/50."

"Processing…"

"This should show us if my hunch is correct," he said.

Markham scratched his head. Margaret did not say anything but scooted up on the blanket.

"Complete," Sys said.

A light burst appeared near the screen's center and formed a green cloud. Seconds later, the ghostly green image fanned out as if influenced by wind. As it dissipated, the jetting motion turned the object sideways.

"Look, the main explosion is moving off-center," Will said, aiming the laser pointer at the main plume. "If this is what I think it is, then we're the first to see this phenomenon."

Scientists had long speculated that cometary bodies outgassed exotic ices in the outer solar system, but until now, it had been pure speculation.

"Sys, please overlay all 2092312 events into the same block with equivalent playback parameters," Will said.

"Processing…"

"I think we're seeing gasses exploding on the surface of an incoming object and jetting out into space," he said. "They have a rocket-like effect on the object, making it dart and spin. Kind of like a pitcher throwing a curve ball."

Margaret glanced at Markham and back at Will.

"Comets are basically big ice balls, but not just water ice. The tails we see in pictures are water ice blowing away closer to the sun," he said. "But this is too far out to be heated by the sun."

"Has Sys located the object at times other than these events?" Markham asked.

"I doubt it; we can check," Will replied. "But it's probably been too far out to be affected."

"Even so," Markham added, "these events can be plotted on a curve. Sys should be able to project velocity and orbital motion."

"And diameter," Will added. "The object should rotate away from the force of the explosion. The explosion should always oppose the direction of travel. If we find the center of the explosions, we can measure the distance it moves as the nucleus rolls to its horizon. In other words, it should go from full to crescent shape, similarly to our moon."

"That might work," Markham said. "Then you could check it against the known orbital elements for comparison."

"Right, then Sys should be able to tell whether the orbit is elliptical or parabolic," Will said. "And back out the mass and diameter from that calculation."

"You two have lost me. Now you are convinced this is a comet?" Margaret asked and borrowed a sip of tea from Will's glass. "But a few minutes ago, you said it didn't make sense because it would have to be very big."

"Well, if it's a small-diameter object, then we wouldn't see it rotate this far out," Will answered. "There would not be explosions. Also, the type of gasses. One pass by the sun at a million degrees would vaporize most exotic ices unless they're buried deep inside the nucleus. To see five or six such events in less than twelve hours means there is a lot of ancient ice on that thing."

"So, when you combine the fact that it has ancient ices and it's rotating as they're outgassed, you can conclude it's probably something massive that has not been to the inner solar system for a long time."

"Complete," Sys said.

Once again, the objects appeared one at a time, each overlaying the previous. The images were exposed for the same duration and formed a puzzling flower shape with petals arching in all directions.

"Yeah, that tells us a lot." Markham snorted.

"Just for grins and giggles," Margaret said. "Can you have the picture ordered sequentially."

"We can," Will replied.

"Sys, please order all 2092312 events with equivalent playback parameters and show them in separate blocks," he said.

"Processing… Complete."

The pictures appeared side by side with blast points and ejecta plumes radiating in all directions.

"From this collage," he said, "there's enough information for an estimate of the orbital elements. Sys, please display orbital elements for 2092312 based on a combination of all events."

"Information for tracking procedure incomplete," Sys replied.

"That doesn't make sense," Will said. "There has to be some information available. Please display any available tracking information for 2092312 based on a combination of all events."

"Processing…"

"Isn't that what you just asked for?" Margaret asked.

"Not exactly. Orbital elements are a complete set of parameters that define the shape of an orbit. Now I'm asking for bits and pieces."

"Complete," Sys said.

Charts of data streamed across the sky, listing times, radial distances, and their corresponding velocities.

"This looks like good information; at least it's not garbage," Will said. "Let's see if Sys can fit a curve if we fudge in some numbers."

"Sys," he continued. "By using the confirmed data for the object, assume a parabolic orbit, a diameter of twenty kilometers, and water-ice density."

"Processing…"

"I hope we can figure out what this thing is doing with a few iterations of guesswork," Will said.

"A *few* iterations?" Margaret remarked.

"This could take a while," he confessed.

"Complete. Plotted coordinates cannot fit standard parabolic orbital path," Sys said.

"Understood," Will said. "Sys, using the same confirmed information, estimate the object's path without regard for standard parameters."

"Processing… Complete," Sys said.

An extraordinarily elongated and elliptical orbit then appeared. The long axis ran through the ecliptic plane of the planets but tilted at nearly thirty degrees.

"Sys, display all orbital elements for the above-referenced elliptical path."

"Processing… Complete," Sys said.

The orbital elements results displayed in the night sky included: inclination, major and minor axes, perihelion near the sun, and an orbital period of 1,682.12 years.

"Sixteen-eighty-two," Will curiously murmured.

"If this orbit is right, then Earth should get a good look at it," Markham said.

"Too good," Margaret interrupted. "Will, how close is that to the planet?"

"Sys, please locate Earth as the object crosses the ecliptic plane," he asked.

"Processing… Complete," Sys said.

The screen showed the two missing by nearly half a million miles as the comet crossed the ecliptic.

"If this information is correct," Will said, "then it's well outside the Roche Limit, so it should pass without incident."

"Roche Limit?" Margaret asked.

"If an object gets too close to a larger body," he continued, "it can break apart and get pulled into the planet. It happens a lot with comets getting too close to the sun or Jupiter. And this object reaches perihelion just behind the sun."

"Okay, what's the time frame?" she asked.

"That information should be in there," he replied. "Sys, based on these orbital elements, please estimate time to Earth passage and velocity at that point."

"Processing... Complete," Sys said. "Object, 2092312, Orbital elements results: date – 06/09/96, time - 15:32:12 hours, velocity – 13,443.15m/s"

"Looks like they have plenty of time to get ready for good fireworks."

Markham nodded.

"Well, whatever the case," Margaret said, with a proud motherly smile, "your curiosity has turned into a discovery."

"So, it would seem," Will agreed, focused on the table of numbers in the sky. "Sys, have you estimated the mass of the object?"

"Affirmative—5.2367E20kg," Sys said.

"E-twenty!" he gasped. "Okay, there's the problem."

"What's the problem?" she asked.

"All this analysis is based on an object that's *way* too big for a comet," Will replied.

"How big?" Markham asked.

"Sys, assume the density of water-ice and calculate object diameter," Will directed.

"Acknowledged, diameter equals 987 km," Sys said.

"That's moon-sized!" Markham exclaimed.

"As I said, there's a problem." Will sighed. "That needs further investigation."

"Sys, please save all data from this session under 2092312A."

"Processing… Complete," Sys said.

"If these calculations are true, then this object would be classified as a *major* Kuiper Belt object," Will said. "Possibly even from the Oort cloud. But I think we're back to a curiosity for now."

Margaret smiled.

"Sys, please playback standard tracking information recorded since the previous session. Use enhanced speed at 48/1," Will said, then turned to Margaret. "This isn't the only object in the sky. I need to keep up with everything else."

The grid lines and overlays vanished as the sky returned to its natural appearance.

Margaret stretched her arms and picked up the blanket. "Is that it?"

"That's it."

"Damn thing," Markham grumbled, smacking his flashlight.

"Here," Will said, grabbed it, and guided them down to the beach. "Tomorrow, I'll study these results a bit closer and let you know if I come up with anything."

He glanced up at the stars and the green world around him. Throbbing pulses of insect sounds echoed off the ceiling, amplified to an unnatural level. Sys signaled the enhanced playback had finished, and no other unusual movement was detected.

"Sys, please return to standard star simulation," Will sighed. "I've had enough for one night."

Will sat back in his chair and looked up at the stars. It felt good to spend some quality time with his mother. Hopefully it would continue.

***

Back in his room, he got undressed and lay down. His mind was caught up in the enigma of the mysterious object. No matter: there wasn't much he could do now but sleep. Just the same, he fought it; there had to be an answer.

Will's head bobbed, and his body leaned forward as the bus driver shouted, "Hey, kid! This is your stop!"

He recognized the aging bus driver. He thought they must have stopped at his dormitory, but how could he have dozed off on a two-minute bus ride? No matter. He'd be up to his room in no time. His vision blurred as he stepped off the bus for the sidewalk, but instead, his foot sank into soft sand, and he stumbled to the ground.

The sky was so bright he covered his eyes and felt the heat of desert sand penetrating his clothes. As the painful sensations pulsed through him, he heard a voice.

"Where is it?" a man shouted, in an Arabic accent.

Before he could answer, another man with a strong back lifted Will to his feet by the scruff of his neck.

"Where is it?" the lead man shouted again.

Will squinted to see a dark-skinned man with a beard dressed in military garb. He couldn't make out the man holding him but knew he was big; his hold was powerful as the lead man's gaze switched between Will and the big man.

"I don't know what you're talking about," Will replied.

The lead man jerked him toward a tent a few meters away. The setting was vaguely familiar now that Will's eyes were adjusted. When they stepped inside, Will realized he was standing inside his tent at Kos Island where he'd spent a college summer nearly a decade ago.

The lead man crossed the room, where a staff of plain-clothed men stood behind a table. Will felt like he was a captured criminal standing before the judge and jury. The big man pushed him across the room until he stood in front of the table. One of the plain-clothed men pulled a canvas cover off the table to reveal an ancient stela.

"The stone is missing from the king's eye," the lead man said. "You stole it. Where is it?"

"I didn't steal it!" Will cried.

The lead man hit him across the face, knocking Will to his knees. The big man pulled him back to his feet.

"I told you," Will growled back. "I didn't steal it, but the man who did sent it to me." He held up his hand, showing him a ring. Then pulled it off and laid it on the table.

"The guardian's eye!" one man shouted.

The lead man snatched it up, laughing.

"So, what is it for?" Will asked.

"You really don't know?" the lead man boasted. His smile collapsed to a scowl, then he nodded to the big man who put a gun to Will's head and pushed him out of the tent.

PART II

Chapter 4
BIOMESS

"Blast this thing!" John Avery shouted.

The others at the table turned to see him through the window, fooling with the entry control pad.

"Still can't figure out how to open doors around here?" Markham jabbed.

Avery crossed the conference room and grabbed a seat. "To me, *enter* means proceed into the room, not a secondary operation. And I don't see why there is a security lock on this door."

"Besides, I'm not the one who has trouble interpreting data around here."

"What in the hell are you talking about?"

John Avery was dark-haired, handsome, well-educated, and cultured. Even though he'd mastered everything he took on in academia, he still thought the world had not given him his due credit. This made him arrogant and confrontational. He didn't have a lot of patience for anything, or anyone, that got in his way, especially in matters of technical opinion. And maybe that was his problem, pushing through people to keep moving ahead.

***

"That's enough!" Margaret interrupted. "You know the rules, John; if a door has a lock, it needs your access code. Now, we have work to do."

She had called a meeting to discuss the low oxygen level in the Living Hemisphere. The command room was just large enough to seat ten comfortably. Will had completed the air circulation diagnostics with Sys and was asked to sit in on the meeting.

"Now, I'm going to start this discussion, and I'm going to finish it as well," Margaret ordered, her blue eyes flashing around the table. "I've called you this morning to discuss the low oxygen situation and determine an appropriate course of action. I have reviewed information from command and mechanical systems, and it appears that the problem was caused by the recent harvest. We have to ensure proper action to correct the problem. We've been pumping oxygen for two weeks, which is eating up our reserves. Before we continue this, I want to make damn sure we're right. Richard, let's start with you since the mechanical systems seem to be functioning properly."

"That's correct," he said. "We first checked the equatorial plate for leaks between the Living and Dead, but they balanced. Then we proceeded to a mechanical check."

"What about the exterior superstructure?" Margaret interrupted.

"With the positive pressure situation outside, I can't see how a leak is possible," Markham said.

"Good point."

"Like I said," Markham continued, "we proceeded with a mechanical check. The supply and return air systems were functioning properly. We performed a complete diagnostic check of air handlers, pumps, compressors, ductwork, you name it."

"Why ductwork?" Margaret asked.

"The monkeys have been stuffing leaves and sticks through the grillwork on the back of the mountain, setting off sensors all over the place. Anyway, Will had Sys look at everything, and it all checked out."

"Anything else?"

"No, not really," Markham said. "I would add, though, we've used less than two percent of our total oxygen reserve at this point. I don't think this situation is anything to be alarmed about."

"But the total reserve is less than fifty percent capacity since we used the majority of it bringing the station online," Margaret pointed out. "We're supposed to extract excess from the natural cycles to fill that tank instead of draining it. That's why I'm concerned."

"Understood."

"Thanks, Richard," she said. "Will, do you have anything to add?"

Margaret's face changed from supervisory to irritated when she saw Will daydreaming, pondering the unusual sitting from last night's observation.

"Will!" she shouted. "Do you have anything to add?"

"I'm sorry," he replied. "No, no, I don't."

Margaret jotted the comment down.

Will switched gears to the weird dream from last night. Why was he having an anxiety dream about something that had happened so many years ago?

"Okay, Libby, let's discuss this harvest," she continued. "The low oxygen levels began after we harvested the three plots in the agricultural area. That's two hundred and seventy, nearly three hundred square meters of surface area. Losing that much biomass suddenly could cause a problem."

"Yes, but standard practice is to turn three plots at a time," Libby replied.

"I understand," Margaret said. "I'm just trying to trace our steps. So, we're pumping oxygen to compensate, which is standard procedure."

"That's correct," Markham said.

"The thing that concerns me," Margaret said, "is the fact that the data indicates no change in the situation since we began pumping. If you compare volume per day, there is practically no change. In fact, we are pumping more now than at the beginning."

"But the plants are not matured," Libby said. "So, we shouldn't expect them to carry the full burden yet."

"That's just it," Margaret said. "On Mars, we planted from seeds so that this problem was expected, but we didn't experience such sharp drops. On Gaia 3, we're pulling the young plants from cryonic freeze, replacing biomass with biomass. This was intended to curb the oxygen problem, but it doesn't seem to be working."

"I think we should clean the moat," Libby said.

"This has nothing to do with the microcity!" John Avery interrupted. Libby's face went blank. Confrontations were not her strong suit, but she had gotten into it with Avery several times. The trouble was that Avery was brilliant and had a nasty habit of letting people know.

"Wait." Margaret pointed to Avery.

He respected Margaret, and that *thing* still lingered in the back of his mind, so he held back.

She admired Avery's problem-solving ability and knew how to play him. She was just about the only person Avery had not gotten his claws into.

But why had she invited him to join the crew out in the frozen abyss? Sure, he was the best in his field, but there was another reason, an old lurking passion that had never played itself out. She was playing with fire, and it was not like her to make a decision that even partially dealt with personal feelings.

"Libby, why do you think the moat is a problem?" Margaret asked.

"It's centrally located and at the lowest point in the Living Hemisphere," she replied. "So, it receives water from all other biomes. Under normal circumstances, it functions properly, but with the kick-starting we went through to bring the station online, it's just been overstressed. We should drain the water to a low level and replace all the filters."

"So, you think it's a combination of two effects, the harvest, and the water?" Margaret asked.

"I think a more appropriate term for the moat right now is soup," Libby replied. "There are no tests that I'm aware of that support this position, but that's exactly what I think. You measured the pH levels yourself, Margaret."

"Have you checked the subterranean insect population?" Margaret asked.

"Ants, termites, earthworms—we sampled populations from each biome," Libby replied. "All species appear healthy and doing the job of breaking down decomposing vegetation."

"Okay, then let's—"

"People," Avery interrupted. "Excuse me, Margaret. Sorry, Richard." Avery gestured. "This linear thinking is getting us nowhere."

Markham rolled his eyes; he had endured too many dinner table discussions with Avery. In short, Avery was a scientist, and Markham was an engineer.

"Young Mr. Vandolah," Avery continued. "Did you ask Sys to combine the effects of the Living and the Dead Hemispheres in your diagnostics? To cross reference and search for possible weaknesses?"

"No, I didn't," Will replied and gazed at Markham.

"Well, there you have it!" Avery said, bluntly.

"There we have what?" Margaret inquired.

"Let me explain," Avery responded. "Animals breathe in oxygen and exhale carbon dioxide. Plants absorb carbon dioxide and release oxygen. Now, she—" he pointed at Libby "—is harvesting the fields and lowering the biomass, which in turn, lowers the amount of oxygen being produced. But the animals still require the same amount of oxygen, so you—" he pointed at Markham "—start pumping oxygen to compensate. The system never learns or adjusts; it doesn't have to because you are nurse-maiding it. You aren't forcing it to grow and produce more oxygen. It stays stagnant until she has a full-grown crop."

Markham could not get in a word edgewise.

"Are you saying we should sit and do nothing?" he asked, spitefully.

Margaret recalled a similar situation on the Mars station that took a long time to work itself out. Nurse-maiding the system might be a good idea, and she didn't want to take chances with oxygen reserves this far from Earth.

"There's no *strain* on the system," Avery continued with a full head of steam. "If you don't work your muscles, they get flabby.

Consider Earth's biosphere. If volcanos of the Mesozoic aren't working on it, then industrialization of the Cenozoic is. Nature has to fight to stay strong; that's why our environment is so resilient. You can't be nice and try to domesticate it the way you want to."

"What happens to the increased biomass of the forest and wetlands when the new crops are fully grown?" Libby asked.

"Some overgrowth will die out to compensate," Avery responded. "You would have a period of excessive oxygen output. Speaking euphemistically, the system would adjust its own metabolism."

No one said a word. What he was talking about went against standard procedure, and everyone knew it.

"So, to answer Mr. Markham's question, yes, I believe we should just sit and do nothing," Avery said. "What have you got to lose, Margaret, besides a little sleep?"

It was a no-risk experiment. Markham hated to agree with Avery, but this proved that his research was correct and agreeing was not an admission of defeat.

"Robert, how long can people be subjected to a sub-twenty oxygen level before side effects are noticed?" Margaret asked Doctor Lewis.

"Depends on just how sub-twenty it is. At seventeen percent, you should not experience any ill side effects for days, maybe weeks," Robert replied.

He was the oldest of the Gaian team and had spent time on the Gaia 2 station. A thin, gray-haired man, he was delicately built and spoke softly.

The team members were all tops in their field, and also people she had worked with on other assignments. Most importantly, they were people she trusted. A big concern of hers was being this far out, where help was years away, not days or weeks as with the other stations. And a trusted physician was one of the most important crew members on board.

"So, the worse we should expect is loss of sleep and a few choice nightmares?" Margaret asked.

"Sleep deprivation would be a common side effect," Robert said, sipping his coffee while staring down Avery. They worked together in the cryonics lab, thawing the inhabitants of the station. But the thought of allowing the system to go substandard disturbed him.

"Okay, then let's do it," she said. "Richard, cancel the oxygen supplements immediately. We will proceed for the next few weeks with only what the Living Hemisphere provides and see if it kick-starts itself."

"What!" Markham said, then caught himself. His performance in this situation was borderline, and Margaret's affronted expression was a testimonial.

"Understood. Will, can you help me with this?"

"Sure, I can get started right away," he replied.

"Margaret, we'll need your voice authorization to get this past Sys," Markham added. "In fact, you should just give the cancel order yourself; there's really nothing to it."

"That's true. I'll take care of it right after the meeting," she said.

"The only hard part is shutting off the supply air grills," Markham said. "We have to do that manually. Some of them are hard to access."

"Margaret," Robert interjected, "I should caution you that people around here are performing some complicated tasks, and we can't afford to let them get disoriented. I recommend periodic examinations for all personnel during this operation."

"Noted," Margaret said, writing down the comment.

"Thank you," Robert said.

"That should handle things for now," Margret said. "I'll schedule a progress meeting next week to review the situation further. Thank you all for coming."

Avery was out the door before Will and Markham were out of their chairs. That bit of chest pumping was an ego boost, and it was in front of Margaret.

There was a time when he'd fallen for her, but she just wasn't ready for that kind of relationship in her life. It was many years ago, but his feelings for Margaret still lingered. In fact, that was one of the reasons he'd agreed to her request to be here. Setting up an Earth-like facility in one of the most hostile environments in the solar system was also a big enticement.

John had always considered himself an adventurer at heart and this was a chance to prove his worth.

"I hate it when he's right," Markham said.

"Do you think he'll push *Enter* twice to get out of the room?" Will asked.

Markham chuckled.

Chapter 5
AIR CYCLES

"No, I don't," Will grumbled, working his way through the foliage of the tropical forest. "What a brilliant response, so concise, so descriptive. You idiot! Back in the doghouse with Mother."

"Excuse me?" Jim Miller said. He was crouched near a banana tree, holding a snake cage in one hand and a retractable claw in the other.

"I really screwed up in a meeting this morning," Will said.

"Oh, I thought you were talking to me. Two days to relocate nearly a hundred snakes isn't too bad, is it?" Miller asked. "I mean, as quickly as they move up here."

Will chuckled. "My mother's concerned about the oxygen level in this place, and I'm too busy daydreaming to take notice. I doubt that I'll ever be asked to another meeting."

"That's all right," Miller said. "I've never been asked to a meeting in my whole life, and just look where it's gotten me."

Will stared curiously at the cage and claw he was holding.

"I'm the head zookeeper for the largest damn zoo in the solar system, other than of Earth."

"She thinks I'm never going to amount to anything," Will said. "Unless I concentrate my efforts in one direction."

"She thinks I joke around too much and don't take things as seriously as I should," Miller said.

"I don't think there's anything wrong with more than one interest," Will said.

"I don't think there's anything wrong with adding a little spice to life," Miller said.

"So why are you here?" Will asked.

"Because I get the job done, and she counts on me for that," Miller answered. "It's good to expand your horizons, but first, you must build a foundation. Prove yourself first! You idiot!"

"So, your zookeeper and part-time psychologist," Will said. "Interesting combination."

"My point is that all she wants from you is to perform your assigned duties. After that, it doesn't matter."

"Speaking of assigned duties, I have to get busy closing these supply air grills," Will said. "I need ropes and climbing equipment. Are they still stored at the base of the rock?"

"Yes, they are. By the way, if you see any snakes back there, let me know," Miller said.

Will turned and waved assuredly as Miller's purple outfit disappeared into the woods. Heavy leaves and undergrowth scraped past his legs as he made his way around the island to the rear of the faux rock. He craned his neck and saw the supply air grills mounted high on the back of the mountain.

In the maintenance room, Will noticed no security lock on the door. The door was stuck tight inside its jambs, so pulling the handle made a noise that rumbled through the hollow concrete mountain. The sound carried up through the rock to the caves. A dozen capuchin monkeys darted out and ran around the top of the rock like ants on a hill.

"At least it wasn't bats." He sighed.

Will sifted through the cluttered storage room. He found muddy boots, shovels, and seed bags. Momentarily, he found a rope, a suspension belt, and some tie-off clasps stuffed into a box under a workbench.

"Head zookeeper," he scoffed. "No wonder there are no locks on the door."

He threw the bag onto a workbench and began sorting the mess. He found metal inserts for tie-off points, then started his way up. Most supply and return air grills were located about five meters from the top. Closing them was easy; each grill had to be manually shut and then deactivated by simply pulling pins on all the lock mechanisms.

One-sixth gravity or not, thirty-five meters was still thirty-five meters. When he reached the top, Will was sweating, grunting, and out of breath. The place seemed contained, a scale model of the real world. The sky simulation was distorted and reminded him of a ship in a bottle.

He tied-off his ropes to metal climbing inserts, tossed the ropes over the side, and started toward the air grills. Directly below, he noticed something peculiar about the uppermost grills. He slowed his descent to stabilize himself against the concrete. When he finally reached the grill, he saw the locking pin was missing, and there were scratch marks and muddy paw prints around it. Spider monkeys, no doubt, were trying to get inside the mountain.

***

"Sys, we need to make a voice-authorized change to established procedures for the air cycles. Do you need voice verification?" Margaret asked from command.

"What specific change is requested?" Sys replied.

"Discontinue oxygen supplements to the Living Hemisphere," she said, with Markham sitting nearby.

"Acknowledged. Voice verification is not required, and a record of the proposed change must be transmitted to Space Council. Would you like to proceed?" Sys asked.

"Yes," Margaret said.

"Understood," Sys responded. "Before execution, I should provide you with a complete estimate of possible problems that might accompany this change: *This would reduce the system-wide oxygen content to 16.93% by volume. Prolonged exposure to—*"

"Stop," Margaret interrupted. "We have evaluated the possible risks and side effects. Please proceed with the change."

"Processing… Complete. Would you like to make any additional changes?"

"No, thank you, not at this time," Margaret replied. "Okay, Richard, that handles the software problem. Find Will and work on the hardware problem."

"He's shutting the supply air grills in the Living," Markham said. "I'll get up there and check on his progress right away."

"Richard, I really want you to stay on top of this thing. Let's keep track of the progress constantly. I don't mean daily. I mean hourly. We're breaking established guidelines here and need to be careful."

Markham stopped short of the door. "Then we should get Sys involved."

"That's fine, and Will, too, if you need him," Margaret said. "I'll get pressure from the Space Council, and I want to ensure all our ducks are in a row."

"I shouldn't need him," Markham said. "But I'll let him know if I do."

"Stay on top of him," Margaret said. "I don't want to push him too hard, but I don't want him to get comfortable. You're the only one who gives me honest input about his performance."

"What about Libby?" he asked.

"I think Libby wants to jump his bones," she said.

"With the schedule, you keep for him she'll never get the chance. And believe me, Margaret, after that look you gave him this morning, he'll be on his toes for a while."

Margaret watched him walk away, then turned to the view screen, sipped coffee, and drifted off in thought. Her career was the main driver for most of her life, she'd devoted all her energies to that direction. But now she hoped to find something else, things tucked away in the deeper reaches of her mind, like an old book collecting dust on a shelf.

Guilt, perhaps brought on by age, clawed its way up to reality and made her wonder if her son was lost to the mechanisms of her career or if there was still time to find him again.

***

Will pulled at a hinged air grill and swung it open. He aimed a flashlight down the air shaft and saw a dented metal liner covered in mud. The shaft extended back a few meters and dropped straight down. He crawled in to investigate. There were no signs of animal droppings, only dirt as if it were a path used often, and about halfway down the shaft, a side panel was knocked out. He aimed the light through the opening.

He saw the interior of the concrete mountain—structural steel framework, ducting, and piping. The concrete shells of tunnels and caves twisted through the bowels of the mountain. There was no sign of activity, but the tops of most of the artificial shafts were covered with leaves, twigs, and dirt.

"This must be where they hide their food," Will murmured. "As Libby suspected."

There was never a reason to check inside the mountain for problems since there was no access.

"How's it coming along?" Richard Markham shouted from the foot of the faux mountain.

"Just about finished," Will said. "I found a problem up here with the upper air shaft that we'll have to discuss with Libby."

"A problem?"

"Yes," Will continued. "Those little organ grinder monkeys broke into the ventilation system and are down inside the rock."

"Inside the rock!" Markham shouted.

"That's right." He checked the pin on the last grill and descended quickly. "They've been all over the place in there. It's going to take a while to clean up."

"Damn," Markham said. "We don't have any sensors to pick them up."

"Kirby and Miller cleaned the grills," Will said. "Didn't they?"

"Yes," Markham replied. "At least they were supposed to."

"Anyone who went up there should have noticed the missing pin, the scratch marks, and the mud," Will said. "It wasn't hard to see."

"I'll have to discuss this with Margaret," Markham said.

Will stepped inside the storage room to put his gear away.

"What a mess!" Markham said, following him inside.

"You should see the inside of the rock."

Markham just shook his head as he stared down at the wreck of a maintenance room, a new item on the list of things to do.

"Okay, I'm going to run down and get some lunch." Markham sighed. "And have a talk with Miller later."

Will watched Markham walk down the path and disappear into the trees.

From the forest edge, he saw Markham enter the elevator shaft with Libby. Will ducked out of sight, afraid Libby order him to work in the fields. With that, he decided to head to his quarters and check Sys' progress.

Chapter 6
COMET

The next day

"I'm sick and tired of these dreams," Will told Markham in the cafeteria. "I need to either slow down or start eating better. Is there any chocolate around here? Any kind, it doesn't matter. Do we have any in storage?"

"That'll really help your diet. How about an apple instead?" Markham scoffed and tossed a half-eaten one at Will.

"Chocolate-coat it, and I'll eat anything," he replied.

"Are we talking male now?" Libby interrupted and dropped a lunch tray next to Will. "Do you mind if I sit here?"

"Oh, we were just..." Will stuttered and held out the apple awkwardly. Libby easily got to him, and she knew it.

"Please do," Markham gestured.

"So, am I interrupting?" Libby asked.

"No, not at all," Will replied, hoping she didn't hook him into another rodent hunt. "We were talking about the object Sys is tracking, then it turned into a chocolate discussion."

"You know, there is a small Cacao tree in the tropical forest," Libby said. "If you want chocolate, you just have to work for it."

Will perked up curiously as Markham pushed his chair away from the table.

"Libby," Markham said. "Will came across a situation yesterday on the rock. The capuchin monkeys have broken into a supply air grill and gotten down inside the mountain."

"You're kidding, right?" she asked, her spoon mid-air.

"No, they really have, and it's a mess in there," Will added. "But there doesn't seem to be any serious damage, just a lot of leaves and twigs scattered around."

"Well, that explains their behavioral patterns," Libby said. "I assumed they spent more time in the trees than expected and didn't give it further thought. Those sneaky little shits."

"I found that, too," Will said. "There is a parch-dried field of manure on top of the rock. It appears the primates aren't a good piece of this perfect recycling process after all."

"Evidently not," Libby said. "I'll get Miller and Kirby in there for clean-up and repair. I wonder if there is any way to keep them off the top of the rock?"

"I doubt it," Markham said. "They won't let us use chemicals, and Margaret probably won't allow barbed wire."

"I'll get with Jim after lunch and bring Margaret up to date," Libby said.

"Thanks," Markham said. "I can scratch that off my list."

"So, what's the scoop on this object I keep hearing about?"

Markham excused himself and started away. "Will, we need to start monitoring oxygen results this afternoon. See you in command."

"Okay, thanks," he replied, turning to Libby, still trying to avoid discussing the biosphere. "We think it's a huge cometary body or possibly an asteroid. But some conflicting data needs to be reviewed.

I'm going to be working on it later this afternoon. Would you like to help?"

"Help?" Libby grinned.

"Sure, the test shouldn't take long," he said. "I had an idea this morning that could help solve our little mystery. If it doesn't work, we're just stuck and have to wait until Sys can get more tracking information."

"Why not? My schedule is light today," Libby replied.

"Good, see you then," Will said. "I don't mean to be rude, but I must get back to command. Besides, I try to avoid smelling this food as much as possible." He picked up his plate and started away.

"Four o'clock, right?"

"Right."

***

Will and Markham spent the afternoon checking the status of sensors and reading the various gas levels, specifically oxygen. The myriad of sensors in the Living and Dead Hemispheres continuously detected changes station-wide to a fraction of a percent.

"This is pretty much what we expected," Will said, pointing to the graphics display on the monitor. "The levels already decreased almost half a percent in the Dead Hemisphere; the Living not quite as much."

"Jesus," Markham sighed. "It hasn't even been six hours, and its below twenty percent. We should check the recirculating system tomorrow. Fresh air from the Living should be distributing itself better than that."

Markham served with Margaret on Gaia 2 and had diagnosed many technical issues there, some life-threatening. Margaret considered him indispensable and had demanded he be part of the crew. Richard chuckled at the rhetoric but jumped at the opportunity. He could fix anything and looked forward to this new challenge billions of kilometers from home.

Will pushed against the tabletop, and his chair quickly rolled across the floor toward the main terminal.

"Have Sys start checking flow capacity," Markham said. He sifted through a control manual for the proper voice command. "We probably have to recalibrate the pull on the pumps. I bet it's still set for a certain percentage, assuming pumps from the reserve tanks are also pulling."

"There are still a few bugs to work out with all the jury-rigging we've done," Will replied. "But the operation shouldn't be complicated. Sys, please check air handlers for recycling capacity versus current usage."

"Processing… Complete," Sys said. "Analysis as follows."

Sys displayed specifications on air pumps serving the Dead Hemisphere. The command to cancel oxygen supplements that day inadvertently shut down all recycling pumps since the Dead and Living worked hand in hand.

"Sys," Markham said. "Reset pumps serving the Dead Hemisphere to draw independent of the storage system pumps and balance oxygen levels throughout the station."

"Processing…. Complete," Sys said.

"That should do it, for today anyway," Markham said. "Tomorrow could be another story."

"So, we're finished?" Will asked.

"I think so," Markham replied, checking the time. "It's going to take a few hours to readjust. Let's pick this up in the morning."

"Good," Will said. "I want to see if Sys has any new information on the object."

"Don't you want to take a break?" Markham asked, as Libby crossed the room behind him. "I'm going over to the recreation lounge."

"Hi, you about ready?" Libby interrupted.

Markham furrowed his brow.

"If he has more to do, I can come back later."

"No, that's pretty good timing, we just finished up." Markham noticed a pleasing odor in the air, and Libby wore a slightly different expression on her face, or maybe it was her hair.

"See you at dinner?" Markham followed.

"Sure," Will replied.

Libby just nodded with a simple smile, hoping Markham held his tongue.

"Have you talked to my mother about the monkey issue?" Will asked.

"Oh yes, she was a real happy camper, too," Libby said. "She cornered Kirby and Miller in the storage room on level fourteen right after lunch. I've never seen Jim Miller speechless in my life. All three went up there about three hours ago, and I haven't heard from them since."

"I'll save that for the next time he starts one of his *Head Zookeeper* stories." Will chuckled.

Libby pulled up a chair next to Will and flipped through the piles of papers and manuals. "Is any of this related to your research?"

"No," he said, gathering things to clear the table. "I keep most of that in my quarters. This mess is what we've piled up on the recent oxygen problem. Sys, please recall information saved from session 2092312A."

"Processing… Complete," Sys said.

"Sys, please use events one through five," Will said. "And plot locations of ejecta plumes onto a spherical surface. Assume that the object rotates opposite the center of mass for each event."

"Processing…"

"This could take a while," he said and leaned back in the chair, brushing his hands through his hair.

"Where did you get that?" she asked, reaching for the ring on his finger. "You're always fiddling around with it."

Will pulled back at first but then put his hand on the table for her to see. "It was sent to me long ago by an old friend," he offered.

"It's beautiful. Is it real?" she asked, rubbing the inset stone.

"Oh yes. It's the real thing, all right," he said. "But it's kind of a long story."

"I see," she said. "Did she break your heart?"

"There was no *she*," Will mumbled. "It's just a long story. Besides, I don't fiddle around with it."

"There, you just did it again," she said. "That's what you always do. You spin it around like it's too big or something."

"Complete," Sys said.

A plot showed a circular globe with longitude and latitude lines and five patchy shapes.

"Damn, that agrees," Will whispered.

"Is that bad?" she asked.

"Sys, what is the estimated diameter?" he asked.

"Processing… Complete," Sys said. "Diameter equals 1027 km."

"It's not the same as last night," he said. "I don't know if that's good or bad, but two independent checks are putting that object at one thousand kilometers in diameter."

"What?"

"And it's outgassing exotic ices," he whispered. "This is amazing."

"Is it visible from Earth?" she asked.

"Probably not, at least not to the naked eye. But it will be when it passes."

"What's going to happen then?"

"Nothing," he replied. "It's going to pass close by. They'll get a pretty good look at it."

"Comet Vandolah?" she asked.

Will chuckled. "Comet 2092312 for now, but maybe?"

Libby put a thought in his head that he hadn't considered during this two-day mystery. He had been so driven to make a name for himself that when he finally found the vehicle, it was going right past him. This was something unique, and he was only concerned with finding out what it was, not what it could do for him.

"Sys, please discontinue the ongoing search routines and start continuously tracking object 2092312," he said. "The orbital elements and spectral analyses determined from the previous session should be updated with each new ejecta event encountered."

"Processing... Complete," Sys said.

"This is something," he said, jiggling his ring while Libby pretended not to notice. "I think we really found something. Last night I didn't believe it, but this confirms it. I'm going to ask Mother about informing the Space Council."

"The Space Council! Don't you think you're getting ahead of yourself?" she asked.

"No, not really," he said. "We could do a few more tests first, but the bottom line is this is a massive comet, possibly a planetoid. Earth-based observers need to start tracking it—if they can—to help with orbital elements."

"Well, then, I guess that takes the heat off me," she said.

"What heat?"

"First, we tell them that we're breaking standard procedure by canceling oxygen supplements, and now we're telling them that we've found a moon-sized comet," she said. "What's next, the bogeyman?"

"They'll get over it," he said. "Besides, that's my mother's problem, not ours. I feel like celebrating. Did you say earlier that we have a tree that makes chocolate?"

"Makes chocolate?" she laughed. "Not exactly. We have a *Theobroma Cacao*. You get chocolate when its seed pods are roasted and ground to a fine powder."

Will deflated a bit. "Why exactly do we have this tree?"

"Because the smaller primates like the seed pods," she said. "And it's not the only unusual plant in the Living, you know. There are hundreds of different species, and they all have a specific purpose."

"Oh." Will nodded, trying to sound interested. Until recently, he couldn't have cared less. "That leaves my options at reading a good book or shoemaker tech manuals."

"Tech manuals!" she blurted, not really happy with his poking at her biosphere or dissing her. She also wondered if he was indirectly trying to be nice. "I don't want to burst your little bubble, but what if Margaret decides *not* to inform the Space Council of your discovery?"

"Maybe you're right," he reflected. "Chances are I'll have to summarize my findings into a report of some kind, and that'll take a while. In the meantime, Sys and I will continue tracking and refining these numbers for additional backup."

"Well, this has been interesting, but I have a lot of work to catch up on this evening," she said and pushed her chair back. "I'll take a rain check on the tech manuals. See you tomorrow."

"Okay," Will stuttered, not understanding her abrupt exit. "If you need any help up top, just let me know."

PART III

Chapter 7
RINGS OF FIRE

May 2092

Four months of research and headaches had gotten nowhere, and the problem worsened. Margaret was so concerned about the oxygen deficiency that she requested approval from the Space Council to delay Phase II by six months. She was nervous about the new crop since it was not helping the situation, and no one knew why.

She would hold on to her oxygen reserves even if it meant loading them on the shuttle and flying back to Earth. But the Space Council pressured her to rectify the situation. So, for three months they pumped oxygen at two percent to bring the levels up to eighteen.

Will had another problem. Comet 2092312 turned out to be one of the most exciting comets ever studied. But Margaret did not want to release information on that discovery. She was leery about making bold statements on two unrelated topics, but the comet was nearing the Saturnian System.

***

"Too rich for me," Jim Miller said, and threw in his cards.

Robert stared across the table with a raised eyebrow. They were matching wits with Will and Markham in poker for about the hundredth time. Libby and Avery were also in the rec area, catching up on reading.

"Let's see what you have, boy." Robert sighed. "I'll raise ten."

"I call," Will replied with a cocky grin and threw out a ten chip.

"I fold." Markham shrugged.

Robert tossed out another ten chip.

The turn was around to Will, who smiled and did the same, then they turned up their cards.

"Another flush," Will gloated. "That's three in a row. How about another round, Gentlemen?" He gathered up the cards and started shuffling to reluctant nods.

Card playing was the only bastion of recreation left, and poker was an easy game. Tension was mounting on Gaia, and Robert Lewis was concerned about the crew's behavior.

"If your mother can't solve this little oxygen mystery in the next two or three months," Robert stated inquisitively, "then we're going to have to leave this place."

"Don't worry," Will said, shuffling. "We'll get it fixed. But it's *our* problem, not just hers."

Robert's face was expressionless. He had been asking the crew questions lately that were indirectly geared toward invoking emotional responses.

"I'm not accusing," he said. "Just stating a fact."

"The fact is," Markham interjected, "we might not be in this mess if we'd stuck with standard procedures from the beginning."

"Oh, there's that hindsight thing again." Avery's voice came from across the room. "Whatever happened to *You make choices and live with them?*"

"Live or die with them, don't you mean?" Markham said.

"Oh, come on, Richard, be a good sport," arrogant Avery responded. "I'm sure we'd all like to hear your solution to this inconvenience."

"Inconvenience!" Markham shouted. "You jackass."

"Hey!" Robert placed a hand on Markham's shoulder.

"Gentlemen," Robert said. "Please, calm down. I didn't mean to start an argument."

"Oh, please!" Avery shouted. "You can stop with the Pavlov's Dog statements."

"Let me bring you back to reality. We're a billion kilometers from home, running out of the basic necessities of life, and there is no scientific explanation for it. And guess what? People are getting on edge. Does that surprise you?"

"All right then, a straightforward question," Robert said. "Has anyone else been experiencing strange dreams lately? I have, twice."

A sort of hush hung in the air—no response.

"That's what I thought. We're all showing the first signs of fatigue from oxygen deprivation."

"I recommend that Margaret let this research work rest for a few days. I'm no expert in what you people do, but it doesn't take a genius to realize that everyone is exhausted. Besides, we have one of the most advanced computers in the solar system at our disposal. Let's set it on automatic and let it run for a while. Any arguments?"

"Robert, we all appreciate your concern," Markham said. "Maybe you're right."

"I don't care if either one of you are right," Will said. "But I know my mother, and she'll stick with this thing until hell freezes over."

"I hope that's not a prediction." Avery scoffed. "Have you checked the weather outside lately?"

"Why don't we all talk about something else," Libby said, noticeably upset just listening. "I can have this much fun cleaning animal cages."

Silence again while Will dealt cards. The good thing with cards is you don't have to talk; just play. But it didn't matter, they were too exhausted to come up with light-hearted discussion.

The four patiently and stealthily studied their cards.

"So, has anyone heard the latest—"

"We don't want to hear about that bloody comet," Miller interrupted.

"Call or fold?" Will asked, still holding his last question.

"Fold, fold," said Miller and the doctor.

"I'm in," Markham said and tossed out one chip.

"Not by much." Will chuckled as he added a ten chip to the pot. "I was going to ask if anyone has heard the latest on the disturbance in the rings?"

"Disturbance?" Robert asked.

"Yes," Markham said and tossed in his cards with a deep sigh. "Lightning occurrences are up significantly."

"Lightning?" Robert asked as if he were being toyed with.

"You know," Will said. "Discharges of electricity sometimes occur between moving objects—clouds, for instance. It happens in the rings, too, just not very often."

"Lightning?"

"But recently," Will continued, "it's been picking up. The Space Council transmitted a message asking that we try and turn Shoemaker on and aim its cameras toward the rings."

Will gathered up the pot. "I can't wait to see my mother's response."

"They should be excited to find out we already have Shoemaker operating," Robert said.

"Maybe, maybe not," Will said. "We aren't even supposed to be using it, especially not how I've been. All that interfacing with the view screen above the Living are special modifications."

Miller started a new deal-out. Robert and Markham grumbled something about calling it a night.

"One more, and that's it," Miller said.

Oh, the high stakes finale. Will rolled his eyes.

"So, when is her response due?" Robert asked.

"This week," Will replied. "She'll probably just tell them we can do it since I already am, but she won't mention the comet yet."

"What have you found out?"

"Nothing," Will answered. "I realigned the satellite this morning. Sys should have something on it tomorrow."

Miller checked his cards and tossed in a fifty piece.

Robert rolled his eyes. "Call." He matched the donation and drew a card.

Markham threw his cards down.

Libby approached the table. "What do you think is causing the disturbance?"

"I have no idea," Will said. "The only thing we can say is that electrical discharges are caused by objects rubbing together. The rings are made up of billions of ice-covered rocks tumbling in orbit. The lightning is caused by their interaction, and now, for some reason, they are interacting more. This is all the more reason we fly out and look around."

"Now, wait a minute," Markham said. "With the problems we're having here, there is no way in hell that Margaret will let anyone on that shuttle."

"To see two of the most interesting astronomical phenomena of this century?" Will interrupted. "I can assure you, Richard, even if we pack up and leave, I'll get up and see that comet firsthand."

Will took a deep breath and pushed out all of his chips. Jim Miller shook his head and pushed in his pile.

"I don't feel lucky," Robert said. "But here goes nothing."

He pulled a card, sighed, and threw them at the pot.

Miller smiled, drew again, and laid down a full house.

"Gotta draw more cards, boys," Miller said, rounding up the chips.

***

Will could hardly sleep. He hated to admit it, but insomnia was taking its toll. He paced his living quarters into the early morning hours. He would doze off for a few minutes, dream strange dreams, then wake up exhausted.

He tried to make the best use of the time and went through it repeatedly, mulling over the unusual activity in the rings. What was different now that hadn't been there before?

Then it hit him. This was a year when the plane of the rings was at its widest angle to the sun and received more light than usual. The increased heat energy was surely exciting the dust particles in the rings. That had to be the source of the lightning!

Will lay back on the couch and curled up with a pillow. As he drifted off, the problems with the comet occupied his mind, piled in with anxiety from the oxygen problem. All those thoughts bubbled and brewed in the dark cauldron of his subconscious.

***

"C'mon, Will!" Murphy shouted. "We have to make a run for it!" Murphy tugged at his shirt, but Will resisted and sat, motionless in the hot sand, staring at a bright sky.

"What is that?" Will asked.

It didn't seem as bright as the sun and appeared to have handles.

He placed a hand above his head to shade the glare. Maybe it was Saturn, except the rings were glowing and pulsing as they lit up the sky.

Before they could move, a small unit of military police corralled them. They materialized from nowhere and led them back to a tent in the middle of an endless sandy desert. Murphy scowled at Will as they were pushed at rifle point into the tent. *Why didn't I run before they got here?*

"The stone, Murphy!" the lead man shouted, standing next to a table where the stela lay. "Where is it?"

Murphy's stern expression and unmoving eyes yielded no answer.

He was hit in the back of the neck and nearly collapsed to the ground.

"Where are you hiding it?" the man shouted again.

"The boy has it." He grimaced, rubbing his neck.

The lead man turned to Will, who wore a surprised expression.

"Talk," the man shouted, holding the butt of his weapon above Will's head. Murphy reached up and grabbed the man's wrist in mid-motion.

"It's hidden on him," Murphy said. "I didn't tell him about it."

Will instinctively lifted his hand, staring at the ruby ring. As if awe-inspired, the lead man grasped his hand and pulled the ring from his finger.

"This is it!" he boasted. He held the ring close to the relief surface and compared its shape to the king's eye.

"You've got what you wanted," Murphy said. "Now let us go."

The man didn't respond, but his teeth shone as he smiled. His smile quickly turned to a frown as he studied the ring more closely.

"What is this?" he shouted, pointing to the numbers inside the ring. "A clever clue to the past!"

Murphy did not respond. The man pointed his gun at Murphy's temple and fired. Will watched helplessly as his friend fell to the ground. Then he saw the barrel of the gun turn in his direction.

Will sprang up in bed, rubbing his eyes. Then it hit him, sixteen-eighty-two, that's where he'd seen it before—inside the ring! From the first day he'd seen them on the bus two years ago, he had just read the numbers wrong. Sixteen-eighty-two was the sum of years it took that comet to orbit the sun. The numbers had been floating around in his mind as separate issues; he'd never considered them related.

***

"Morning," Markham said, passing Will in the hallway.

Will grumbled something, his words muffled by clanging metallic footsteps.

Markham paused, raised a concerned eyebrow, and then watched him enter systems command. "Sys, please access Shoemaker file; ring test," he ordered from the main terminal.

"Processing... Complete,"

"Sys, please playback the entire visual sequence at normal speed," Will said.

"Accessing," Sys said.

Will was stunned by what he saw. They had always shown up as a pink overlay in the past. The rings were bothersome to his motion-sensitive search programs, so he had them graphically frozen. For months, he had not seen Saturn, its rings, moons, or any other moving objects. There was no other source for comparison; no one else in the entire system, and cloud cover blocked the view. But there it was, like nothing he'd expected. The rings were alive and crackling with lightning.

Great arcing flashes resembling a solar prominence above and below the ring plane. The ring plane was also thickening; the one-kilometer-thick sea of whirling ice was bulging at the center.

Markham entered the room and stood behind Will at the computer terminal. "What are you doing?" he asked. "Playing with your overlays again?"

"This is no overlay," Will murmured.

"Then what is it?"

A confused Will held up his hands. "It's supposed to be the rings."

"Okay, so what's the joke?"

"No joke, everything's working correctly," Will said. "I can't believe this went unnoticed. I mean, this is unbelievable."

"You use this simulation every night," Markham said. "Why haven't you noticed it before?"

"Because it's always in the form of an overlay," he replied. "This unusual activity is just an enhancement of normal motion. So, this light show just went totally unnoticed."

"We should notify Margaret right away," Markham said.

Will stared at the view screen and fiddled with his ring. In the split second that it caught his attention, he remembered his dream.

This strange event was not something that happened once every fifteen years. Widest face to the sun or not, this phenomenon had never been reported. The excited rings were the victim of another kind of force, which is still unknown.

"We need to do more than that." He turned to Markham. "Feel like taking a ride on the shuttle?"

"Out there?" Markham pointed at the view screen.

Will turned back to see another massive prominence rising above the rings.

***

Robert and Margaret finished a discussion regarding the side effects of the low oxygen problem. Robert now had proof of nervous behavior and anxiety dreams from most crew members. He'd confronted her to suggest they contact Earth, and her calm composure and iron-clad will showed signs of fatigue.

"Robert," she said. "We've gone over this again and again. The fact remains that this station was meticulously designed. Therefore, the low O2 problem will correct itself in time. But I'm not going to jeopardize the lifeblood of this station just because we are starting to show signs of fatigue."

Robert paused momentarily, then offered, "Let me put it to you another way. These problems we're having will grow progressively if they aren't corrected. In the next phase, we'll have people hyperventilating and passing out. I'll end up with an entire crew of basket cases in the med lab, and you won't have enough healthy people to run this base. Let alone solve this kind of a problem.

"We can, however, head this thing off before it gets any worse. If you initiate potent supplements for two or three days, the crew can get back on its feet. That will allow them to regroup and have a fighting chance to solve this problem with clear heads."

Margaret rubbed her forehead. Maybe she was working the crew too hard. Perhaps she should give this thing a rest. She was about to answer when a voice came through her desk speaker.

"Margaret, it's Richard and Will," Markham spoke. "We have something important to talk about."

She rolled her eyes and made a waiting gesture to Robert. "Come in, please."

They hurried into the room and stood across the table from Margaret. Whether it was the lack of oxygen or the quick pace down the hall, they were both out of breath.

"Mother, the Space Council was right," he said. "I don't know what's causing it, but what's happening out there is unbelievable."

Margaret's cool gaze bounced between them as if they'd been drinking.

"We're too late, Margaret," Robert joked. "It's already gone to the second phase."

She shot him a look.

Will and Markham went on in stride.

"Mother," Will said. "We have all seen intermittent lightning in the rings, right?"

She nodded.

"What's happening now is unbelievable; it's constant and encompasses the whole ring system."

"They appear to be on fire, Margaret," Markham added.

"On fire," she said.

"Has the Space Council sent any new messages?" Will asked.

"Not that I'm aware of. Why?"

"Because—and I know this sounds crazy—but the amount of electrical turbulence increases almost exponentially on a time scale. Three weeks ago, there was nothing. Three days ago, there was only slightly more than normal. And now, this has to be the brightest planet in the solar system. I'm sure astronomers on Earth are pulling their hair out over this one."

"Richard?" She raised an eyebrow at Markham.

"I saw it, too, Margaret," he said. "I'm no astronomer, but I've never seen anything like this. I've never heard of anything like this."

"Mother," Will said, "this event is unprecedented in recorded history. Let's investigate in the shuttle."

"What do we gain from a shuttle trip that Shoemaker can't give you?" she asked.

Will paused.

"Two things," he said. "One, Shoemaker can't see the whole ring system. At least thirty percent of the ring is behind the planet at any time. We could get above the rings and get a better insight into the expanse of the phenomenon."

"Two, comet 2092312 is on its way to a near-Earth flyby, but it'll pass the opposite side of Saturn in just two days. We need detailed observations of that object, and I want to see its effect on crossing the ring plane."

Margaret sat calmly, eyes fixed on the books at the edge of her desk. For a moment, the room was still and silent.

"Robert," she said. "You've got your supplements again."

He let out a grateful sigh.

"But for three days only, no more." She stood and moved quickly toward the door. "You two, come with me to command," she said. "I want to take a look at those rings."

***

Margaret followed Will to his station and saw what she didn't have time to think about, let alone take seriously. But there it was—she couldn't even picture what he was trying to describe. Chaotic bands of light crackled and spit their way through the rings. He could swear it looked worse now than just an hour ago.

There was no question it was real. The lack of color enhancement, the dry, unenhanced image on the screen, and a time-lapsed clock speeding in the lower corner. For the first time in months, her mind was not preoccupied with an oxygen problem.

"What has Sys told us about this?" Margaret marveled.

"I haven't asked Sys to do an analysis yet." Will shrugged. "We're taking pictures and saving images."

"What can Sys analyze from that?" Markham asked.

"All we could do," Will replied, "is start running a crude spectral analysis across the entire electromagnetic spectrum and see what frequencies are affected."

"The color is so odd," Margaret said. "The flashes are a kind of bluish white, but the overall glow is yellowish. A lot lighter yellow than their normal color."

There was quiet anticipation in the room. Meanwhile, a middle-aged man sat silently on a table in the back. His light build and well-groomed hair blended nicely with his flight suit.

"Gerhardt," Margaret said. "What do you think about taking the shuttle up for a look around?"

Gerhardt Krauss was the flight engineer in charge of the shuttle and hovercraft. He and Margaret had flown the Mars mission together three times.

***

"If you mean, does that worry me?" Gerhardt spoke in a half-German accent. "No, it does not. We should be fine if the shuttle hull can handle the stress of getting out of this heavy atmosphere. Beyond that, it protects us from any radiation out there."

Margaret trusted Gerhardt's opinion. She was hopelessly ignorant of his job, and he never let her down. He was a quiet, reserved man who didn't boast about his abilities.

"Will, you just might get your wish after all," Margaret said.

"It's not a bad idea either," Gerhardt went on. "We need to get the shuttle up for a test flight and break it in, *ja*?"

He turned to Will, who took a deep breath.

"We can't afford to take one strike from that lightning," Gerhardt said. "So, we won't come within a hundred thousand kilometers of the rings or that volatile ice ball of yours. You can bring all the equipment you want, but I'll say where the ship goes, okay?"

"*Ja*," Will timidly replied.

***

Margaret was at the entrance to the sky bridge on level five of the Dead Hemisphere. She engaged the airlock control panel to the rumble of air pumps filling the sky bridge with breathable air.

"That's precious air we're pumping in," Margaret said. "Let's make good use of it. Once you return, I'll recover all of it for supplies. Be careful boarding the shuttle; we don't want to get any methane into the mix."

The panel flashed green, and the Gaians proceeded into a circular shaft, wearing environmental suits. Will pulled a trolley cart with reserve oxygen, food, and a portable terminal for up-linking to Shoemaker.

The triple-layered, clear-tempered glass separating them from the near-absolute zero world was a dead giveaway. They'd not seen the real Titan sky for months, and Gerhardt stopped halfway down the hundred-meter sky bridge.

"You people weren't joking," he said. "I've never seen it this bright before." About once a month he crossed the sky bridge with carts of maintenance equipment. But until now, the sky of this frozen world had never changed.

"You're right," Will said. "It is noticeably brighter. Look at the horizon. I've never seen that outcropping of ice before. Visibility must be doubled."

Margaret didn't bother to stop or take note; she was already at the secondary chamber engaging the air pumps.

"Now remember," she said. "When boarding or leaving the shuttle, check air quality in the secondary vessel. Leaks were designed to be trapped there first. We don't want methane in this shaft or the shuttle."

"That's just in case I get struck by lightning," Gerhardt joked.

The panel flashed green. The three men latched helmets and proceeded inside.

"Good luck," Margaret said and gave Will a reassuring nod.

Gerhardt opened the shuttle doors. Will rolled his supply cart into the shuttle and parked it near the exit door. The twenty-five-meter-long shuttle had plenty of storage compartments and a dozen seats, four in the front cabin with a partition wall separating the other eight. The clean white interior was almost devoid of navigational monitors and other electronic equipment.

Will ducked his head and stepped through the threshold to the cockpit where Gerhardt was busy at the pilot's station. He took a seat next to Gerhardt. Markham was already seated in the rear of the cockpit.

"This really is not hard to fly," Gerhardt said. "Want to see?"

Will nodded.

Gerhardt reached overhead and pressed a button marked *Heat Shield*. "I don't know why we need this thing; I never use it."

A segmented metallic shield covering three sides of the cockpit began winding to one side in a coiling motion. As it crossed the front window, the hangar doors opened in front of them. An eerie cold rushed inward that caused the shuttle's hull to creak and pop as it adjusted to the new temperature.

"You start the computer on routine status checks of the hydraulics, fuel supply, and standard system functions," Gerhardt said, then went to the shuttle's rear. "Disengage the docking tube."

He pulled a lever next to the exit door. A red light flashed, the secondary chamber collapsed like an accordion, then the light turned green.

Gerhardt reseated himself in the pilot's chair and strapped in. "Are you both fastened in?" he asked. "Good. Now it's thrusters and ramjet until we get out of the atmosphere."

"Then what?" Richard asked.

"Then the modified ion propulsion kicks in," Gerhardt replied.

"Just like that?" Richard snapped his fingers.

"Huh, *ja*." Gerhardt chuckled.

Gerhardt taxied the shuttle out of the hangar and initiated vertical thrust. The high-pitched sound of engines whined, lifting the shuttle craft a few meters in the air. The metal alloy hull hummed and vibrated as thrusters rotated to a forward position and accelerated the ship. Within minutes, the shuttle reached an altitude of three hundred kilometers and cleared the misty aerosol layer and cloud tops. The sky was incredibly bright. Will looked for a glimpse of Saturn.

"Now the fun begins," Gerhardt said, throwing a damper on Will's moment of anticipation. "We need to engage the ramjet to catapult to escape velocity." He reached up and pushed the heat shield button again.

"I thought you didn't use that thing." Will gasped.

Behind them, Markham sat eyes closed, teeth clenched, gripping the arms of his chair.

"I was just teasing." Gerhardt chuckled. "You can get out of the hangar blindfolded, but up here is a different story."

As an astronaut he had as many piloting hours in space as anyone alive. Even on the journey from Earth he had been the only crewmember awakened by Sys, many times, enroute to Titan. All told, he'd logged an additional four months to his ledger with flight corrections, routine engine checks, life support monitoring, and orbital approach.

Gerhardt felt like the hard part was over when they finally reached Gaia 3 and was relieved to see the station and hangar perfectly deployed and operational. Once he'd located and loaded all supply drop modules into the Dead Hemisphere, it seemed like his job was done.

But ongoing recon missions through the orange haze and absolute zero atmosphere were the most spectacular and exciting things he'd ever done.

He never wanted to leave.

The cockpit darkened except for the light of the navigational screen in front of Gerhardt. The onboard computer signaled ready, and the screen flashed *Ramjet Functional*. A red bar appeared in the middle of the screen. One end read *0%*, and the other read *100% - Engage*. The counter moved to *50%* in just a few seconds. Will leaned back and closed his eyes.

***

"Will! Will! Up here," Libby shouted, waving from a cave on the side of the concrete mountain. "I need your help."

"Okay, I'm coming," he replied, stepping out of the elevator. He struggled to walk through the sand, his feet as heavy as lead. He was so tired he could hardly keep his eyes open. It seemed to take forever to reach the foot of the mountain. Seconds later, as if he'd imagined it, he was up in the cave with her.

"Oh great, another monkey chase, right?" Will sarcastically commented.

"It's over here," Libby anxiously said, pointing to a pile of debris in the corner. "The primates haven't been using this cave for a while, or so I thought. See, all these leaves and branches were packed tightly into the corner. I managed to pull most of them out, but the farther I got, the more mud and manure I found. So, I thought I'd get you to help dig."

"Wonderful," Will said. "So, what do you expect to find buried back there?"

"I have no idea," she said. "Maybe nothing."

Will didn't say a word and started digging. The matted leaves and manure formed a hard, dry shell, but underneath, the mixture seemed sloppier as they searched. Before long, Will scooped the mess through his legs, digging away like a dog. Until they finally reached hard concrete.

"God, it stinks in here." He gasped.

"I know," she said. "Great, isn't it?"

Biologist or not, Will was done with this little chore and backed away. Libby moved closer and scraped away at the concrete surface to see where the cave had led.

"You'd better come to take a look at this," she said. She'd uncovered a stone slab propped up against the cave's back wall. The rough face of the stone was covered with red paint or blood. Saturn was drawn in the middle, with wavy lines shooting in all directions. The wavy lines all had heads with rings through their noses. Will had seen this image before.

"What is this doing here?" he asked. "And why did they cover it up?"

"Primates would only have buried it if they were afraid of it," she said.

"Afraid of it?" he asked. "Didn't they paint it?"

"Are you kidding?" she replied. "Of course, they didn't paint it."

She reached around the corners of the stone, pushing at the manure around it. Clumps fell away behind the stone and disappeared.

"Hey, it looks like there's an opening behind here," she said. "They must have pushed this stone up to cover it."

"I'll give you a hand," he said and leaned in to grab the edge of the stone.

With one great tug, they dislodged the stone. It slurped open with a grotesque suction noise as wet manure and urine were dislodged. Libby screamed and covered her eyes. Will tucked her head against his shoulder. There lay Jeff Kirby, his rotted face fixed in a rigor pose as if it were still pressed against the stone. His bloody, red and swollen eyes bulged from their sockets, and the pupils were dark as night, completely dilated.

It was one of those dreams that, sleeping lightly enough, you can wake yourself from. But try as he might, Will just sat there scared to death. He couldn't move. Just then, Gerhardt nudged him on the shoulder.

***

Most Gaians had broken for the day after completing their daily chores. The dining area and rec hall were filled with hungry stomachs and headaches. Systems command and testing labs were empty; only the lights of the active electronics cast shadows.

Margaret contemplated the day's events from her chair in the admin office, where a half-full cup of coffee had lost its steam an hour ago. The wall behind her was covered with diplomas, degrees, and photos of her achievements. She took a deep breath and called up the System Operator.

"Sys, please accept Voice Authorization Code—priority one, Vandolah, Margaret A., Administrator, Titan Base, seventeen May 2092," she said.

"Processing… Complete."

"Please transmit the following information to the World Space Council:

Item one - Image data file, Ring test.

Item two - Message regarding the same: Shuttle carrying three personnel to investigate ring phenomenon from high Saturn orbit. The closest approach to the ring plane or object is 100,000 kilometers.

Item three - Crew members are showing the first signs of fatigue from oxygen deprivation. We must initiate complete O2 supplements to compensate. The staff physician recommends a minimum three-day trial period.

End transmission."

"Acknowledged, accessing information," Sys said. "Transmitting message."

Margaret walked through the room. Even *she* was getting exhausted. The start-up phase had been extended to six months, which was enough time, plus a buffer zone. Four months into their extension, the main problem was getting worse. The one-year start-up schedules were complete except for the most critical item—balancing the oxygen level.

When Margaret requested the extension, she had been out of answers and excuses. The Space Council took the news well and granted the extension as if it were expected. But the anxiety leading up to that request was nothing compared to this. Now her judgment would be questioned, tempers would flare, and the project's credibility would be on the line.

Her worst nightmare was turning into reality. She'd have to send for supply ships if nothing was resolved in thirty days. Her self-sustaining world would have to be stocked regularly with new oxygen.

"Sys," she said, pacing. "Have you completed transmitting the message? Acknowledgment statements are usually immediate."

"Local interference is disrupting the signal," Sys replied.

"Excuse me?" Margaret asked. "Sys, have you tried accessing Shoemaker to compare signals?"

"Shoemaker signal clear, online, and functioning," Sys replied.

"Can we change frequency to match?"

"Interference is not atmospheric," Sys said. "Transmission complete."

"Sys, please explain the problem?" she asked.

"Electrical interference from the main planet is scrambling the signal," Sys said. "Signal boosted sixty percent to compensate. Would you like to transmit additional messages?"

"No, thank you, not at this time," Margaret answered.

***

"Hey, we made it," Gerhardt said, shaking Will's shoulder.

Will came around, startled, confused, and wiping the cold sweat from his brow. Markham did the same.

"Jesus, what a dream," Will whispered, taking note of the fiery rings before him.

"Don't worry, they're almost a million kilometers away," Gerhardt said.

The gas giant and its fiery rings snapped and crackled in the dark void. The dark Cassini Division was more prominent than ever as the two leading bands danced in a vibrant glow. The massive planet in the middle seemed insignificant as a lightning storm blasted away on its perimeter.

The incredible spectacle in the distance was more than he'd prepared himself for. Despite his drowsiness, Will tried to gain control by turning his attention to flight control. "How are you tracking distance?" he asked.

"Radar," Gerhardt replied, pointing to a circular screen.

"And velocity?" Will asked.

"Fourteen thousand meters per second," Gerhardt said, pointing to another gauge. "But we must improve that by another eight thousand to reach your rendezvous point. We have nearly two million kilometers to cover in the next sixteen hours. That's why I had you cart food and water on board. This is basically a two-day flight. The good thing is we'll be breathing high-quality air for the first time in months. No bad dreams, *ja*?"

"But at that velocity, we'll blow past the comet," Will said. "It'll be cruising at about thirteen thousand meters per second."

Will checked the Shoemaker uplink terminal, and it looked fine.

"Wait a minute," Markham cut in. "Are we actually going to be in here forty-eight hours?"

"No, closer to thirty-two," Gerhardt responded. "If that rendezvous point is accurate, it's about sixteen hours each way."

"And no playing around either. We approach, pass, and return home. We'll blow past it all right, but you'll see enough of it.

"Understood," Will said.

***

The shuttle navigated across the ring system in an arching path over the planet. Gerhardt set the helm to autopilot and instructed Will on flight operations: lift-off, boost, and maneuvering in space with the onboard simulator.

The storm raged on, and electrical equipment on board began to feel the effects. Gerhardt dispatched a message of their safe ascent before waking Will and Markham, but communication with the parent base was lost shortly after. The orbiting Shoemaker was still accessible, and Will managed a communication link.

***

"Keep that kind of thought out of your mind," Gerhardt said. "We need to focus on the mission, *ja*?"

"I'm trying to," Will replied. "I just hope she knows we're all right."

Having Margaret in his immediate thoughts was something Will had not experienced for a long time, and it felt good.

"Your mother doesn't worry about things she can't control," Gerhardt continued. "She knows we made a safe ascent. She also knows the most dangerous parts are take-off and landing. I'll bet she's waiting in the sky bridge fifteen minutes before our arrival and not a minute sooner."

"This is going to be difficult without Sys," Will said. "I can't remember all the command codes to request information."

"Don't worry, you have plenty of time," Gerhardt said. "I have your comet on radar. We should rendezvous in three hours and thirteen minutes."

Markham unstrapped and knelt between the two.

"We're not going to rendezvous, right?" he asked. "You said something about one hundred thousand kilometers."

"I think we can get a little closer than that," Gerhardt responded. "I've been monitoring the storm, and nothing has projected more than twenty-thousand kilometers. So, I've adjusted our telemetry a bit. We'll approach at fifty thousand kilos. Does that work for the comet?"

"Excuse me?" Will asked.

"I'm planning to approach at fifty-thousand kilos from the rings," Gerhardt said.

"The closer, the better, as far as I'm concerned."

"What about the comet?" Markham asked. "Aren't we worried about these surface explosions?"

"Probes are sent through comet tails all the time," Will said. "It's basically dust—don't worry about it."

"Dust traveling at about twenty-thousand meters per second," Markham followed.

"Richard, we're staying clear of that, too," Gerhardt interrupted. "You see?" He pointed to a graphical display of their flight path with respect to the comet. The image was sophisticated but was still the product of radar imaging. Background distortion was present from the ring disturbance while the planet and rings were shown in full color.

"The large, arcing yellow line is the comet's path," he continued. "The blue line with the smaller oval shape is the shuttle. You can see by the scale that our path is clear of the rings and the comet."

"So, this is to scale?"

"Yes."

"That thing is big, all right," Markham said, studying the circular screen.

"Second largest moon around Saturn right now," Gerhardt said. "What do you estimate its velocity at ring passage?"

"I've been studying this thing so long," Will responded. "Like I said, just over thirteen thousand meters per second."

"That's pretty close to the value from radar tracking," Gerhardt said. "We'll be in its vicinity for about twenty minutes while it crosses the ring plane. At a distance of fifty K, we should get a good look at it. So, if you want to set up your portable telescope and camera, we'll be in position in about two hours."

"Good," Will said, checking the time. "That still gives me time to get Shoemaker set up to analyze the ring disturbance. It's the only piece of equipment we have that can."

"Gerhardt, what is that dot?" Markham pointed to a small, off-color mark on the screen. "There, near the edge of the ring, just past the yellow line."

"It's difficult to say with all the distortion," Gerhardt said, adjusting image controls. "But it's too large to be a part of the rings. What do you think this is?"

"Give me a minute," Will replied, keying in commands. "I've just about got Shoemaker started in the right direction.

SCAN ELECT SPECT WAVLGTH
2 CENTIMETERS TO 1 ANGSTROM
Enable

"There, that should do it."

He turreted his chair to face the circular radar screen. Markham and Gerhardt's untrained eyes saw something unusual they couldn't identify. Will's was a different response that leaped from his subconscious like it was hiding there, just waiting to pounce.

"Damn," he whispered. "I didn't think to check the orbits of the other moons, but it should have shown up somewhere."

"What should have shown up somewhere?"

"Mimas."

***

Libby marked her book and made her way out of the rec hall. She noticed a footlight reach across the hallway from under an office door. The door was ajar, so she peeked in.

She saw Margaret across the room; her inanimate gaze did not notice Libby's entrance. Her unmoving eyes locked in place in the direction of a blank wall. Libby was hesitant to cross their path but wanted to talk.

"Hey, are you okay?" Libby asked.

No response, but Margaret's eyes moved a bit, and a relaxed expression came over her face. She felt more at ease and slowly crossed the room.

"Do you mind if I sit down?"

"No, go right ahead." She gestured.

Libby seated herself at the oversized desk across from Margaret. "Is there anything you'd like to talk about?" she asked.

"You know, when there's one big problem in your life, it kind of overshadows everything else," Margaret said. "Until it becomes nearly impossible to deal with even the simple things."

"Well, I know the big problem," she said. "So, what's the simple thing?"

"What?" Margaret was silent for a moment. "I've lost contact with the shuttle. I don't think it's anything to be alarmed about, but no communication."

"Nothing to be alarmed about?" she said. "Your son is up there!"

"With one of the best pilots alive," Margaret added. "I've been going over this in my head, and there is no reason to panic. But we might not hear from them for two more days."

"I don't understand."

Margaret took a deep breath. "Gerhardt signaled that they had achieved orbit safely. Which is, by far, the most dangerous part of space flight. Their signal was lost after that, but the ring disturbance is probably the cause. I had trouble sending a message to Earth because of it."

"Has the Space Council figured out what's going on out here?" Libby asked.

"I don't think so," Margaret said. "Even if they do, we might not find out for a while. If this electrical interference gets any worse, we'll be cut off from them indefinitely. Besides, I'm not sure I want to hear from them for a while. I sent up the shuttle without their approval." Margaret chuckled. "I would just as soon get the shuttle safely home before that call."

"So, you think Will is all right?" Libby asked.

"There are three people on board, you know." Margaret raised an eyebrow.

"I'm just thinking of you."

"I know, but I sent all of them up there, and I feel responsible for their safety," Margaret said. "For now, all I can do is wait twenty-six hours for their return. In the meantime, we need to continue working on the O2 situation."

"Margaret, you've let up a bit on the supplement issue," she said. "Don't you think it's a good idea to let up on research, too? I mean, this thing is driving everyone crazy. I'm letting a lot of other things slide, and I think it would be therapeutic to give it a rest for a few days."

"I can't let up, or the future of this whole goddamn base could be in jeopardy," Margaret burst out. "This problem won't just disappear. We are on a critical path ending in two months. If you need time off, go ahead, but we'll stick with this thing until it's finished."

"Margaret." She jumped to her feet. "Don't be condescending with me. I can hold my own. I'm just giving you a piece of friendly advice. And here's another one—get some sleep, you look awful."

Libby stormed out of the room. Margaret leaned back, stared at the ceiling, then walked to the couch and lay down.

***

"Open the goddamn door!" Markham shouted.

Will and Gerhardt were humped over, gasping for air, their flesh turning a pale shade of blue. The shuttle's oxygen reserves were depleted, and the resources of their environmental suits were exhausted. They were disoriented but managed a shaky landing in the hangar bay.

"The secondary chamber was damaged when we landed." Markham peered through the double-glass porthole. "The outer shell is ruptured and leaking. Can you engage the air pumps?"

"I'm trying, but the override won't allow fresh air to be pumped into a contaminated zone!" Margaret frantically entered every option she could think of on the control panel. A smokey discoloration filled the chamber and muffled the gasping sounds of death on the other side. She looked back at the thermometer. It read -175 degrees Celsius.

"The temperature gauge is dropping off the scale. Get back into the shuttle! Get to your E-suits!"

There was no response. Margaret looked through the porthole. Three men lay on the floor with their hands clutched to their throats. No one moved, and their skin appeared crystalline. They were rock hard and brittle.

"Will!"

The word had hardly left her mouth when she went limp and collapsed at the foot of the airlock door. Avery ran down the sky bridge toward her.

"Margaret!" he shouted. "Where are they? Open that door!"

"I tried, but it's jammed," she cried.

Avery turned and saw the frozen bodies through the porthole. Margaret was flat on the floor; she tried but couldn't move a muscle.

"Well, I guess we'll just have to throw these three into the cryonics lab," Avery said. "That is if I don't break off their arms and legs dragging them there. "

"What?"

Avery leaned over and put a hand to her cheek. "My dear, you look pale."

"I feel so weak," she whispered. Chills came over her, and she started sweating. "This is sucking the life out of me."

"That's all right," Avery said. "I'll take care of it. Roll up your sleeve please." He grabbed her forearm and felt for a vein. "This won't hurt a bit."

"What are you doing?"

"Sucking the life out of you, of course," he said. "Isn't that what you want?"

Despite all her efforts, Margaret couldn't manage the energy to move. She couldn't even talk and just lay helpless.

Avery stuck a syringe into her limp, outstretched forearm, taped it down, and pulled the plunger from the end. Margaret watched her blood spurt out in waves with each beat of her heart until her field of vision faded to black, and the beating finally stopped.

She woke up startled and confused; everything had seemed so real. Then she swung her feet to the floor and buried her face in her hands.

"What's happening to me?" she sobbed.

***

"What's Mimas?" Markham inquired.

"A moon," Gerhardt sarcastically replied.

"This should have shown up before," Will said. "I doubt whether it's a problem. But I should have referenced the orbits of the other moons a long time ago."

"But their paths don't cross. They aren't going to collide," Markham said, pointing to the monitor. "So why be concerned?"

"I don't know," Will replied. "Just a feeling, I suppose. Mimas is a tiny moon. The screen shows their closest approach is a few thousand kilometers, right, Gerhardt?"

"Let's see," he replied, punching away at the controls. "Three thousand four hundred, plus or minus."

"I guess we'll just keep an eye on it," Will said. "It's probably nothing."

He turned back to his computer, where information was already transmitting from the orbiting observatory. The readouts were as expected in the upper range, but some peculiarities appeared at lower wavelengths.

"Damn," he grunted. "This is turning out to be an unusual trip, one surprise after another." He sat silent, manipulating the data.

Gerhardt and Markham were understandably attentive, waiting for the punchline.

"Saturn normally emits radio waves in the microwave range," Will said. "That's why we started out at two centimeters. The false color image of the planet and the rings read the same as normal at that wavelength. The strange thing is the lower range. An odd wavelength bordering ultraviolet, and x-ray is pouring out of the rings, but the planet is black."

"Black?" Gerhardt asked.

"The false-color images show the intensity of the electromagnetic radiation." Will pointed to the view screen. "Orange is the strongest, blue is moderate, and black is nothing. See here, at two centimeters, the planet is orange, and the rings are blue, meaning they both emit low-level radio waves. But now we are only getting lower-level waves—in the ultraviolet range—from the rings."

"Do you know what's causing it?" Gerhardt asked.

"Only thing I could say is that it has something to do with the lightning," Will responded. "Maybe I should instruct Shoemaker to start mapping the storm's intensity."

"You could have it plot density and brightness to see if there are any concentrations or if it's uniform," Markham said. "Maybe there's a correlation between the properties of the lightning and the radiation."

"Hopefully, this won't take long." Will turned and punched away at the keyboard. "I need to set up the onboard telescope, or I'll miss the comet."

The shuttle continued its picture-perfect run toward the comet. Meanwhile, the ring system changed its complexion hourly. The sea of tumbling ice became a glowing, donut-shaped ring. As if a fusion reaction were taking place, creating a ring-shaped star. The luminosity grew so intense that Gerhardt closed the heat shield covers. But Will was determined to get some visual shots of the incoming comet. So, he talked Gerhardt into rotating the shuttle to face away from the ring and leave the shields open. While Gerhardt adjusted their position, he aligned his telescope for the rendezvous shots.

The shuttle maneuvered into a chase position at better than twenty-two thousand meters per second and closed fast on the lumbering giant with less than ninety minutes to their closest approach.

Will hadn't tracked the comet since the frequent outburst sequences and was anxious to see it first-hand. But when Gerhardt opened the shields, Will couldn't believe his eyes. The comet had developed an atmosphere. Instead of a rocky surface, the comet was shrouded in haze.

"Oh, my god," he whispered while Markham and Gerhardt stared in amazement.

They gazed in awe at the primordial ball of ice and its puffy appearance. The atmosphere surrounded the comet but had some open patches where the surface was still visible.

Will had never seen such a world of scattered ice and inlaid rock. A canyon stretched the length of the visible surface, probably the primary source of the outgassing.

"Unbelievable," he said. "I can't think of the words to describe this thing, but it's definitely planetoid-sized."

He turned to the terminal, and a large flash lit up the cockpit.

"What in the hell was that?" Gerhardt asked.

Will paused, then moved over to the radar tracking screen. "That's too bright for a lightning bolt," he said. Then he saw it, a blur in the middle of the screen.

"Where did that cloud come from?" Gerhardt looked over Will's shoulder.

"Oh no!" Will shouted.

"What?" Markham gasped.

"Oh no!" he repeated, shuffling through telemetry read-outs. "Gerhardt!

Quickly, punch up our flight path!"

"What are you—"

"Just do it!"

The same yellow and blue lines came up as before but were farther along their paths. Their closest approach was set to be fifty thousand kilometers, and they weren't far from it. But in between them, at Mimas' position, was a cloud.

"I'm afraid something's happened," Will said. "We have to readjust our position or abandon the mission."

"Wait a minute," Gerhardt said, pointing to the two lines on the screen. "We've set ourselves out this far to avoid outbursts from your comet."

"This isn't an outburst from the comet," Will said. "I think the moon was just torn apart."

The seventh moon from Saturn, Mimas, was less than four hundred kilometers across. Its distinguishing feature was a large crater nearly one-third of the moon's diameter. The ancient eyeball impact crater was so large that it probably cracked the moon's core and weakened its resistance to tidal forces. Saturn constantly pulled at Mimas, but the comet's passing was the straw that broke the camel's back.

"The moon," Markham interjected. "Mimas?"

"Yes, Mimas," Will replied. "The problem is that it's a rocky object. That cloud you see on the radar screen is a mass of rocks that could be hundreds of kilometers across."

"Oh shit," Gerhardt said.

"*Ja*, oh shit," Will concurred. "And that cloud is getting bigger as we speak. But unlike the comet, we know little about its explosion characteristics."

"But how did that happen?" Markham asked. "The comet didn't hit it."

"No," Will said. "But it came close enough that tidal effects from gravity were too much for it. That planetoid has ten or twelve times the mass of Mimas."

"And?" Markham asked.

"So, it tore Mimas apart," Will explained. "Gerhardt, I think you should get us out of here. We should alter the flight path and make some radical course changes, or we could fly through the shrapnel of that explosion in the next thirty minutes."

"We don't have the fuel to push our orbit farther from the planet," Gerhardt responded. "But we could adjust pitch and yaw rates to veer away from the explosion. Suddenly, the lightning doesn't bother me as much; an electrical surge shuts down some of our systems."

Gerhardt disengaged the autopilot and adjusted attitude control. The brightness of the rings required the heat shield covers to be shut during their closest approach. The blast radius expanded rapidly, but the tiny craft managed to stay ahead of the ever-growing cloud on the radar monitor. The once confident Gerhardt was growing concerned over the progress of the mission.

The shuttle moved in close to the braided F ring. The strand ring followed two small moons like waves behind a speed boat. At twenty thousand kilometers away, the rope-like shape of the rocky ring showed well on radar. Radar also indicated the rings were more than five-hundred kilometers thick, compared to their normal one-kilometer range.

"This doesn't make any sense," Will shook his head.

"What now?" Markham gasped. "I'm really getting tired of all this strange crap. What? What doesn't make any sense?"

"The ring's thickness," he replied.

"Will you two quit bickering?" Gerhardt interrupted. His voice was sharp and accented, and his linguistic guard dropped as he focused on the task.

That got their attention, the man didn't panic, but this was pushing him.

"The only thing I care about on that screen is how close we are to those electrical discharges," Gerhardt said. "Whether it makes sense or not, the storm is getting worse, and we are getting closer to it."

A few minutes later, the vessel took a small lightning shot. They lost communication, but navigation, hydraulics, and life support remained intact. Gerhardt shut down all unnecessary systems and lighting to conserve resources. Within an hour, they'd drifted silently away from the raging storm. The nervous crew sat in darkness, patiently watching the flight clock display the time remaining on the mission. They couldn't wait for the autopilot to kick in and initiate a landing sequence, but that was fourteen hours away.

Chapter 8
A PERTURBING SITUATION

An orange vapor cloud engulfed the sky bridge and the connecting hangar. Loose surface material swirled in a frigid dust cloud while Margaret waited at the airlock door. Robert and Libby joined her, all impatiently awaiting the shuttle's arrival. Her unwavering trust in Gerhardt's piloting ability was shaken but hearing the thruster's blast restored her faith. Bad dreams aside, she was relieved to see the shuttle safely inside the hangar bay.

Margaret watched with anticipation through the porthole. She saw nothing but a frosty surface where the shuttle window should be. But the shuttle's surface was frosted from the temperature change as a breathable environment slowly pumped into the secondary chamber.

Moments later, the shuttle hatch rolled open. Gerhardt stepped through, waving and motioning for the others to follow.

"Gerhardt!" Margaret shouted. "Is everything all right?"

He motioned thumbs up, but the exhausted crew showed little signs of emotion. Will dragged his equipment off the shuttle and waited at the entry door. Libby leaned in beside Margaret to catch a glimpse. Will drew a quaint smile as the control panel signaled green and the airlock door opened.

He hardly made it over the threshold, and Libby bear-hugged him. "Thank god, you made it!" she cried, holding back tears.

Will was caught off guard like his kid sister welcomed him home from college. Margaret cut in, since Libby beat her to the punch. She hugged her son warmly, and Will hugged her back.

Margaret continued her technical discussion with Gerhardt on events of the mission. They proceeded up the sky bridge toward Gaia.

Robert reached to Will's face and placed a thumb under his eye. He held his head medically and shined a light into Will's eye. "You're okay, for now," he said, then turned and followed the others.

"For now?" Will said. "What's that supposed to mean?"

"That means he's also glad to see you," Libby said. "He's been spooking about low O2 issues lately."

"What about the condition of the crew?" he asked.

"Even though O2 levels have been normal for two days," Libby said, "the signs of fatigue haven't let up."

The excitement of returning safely and planting his feet on Gaia absorbed Will. He'd waited hours to tell his mother about Mimas and the UV emissions, but it slipped his mind with the unexpected hugs. Then he heard *Mimas* echo down the corridor. Markham gestured wildly, and Will could swear he heard the word *kafluwie*.

Margaret gave an expression of disbelief and turned to Gerhardt. Will started up the sky bridge with his supply cart but stopped short.

"Look at our feet, Libby," he said. "We're casting shadows."

The bright overcast Titan sky shone through the glass walkway. His comment caught Margaret's attention, who joined them at mid-span of the sky bridge. Beams of light cut through the cloud tops to the ground near the horizon. No one said a word, taking in the strange new appearance of the cold world they called home.

Will was emotionally depleted from the long flight, but a new energy built up inside him. This phenomenon had some relationship to other recent problems. Maybe it was paranoid speculation, but the ring phenomenon was a real threat, and there were no answers.

The excitement of their safe return was lost in those dark shadows at their feet.

Margaret's high spirits torpedoed. "Will, I'd like you to start an analysis of the rings," she said. "Just as soon as you get cleaned up and get a bite to eat."

***

"Now pay attention, everyone," Will said.

He pointed toward the moat near the foot of the terraces. He'd talked Margaret into holding their weekly progress meeting in the Living Hemisphere. If nothing else, it was a good change of pace. The team assembled on the desert plateau for a unique demonstration.

"Three, two, one, and... *thump*!"

The pump system started an underwater wave that proceeded slowly around the moat. The wave picked up momentum as it moved and left a sea of oscillating ripples in its wake. Mud swirled away from the banks in a current of eddies that followed the wave, clouding the water. Every quarter hour, another slow-moving wave circumnavigated the perimeter to prevent stagnation.

"Margaret," Avery said. "If this is the best we can come up with, then you'd better have Gerhardt fire up the shuttle and fly us the hell out of here."

She didn't acknowledge the statement. Will seemed confused by their lack of reaction and waited for another response.

"I have a better idea," Markham said. "Why don't *you* get on the shuttle, and we'll stay here."

"This is an interesting correlation," Margaret said. "Movement in the moat is similar to movement in the rings, right?"

"I noticed it earlier today while eating lunch," Will said. "Pay attention to the wave as it passes a certain point and watch what's left in its wake. The big wave surges along, and it causes a series of smaller ones. If we had more delicate instruments to study this, we would see the wave go around, hit the other end, and bounce back, creating more tiny waves as it goes. It's almost endless motion. If you removed friction and gravity, it would go on forever. Shoemaker found from its analysis that two sources caused waves to oscillate throughout the rings. Similar to the water in the moat."

"Okay, so if I picture wind blowing across a sea of water with waves running about," Margaret said, "then I can start to grasp the concept of what's happening out there?"

"That's right, and the model you'll see doesn't go into much detail either," Will said. "The dynamics of this phenomenon will probably be studied for the next hundred years. We're just trying to grasp the basics."

Will directed Sys to show the model on the sky above. A false color animation was displayed in time-lapsed motion with comet 2092312 highlighted on a simulated path. The comet was labeled *Rogue planetoid*. There was no longer any doubt about what caused the problem in the rings. The great ball of ice that invaded the system triggered an explosion of fire and ice. Its passing brought two changes to the rings. Whether the effects would correct themselves was not known. The first effect was extraordinary, and the second was unbelievable. Only a time-lapse simulation could bring the scope of the disaster into perspective.

"It's first noticed when the rogue is about one month away," he said.

"Rogue planetoid?" Margaret inquired.

"The comet," he replied. "It's too big to be called a comet. The simulation shows it has caused all the problems. So, it's nothing more than a virus in this scenario."

"The object's mass is so great that it causes a spiral density wave to form. Instead of a flat ring system, we get a warped and wavy shape. The passing planetoid acts like a magnet. It attracts small particles of the ring, causing an upward heave, then as it passes below the ring plane, it pulls downward at them. The initial swells then interfere with one another and dissipate to smaller waves."

"Sys has shown that this is actually happening?" Margaret asked.

"Oh, yes," Will replied. "This perturbing effect has been measured before in the rings but not at this scale, so the concept is something Sys can analyze. It's the other effect we're having trouble modeling."

"You mean the moon's destruction?" Margaret asked.

"No," he replied. "That's easy when you consider the relative masses of the two objects and Mimas' internal structure. But when Mimas was destroyed, its gravity well went with it. Look here. Mimas is located at a two-to-one orbital distance from Saturn with respect to the Cassini Gap. That wide gap you see in the middle of the rings was made by Mimas' gravitational presence. Now that Mimas is gone, the Cassini Gap is closing with a bang."

"So, in one direction, we have the waves, and in the other direction, we have the particles of the ring pushing together. The net perturbation is like none ever seen before."

"And the result of all this chaotic movement is friction," Avery chimed in. "Which gives rise to electrostatic energy and the lightning."

"Initially, yes, but now it's more than that," Will said. "The amount of light can't be explained by the lightning alone, and Sys doesn't have an explanation for it either. Ring material is mostly ice, but some fragments are primordial rocks, and other heavy elements are covered with ice. I think all this interaction exposes their hidden identities. Besides bright visible light, there is also an unusual level of ultraviolet radiation blasting out into space."

"A paper published a few years ago discussed the concept of ring mining," Markham interjected. "It disputed the traditional theories of material in the rings. Based on a random sampling of actual pieces, they found an abundance of elements not just water ice. The paper estimated there's enough raw iron in the ring system to supply Earth's demands for centuries."

"Oh, there's a narrow vision," Avery said. "Rape another world's resources in the name of technology."

"Hey, I didn't say I agreed with it."

"You didn't have to," Avery replied. "It's that engineering thing in you. I could see the sparkle in your eyes."

"Anyway, it laid out a pretty detailed plan on harvesting the material in sectors laid out radially around the circumference of the ring," Markham continued. "Enormous harvesters would float along, scoop up debris, process it, and eject the unused material."

"Any material that might be volatile?" Margaret inquired. "We need to know what type of chemical reaction can emanate harmful radiation."

"I don't recall," Markham said. "They only discussed fundamental metals and ices."

"People, this is all a fascinating discussion." Avery sighed. "It really is. And I'm sure it has captured the imagination of the people on Earth, too, but don't you think they should study it? We have a little problem that needs more immediate attention."

"I agree with you, John," Margaret said. "But I can't overlook this phenomenon without everyone's input first. I need to know if this poses a threat to our safety."

"More of a threat than losing oxygen?" Avery asked.

"That's not what I said," Margaret said. "But now that Mimas has exploded, there could be, for instance, meteor showers, or worse, fallout. If we conclude there's no life-threatening issue, we focus again on the O2 issue."

"So," Margaret redirected, "do you see any immediate danger from this situation?"

"If we examine the two issues separately," Will said, "I don't think we need to worry about the Mimas explosion. The debris seems to be hanging in the moon's original orbit. Some smaller pieces move inward and will probably intermix with the rings."

"Rocks as part of the rings?" Markham added. "Maybe that paper wasn't hocus-pocus after all."

"Could be," Will said. "But either way, the debris from Mimas won't get this far into the system. Saturn would suck them up first."

Gerhardt stepped forward after patiently listening. "As far as the radiation is concerned, we have one thing in our favor. From the atmospheric profiles of Titan, we know it has an extensive ozone filtering layer thicker than Earth's. But Earth is also shielded from the solar wind by its magnetism. This moon has no molten core, no magnetism, so that defense is not present."

"We're talking about two entirely different things here," Margaret said. "The sun puts out energy on a different scale of magnitude."

"Maybe, maybe not," Gerhardt said. "Compare our proximity to this energy source versus Earth's proximity to the sun."

"True."

"We need to study the profile of the wave emissions," Will said. "Titan is in the same plane as the rings, but the electromagnetic radiation blasts perpendicular to the ring plane. For instance, if you stand in front of a rocket launcher, the rocket hits you. Behind it, the exhaust hits you. But stand beside it, and nothing happens."

"Since we're not in its path, we get no effect?" Margaret asked.

"Not zero, but a hell of a lot less," Will added. "Earth will view it nearly straight on, but the radiation is dissipated at their distance."

"So, Gerhardt's ozone layer should be adequate shielding," Margaret said. "Do we all agree on that much?"

Avery's voice rose from a crowd of nodding, but apprehensive, crew. "I don't think we have much choice but to wait and see."

"We have sensors to pick any form of radiation," Robert said. "If that's all we're worried about, then medically, I'm not concerned. I can monitor it from command."

"Mother, I'm a little bit confused at this line of questioning," Will said. "Are we taking a vote on whether or not to leave Gaia?"

"No," she answered. "This situation is something I am not prepared to deal with, so I need your input to arrive at a solution."

"So, the Space Council hasn't given us an ultimatum?" he asked.

"That's the second thing we need to talk about today," Margaret replied. "I haven't been able to send or receive messages from Earth for a couple of days. Without instruction, this event isn't in any administrative manual."

"Wait a minute," Markham said. "We've lost contact with the Space Council?"

"Yes," Margaret said. "Does that surprise you?"

"I suppose not."

"What do you want them to do?" Margaret said. "Send the cavalry from a billion kilometers away? The most they could do is order us to abandon the base; that's why we're talking. Now, any questions so far?"

Will cleared his throat. "There is something else."

"Something I don't already know about?" Margaret asked.

Markham and Gerhardt exchanged glances.

Margaret crossed her arms.

"The planetoid has an atmosphere and a vertical tail now," Will said.

No response, but Margaret's look of dismay summed it all up.

"And Sys's initial spectral analysis," he continued, "shows it has the same chemical composition as the rings."

"The *vertical* tail?" she stumbled out.

"Right," he said. "Like most tails that move away from the solar wind, this one is affected by light—or something—emanating from the ring system."

"And there's a compounding effect. The planetoid's gravity excites the rings, and the resulting light and radiation sets off more eruptions on its surface."

Margaret looked over an assembly of distraught faces. The hush in the air and the sun setting in the backdrop were an eerie irony; they were running out of options.

Libby sat behind the rest of the crowd and watched the orange sun fall below the desert rock. The long shadow of the desert rock stretched across the plateau, almost to her feet. A light chill set in the air.

"Are you all right?" Margaret asked her with a calm, inquisitive tone.

"My father used to come home from work, sit on the porch, and watch the sun set," she said. "Almost every night, he'd sit and catch up on the daily news before doing anything else. I was little and didn't understand why he'd do that instead of riding a bike or playing in the yard. One day I asked, and he said it was the only way to clear his mind of the day's worries."

Margaret searched for something to say.

"You know," Libby said. "We should quit tossing this ring thing around and get back to work on the O2 problem."

Her attitude surprised Margaret: she thought Libby was about to break under pressure. Margaret took advantage.

"Good," she said. "Let's get back to work. I want everyone to catch up on where they left off and trace their steps closely. We'll meet tomorrow at nine AM in the conference room."

PART IV

Chapter 9
DILATION

John Early rolled and groaned, then awoke in a feverish sweat. He struggled to shade his face from the light, searching for the source of his pain. He tossed the bed sheets aside and swung his feet to an icy tile floor. As if near a hot fire, he couldn't face it and swatted blindly at the light. Finally, he grasped a metal lamp post and slammed it to the ground. Glass shattered as sparks popped and glided across a slick floor. It was gone. He breathed a deep sigh of relief and rolled back into the sweat-soaked bed.

Robert Lewis burst into the observation room. The opened door cast new light into the darkened room. Once again, Early groaned and rolled over to face the wall.

"Are you all right?" Robert asked.

"Turn off that damned light!" Early shouted. He threw a pillow at Robert, who ducked away and nearly tripped over the broken lamp.

Robert bent over the rails of the nursing bed and shone a pen-light on Early's face.

"Leave me alone!" he shouted. "I just want to get back to my room, so I can get some sleep."

"Not tonight. You're a sick man," Robert ordered. "Now roll over. I need to examine your eyes."

Early tried to compose himself. He clenched his teeth and slowly rolled over.

"Now, take a few deep breaths and relax," Robert said. "What in the hell happened to the lamp anyway?"

"Oh, I needed a glass of water," Early replied, turning away from the penlight.

"I'll send someone in here to clean this up and change the bed sheets," Robert said, drawing a glass of water from the sink. "You know the sink's over here, not on that side of the room. Why did you knock over that lamp?"

Early gulped down the water that ran down the side of his face. "I had an awful dream. Everything was so bright. When I woke up, it was blinding."

Robert returned to the desk where he was preparing a medical journal entry. Another in a series chronicling his investigation into the side effects of oxygen deprivation. The young technician had taken extremely ill recently and required observation. Early worked in the lower decks with Gerhardt. His primary duty was servicing electrical systems on the shuttles.

"Sys, recall the previous entry on patient John Early," Robert ordered.

"Processing… Complete.

"Journal entry - May 21, 2092:

"Patient- John Early. Complained of exhaustion and lack of sleep.

"Symptoms- Lack of REM level sleep, waking continuously through the night. High anxiety during waking hours and nightmares while sleeping. Pupils are slightly constricted and sensitive.

"*Recommendation:*

Tranquilize the condition with medication to promote sleep."

"Sys, please accept the new journal entry as follows:

"*Journal entry- May 23, 2092:*

"*Patient- John Early suffers from anxiety and is sensitive to bright light.*

"*Symptoms- Previous symptoms are ongoing but combined with additional problems. Recent irrational behavior with complaints of sensitivity to light. This photophobia is unusual; not found in other case histories of oxygen deprivation. Extreme dilation and photophobia are combined with unique physical characteristics. Exposed areas of the skin have a burned redness synonymous with radiation exposure.*

"*Recommendation:*

Tranquilizing medication was not successful. Eye problems could be a side effect of radiation exposure. Diagnosis incomplete.

The patient is to remain for further observation."

A frightened eavesdropper hid behind a cloth partition. Robert turned at the sound of footsteps and saw John Early scramble out of the med lab, wearing a hospital gown and a pillowcase over his head with cut eye slits. Robert made chase, but the barefoot man was quickly down the corridor.

Early ran like a mad dog with the cunning of a fox and slipped into a janitor's closet. Robert pulled at the jammed door, but Early was quickly down a maintenance ladder and into the Dead Hemisphere, where he disappeared into the dark maze of piping and catwalks.

Robert made his way back to the med lab. "Margaret," he called to her quarters. "Are you there? We have a problem in medical."

"Robert," a confused voice responded. "Is that you?"

"Yes, Margaret," he said, worried. "I'm sorry to wake you, but we need to talk."

"It's two AM. Can this wait a few hours?" she asked.

"I'm afraid not."

"That's all right." She sighed. "I wasn't sleeping anyway."

"I'll put some coffee on," Robert said. "See you in a bit."

***

Margaret pulled up a chair next to Robert. Her hair was crudely pulled back, revealing dark circles under her eyes. The good doctor skipped past her apparent aggravation and shone his pen light into her unmoving eyes. He pushed her shirt to either side near her breast, pressing a hand against her chest.

"I hope this is leading somewhere important because I'm really not in the mood," she said.

"Just checking eyes and skin tone." Robert jotted down a note and gathered his thoughts.

Margaret could tell wheels were turning in his head but had no idea what he was about to say.

"We have a serious problem," he said.

She laughed; she couldn't stop. She had to turn away to compose herself. "We have an unexplainable oxygen problem, a mysterious phenomenon in space that I can hardly describe. We've lost contact with Earth, and you called me down here at two o'clock in the morning to remind me that we have a serious problem?"

Robert didn't appreciate her mocking tone, and Margaret saw it in his straight face.

He was like a big brother to Margaret, and he was content with being that guy in the background. He was well prepared, studious, and excited to take on anything the outer belt living station could throw at him.

"I'm sorry, Robert, it's just that… I'm sorry. Go ahead."

"John Early just left the med lab," he said quietly. "I should say that he *escaped* from the med lab."

"What do you mean?"

"He has no shoes," Robert said. "He's dressed only in a medical gown with a pillowcase over his head. I chased him down the hall, but he got away and disappeared into the Dead Hemisphere."

"Well, we've got to find him." She reached for the intercom button.

"Wait, there's more," Robert said, placing a hand on hers before she could press the button. "Please."

Margaret relaxed back into her seat.

"I called you here at this hour to discuss this," Robert continued. "We need to brainstorm some ideas that I'm not comfortable discussing around the others. We'll send some people after Early in a few minutes, but first, we need to talk."

"Okay, you've got my attention," she said.

"The problems we're having are more than just a lack of oxygen," he said. "We're getting bombarded by low-level radiation that's affecting some crew members."

"Radiation!"

"Yes, but just hear me out," he said. "All right?"

"All right."

"It's not gamma radiation or anything as lethal as all that," he explained. "It's what Will mentioned today, an unusual frequency near the x-ray and ultraviolet range. It's the kind of radiation that causes skin or eye damage, and John Early's symptoms match it. It's as if he stared at the bright hot sun, naked for twenty minutes.

"We've got internal sensors tracking this wavelength. The exposure inside the Living Hemisphere is negligible; it's slightly higher and growing down here. But it's off the scale in the sky bridge and the hangar bay."

"And Early works out there," she commented.

"That's right, he's out in it," Robert responded. "But here, the levels aren't as high. We must be better shielded. The radiation frequency seems to penetrate glass pretty well, but it bounces off denser materials. The thing that concerns me is the levels are increasing everywhere.

"I should have seen it sooner, but his case progressed so quickly. When he came in the first time, his pupils were slightly constricted, as though he'd been out in the sun or near a bright light. That's why I checked everyone's eyes; it was just curiosity. Now, his pupils are dilated because photophobia has set in."

"I don't understand," Margaret said. "Why do the pupils go from small to large?"

"It's the classic symptom of iritis," Rob said. "You normally get it by looking at an arc weld or the sun too long. You don't even know it, but the UV radiation damages the eye, and it takes a few hours to set in. First, the pupils constrict because the bright light causes pain. Then the patient goes to dark places to ease the pain, and then the pupils dilate."

"Sounds like an easy thing to prevent," Margaret said. "Wear protective clothing and eyewear. What about the treatment?"

"For isolated cases," Robert smiled and spoke, "I can treat the iritis with parasympatholytic drugs. Then we can all walk around with sunglasses, which might handle the iritis issue. What concerns me is the two-fold issue: one, there are no cases on record of iritis and O2 deprivation, and both can lead to hallucinogenic behavior. And two, what if the radiation blasting out in space gets worse? Are we going to have to wear environmental suits?"

"I see your point," she said. "Can Sys help you separate the conditions and find the appropriate remedy? I need to buy some time against the radiation until we get the O2 situation under control. And I think we have a good chance of solving that in the next few days."

Robert just sighed.

"Robert, we can't fight anything if we lose our confidence," Margaret said. "I'll get Kirby and Miller to find Early tonight. In the morning, I'll issue a statement that requires proper dress in the sky bridge and hangar areas. Does that satisfy you for now? I'm in charge of operating this base successfully, but I won't go against your wishes if it jeopardizes people's lives."

Robert didn't seem convinced. "Let me play devil's advocate. This is a huge station. What if they can't find him?"

"Can't find him?"

"Yes, if he manages to hide away for a day or two, his condition will worsen," Robert said. "Cases of iritis can progress to a secondary form of glaucoma that leads to madness. If we can't locate him within twenty-four hours, he'll go blind."

"Okay, let *me* play devil's advocate." She sighed. "We're basically stuck here. Getting the entire crew into a safe orbit and on a flight path back to Earth will be extremely difficult. There aren't enough freezers on the shuttle, and it's a four-month journey. You get it. This base is not meant to be abandoned, so the worst-case scenario of packing and leaving isn't possible.

"If we start saying that radiation is a real threat, we'll create a panic. I'm not worried about a mutiny or anything serious, but this could get out of control. So, give this a couple of days. We'll issue the hangar area statement and locate Early."

Robert took another deep breath. "I suppose you're right. Maybe I'm jumping to conclusions."

"No, I don't think so," Margaret said. "And I'm glad you told me this in private."

"Do you want me to wake up Kirby and Miller?"

"No, I'll do it," she replied. "I doubt if I'll get back to sleep tonight."

"Margaret, don't avoid sleeping," Robert said. "Even if you have bad dreams."

"After that coffee of yours?" She scoffed. "I'll be up all week."

Chapter 10
SCREEN SAVER

"Please note the display will return to sunrise simulation in fifteen minutes," Sys stated.

Will was up before dawn to review the storm's status in the rings, their subsequent perturbation, and the Mimas explosion.

"Damn." He checked the time. "Sys, please playback the explosion event at twenty to one."

"Processing… Complete."

The sky went black for a second, then burst alive with fiery rings covering the entire hemisphere. The image moved rapidly, focusing on object 2092312 as it crossed the ring plane and pulled Mimas apart.

The image stopped where the explosive cloud was brightest, showing ejecta from Mimas colliding with the planetoid, confirming Will's curiosity. The film was shot from the onboard shuttle camera since Shoemaker was out of visual range. The images were salvageable even though the distortion was awful.

He noticed another oddity in the taped display. A stripe crossed the ring near its center, like a jet stream that ran the length of the screen. It was darker than the rest of the image, as if a stick were in front of a camera.

"Sys, please replay the explosion event," Will commanded. "Again, at twenty to one."

The sky went black, and the image proceeded again at high speed. This time he watched the center of the rings. It wasn't in the rings; it was the image itself. Fixed sections passed in and out of a dark stripe. It was strange. Was the film flawed?

"Sys, please discontinue the explosion event," Will said. "Access deep sky object library, Crab Nebula. Display fixed image at ninety degrees of screen width."

In seconds, the majestic blue cloud of the Crab Nebula with its inlaid red and white fingers displayed itself with the same dark stripe projecting through it. His curiosity grew.

"Please note the display will return to sunrise simulation in five minutes," Sys said.

"Sys, discontinue deep sky object. Access overlay files displaying fixed color over the entire hemisphere," Will commanded.

"Processing... Complete."

The sky turned bright pink, and then he saw it. A region lacking clarity faded with respect to the rest of the sky. A stripe extended from one horizon to another like a rainbow across the sky. Will carefully checked the balance of the view screen but saw no other problems. From the vantage point where he'd watched many a sunset, this was obvious. The stripe made an arcing motion across the sky and set almost precisely where the sunset was every night.

"Sys..." He nervously searched for the words. "Please plot the sun's course across the sky in standard daytime simulation."

"Processing... complete," Sys said.

The yellow line laid into the faded stripe like a hand in a glove. Will slumped back in his chair in deep thought. "What have we done?" he muttered in remorse.

Soon, the planetarium-like images faded, and the orange glow of sunrise crept up in the east.

"Wait a minute," he murmured. "Wait a minute. I have an idea."

Will packed his gear and raced down the terraces toward the elevator.

***

The nine AM conference room was a nervous quiet at best. The only sound was that of scratching heads. There were no new answers, at least from all those present. The news of John Early's disappearance spread quickly and smothered the light breeze of hope that Margaret had laid the night before. John Avery seemed more on edge than the rest of the group.

"I'm telling you this is just the beginning," he spoke. "John Early was exposed before the rest of us."

"John, I think you're jumping to conclusions," Markham interrupted. "There's not one effect yet that we can't explain."

"Excuse me," Avery said. "Have you bothered to check the weather outside lately? It's overcast but very bright, and as far as we know, that's never happened before and might never end. It doesn't matter to me if wonder boy can create a computer-generated model to describe portions of the problem. We haven't explained anything!

"And now we're told that communication with Earth is cut off. Has it occurred to anyone that maybe they're trying to contact us and tell us to get the hell out of here? After all, every Earth scientist must be observing the rings by now. And the World Space

Council has a lot more sophisticated sensing equipment and trained personnel to assess the situation. Maybe the UV radiation is just the tip of the iceberg—we could be exposed to lethal doses before it's all over. Has Mr. Vandolah figured out whether the perturbation has reached its chaotic peak yet? Is there any way to tell?"

Even Markham was without response to his favorite adversary. Robert's fingers strummed the tabletop as he took in the conversation.

"This discussion is getting us nowhere," he said. "And besides, we should wait until Margaret gets here to discuss anything."

"You examined Early," Avery said. "What exactly were his symptoms?"

The conference room doors opened, and Margaret crossed the room with a heated expression. "News travels fast, I see," she said.

Robert rolled his eyes and sighed even though he hadn't said a word about Early's disappearance.

"Not as fast as John Early, we're told." Avery nodded.

"I was going to save that 'till last," Margaret returned the cynical tone. "But since you're so interested, why don't we have Robert explain the situation." She gestured to Robert as she sorted through files.

"In a nutshell, I started to notice signs that were not symptomatic with oxygen deprivation," Robert said. "But more in line with low-level radiation exposure, and the sensor readings throughout the facility were good backup for that diagnosis."

"What kind of readings?" Avery asked.

"Negligible in the Living Hemisphere," Robert continued. "Only slightly higher in here, but in the hangar area, they were extreme. His skin was discolored, burnt sort of, and his pupils started out constricted but became dilated. Some forms of radiation exposure can lead to iritis and worse if not brought into check.

"Anyway, he overheard me entering that information into his medical file and bolted out of the med lab. I chased him down the corridor, but he crawled down a maintenance ladder and into the catwalks.

"There is a type of madness associated with extreme cases of iritis. So much pain develops in the eyes that vision is unbearable, so patients hide in dark places. Early smashed the lamp in his room right before I last examined him. He was irrational, talking about strange dreams, fighting back pain to have a short conversation."

"What's his condition now?"

"It's hard to say," Robert replied, checking the time. "He's been gone for seven hours now, and there's no telling if he's been exposed to more radiation. But the worst case is that he could lose sight if we can't find him."

"And the danger to us?" Avery asked.

"Almost nonexistent in here, for now," Robert replied. "I recommend we avoid the hangar areas unless E-suits are worn. Other than that, all we need to do is keep monitoring the sensors."

Avery almost started one of his egotistical orations but held his tongue. The others were too tired to talk about it, looking for something good to talk about.

"Any other comments?" Margaret asked, raising an eyebrow at Robert.

"Yes, just one," he replied. "Gerhardt, I want to see you and your men sometime today for an examination. Your job description exposes you to more radiation than the rest."

"Understood," Gerhardt said. "I'll gather them up later this morning."

"I spoke with Jim Miller right before this meeting," Margaret said. "He and Kirby have covered five levels since this morning with no luck. The problem is this place is so big, and the man is a moving target. I'll expand the search party to six people after we adjourn."

"Gerhardt." She pointed. "I'll need some of your people as soon as they're available. "As I've said, this situation is one we're completely unprepared for, and all we can do is make the best of it. I'm as concerned about this issue as anyone, but we must proceed as if we've seen the worst and get on with more immediate problems."

Will entered the meeting unannounced, with a kick to his step and full of energy that no one else seemed to have. Margaret gave him a blank look, not a dismissal. He took it as an invitation and seated himself.

"Last night, I requested everyone review their previous notes and summarize their findings," she said. "Richard, you're first. What have you got on O2 production and supplements to the Living?"

"We're down to twenty-two percent capacity in the tanks and pumping away at eight percent by volume," he responded. "The Living is generating only twelve percent O2."

"Margaret," Avery cut in. "That gives about a four-week window before the reserves are tapped to critical limits."

"John, I'm aware of that," she replied. "That's why we're here. Can we continue?"

"There's something else," Libby added. "I've noticed unusual animal activity, particularly with the primates. The monkey troop never comes off the mountain or down from the treetops, but I've seen them scavenging about the ground the past few days. I can tell they sense something."

"And they should." Will stood and approached the table.

"Will, we have a lot of ground to cover this morning," Margaret said. "Your help with the ring disturbances has been much appreciated, but we're dealing with other issues right now."

"Thank you," Will responded. "But this has nothing to do with the rings, although it indirectly helped me solve the puzzle."

"What puzzle?"

"The O2 puzzle," he replied. "I wouldn't interrupt this meeting otherwise. But in short, I think the entire problem was caused by the daytime sky simulation. I made adjustments with Sys this morning that should correct it and get us back on track."

A wave of curious energy swept the room. You could hear a pin drop.

"Wait a minute," Margaret said. "What could the daytime simulation have to do with our problem?"

"What do you know about the solar equinox?" Will asked.

"Seasonal changes in the length of the days," she replied. "Why?"

"Exactly. Daytime hours vary during the year," he said. "In summer, we have more daylight. In winter, we have less since Earth rotates about its axis as it orbits the sun. In other words, if you could draw a line across the sky that follows the sun each day, you would find that in the winter its arcing path is lower in the sky than in the summer where it's nearly overhead."

"But here," Margaret said, "the sun shines every day for a fixed amount of time."

"That's right," Will continued. "We have a simulated sun that follows the same path every day, and the artificial screen is getting burned out along that path. I noticed it last night while reviewing ring disturbances—dark bands in a bright background. When I took the time to investigate, it was obvious what the problem was."

"You're getting ahead of us," Margaret said. "Let's get back to this equinox thing—how is it tied to the oxygen problem?"

"I dug up the manufacturer's literature this morning," he replied. "It qualifies that the radiant energy from the sun image can damage the fabric of the imaging screen if misused. The original programmers intended to use the equinoxes, different paths across the sky, to control that problem. Giving the sun different paths to follow distributes the detrimental effects to the screen. Otherwise, the intense light eventually burns out the screen."

"So, you think the screen is already burning out?" Margaret asked.

"Oh, yes, there's no doubt about it," Will said.

"That would cause the sun to dim a bit," she said, "and release less energy, which slows the photosynthesis process. Less oxygen is produced."

"How did this happen?" Avery asked. "This is too important an item to overlook."

"I wasn't aware of the requirement," Margaret said, enlightened. "The original intent was to use standard artificial lighting and a clear sky. But the Space Council decided to go with this system, requiring it to have the same luminosity. They told me that it could double oxygen production if necessary. I was skeptical initially, but this situation never occurred to me."

"It got through all the catch nets because of a lack of communication," Will continued. "Construction records show that the fabric installer had no contact with the computer systems operator. The technology was so new that the original design concept didn't allow such interfacing. The only mention of artificial lighting, beyond the construction phase, was changing light bulbs as a part of general maintenance."

"My god, it never would have occurred to me." Margaret sighed. "Okay, if this is true, then show me. We'll go to command and review your notes. Everyone else, please continue to monitor as before until further notice. This meeting is adjourned."

Markham perked up like a proud papa. "What was all that about wonder boy and computer models?"

Avery was too relieved to strike back.

***

The reason she hadn't slept well for all this time was over; it just didn't seem possible. The months of intense research, reviewing and re-reviewing operating procedures, schedule extensions, co-ordinating efforts among all the necessary disciplines, and explaining problems with the Space Council. If it weren't for Will's use of the viewscreen, they'd still be in trouble. The team assembled for the Gaia 3 mission was the best group of scientists and engineers in their fields, but the mission would have failed if it weren't for the chance decision to bring Will along for the ride.

Margaret couldn't deny him his due credit; he'd solved a dangerous problem that no one else could. There was no more wondering when he'd get on track; he was there. All her feelings of disappointment and unrealistic expectations disappeared.

Chapter 11
THE SKY BRIDGE

Their review took most of the morning, but Margaret was a believer in the end. Will got a pat on the back from just about everyone. Afterward, Will adjusted the sun's path across the sky and restored the original luminosity. No one could believe it had gone that far.

She was eager to reestablish contact with the Space Council and finally had something to discuss. She assigned Will to work with Shoemaker and contact Earth. He quickly made an uplink between the ground-based dish and Shoemaker. The next step was to sort through background noise for anything remotely intelligent.

***

Will punched away at keyboards and heard the unmistakable sound of emergency alarms blasting away from every speaker in the facility. He jumped to his feet and headed toward the door. Sys's voice barely cut through the pulsing alarm, but the only discernible word was *contamination*.

He ran down hallways where strobe lights in the corridor synchronized with flashing sirens. He ran past the elevator shaft where the hallway tee'd into the main corridor. And then, out of nowhere, *crunch*, he fell down, after slamming head-on into Libby. His head bounced off the floor, and he faded in and out of consciousness. Libby was almost unharmed, but Will was on the ground, trying to figure out where he was.

***

John Early nervously stepped into an E-suit. His eyes reddened, and his face blistered, he ducked behind piping near the air processors. Sweating and breathing heavily, he zipped the suit up from foot to neck. The sound of search teams drew nearer, and he stood back as they passed in front of the central air processor.

Technicians Richard Brown, John Phillips, and Mark Jackson passed by with flashlights. Jackson's flashlight caught the glass face of a control panel and reflected into Early's eyes. A searing pain ripped through his body as he squinted to mask the light.

The searchers passed him by without notice. Moments later, they passed the sky bridge entry. Now was his chance.

He stepped out and ran toward the pressure lock. The keypad was a blur. He couldn't remember the sequence, but there was something important to do first—*Pressurize/Enter*. He hit the two buttons and kept an eye out for the search team.

Pumps of the supply oxygen tank engaged, and the entrance to the sky bridge opened. Early strapped his helmet and hurried down the shaft toward the secondary pressure lock. The bright Titan sky beamed all around, nearly blinding him. The pain was excruciating, so he focused on the next obstacle. He finally reached the pressure lock, but there was another combination.

"Hey!" a voice shouted. "Get away from that door, John!"

Three men ran down the sky bridge in full stride. There was no time for a proper entry; he reached for the emergency exit chain. In that instant, he experienced his last moment of sanity. He turned toward the approaching search team and motioned for them to turn back. But it was too late.

Frigid air blasted in with hurricane force at twice the pressure of the inside environment. A wave of methane-enriched air shot through the sky bridge like a bullet through a gun. Early was blown off his feet by the rush of air at liquid nitrogen temperatures. It threw him against the sky bridge, where his suit froze instantly to the steel mullions of the glass window panels.

He regained consciousness a few minutes later to see only frost. An unusual pressure pushed against his body. He was hung from the wall by one arm and leg as if he'd stuck his tongue to a freezer door. The water vapor on his clothing had instantly crystallized and stuck like glue, but one hand was free, so he wiped the frost from his facemask.

Below him was a blue face. At first, he thought it was his reflection in the mask. But it was the face of another man, Richard Brown. He was dead, along with two other men. They lay rock hard and blue-skinned at the foot of a door they could not open. Early had been lucky; his environmental suit was still active and uncompromised.

He pried his arm off the frozen steel and fell onto Brown's body, horrified by its statuesque hardness. There were voices on the other side of the door, so he hurried down the frost-covered sky bridge and made his way into the hover-shuttle.

When Gerhardt secured the secondary pressure lock, Early was away in the hover-shuttle, speeding into the methane wilderness.

***

"Are you all right?" Libby cried.

"I was." Will shook his head. "What happened?"

"Never mind." She pulled him to his feet. "We have to get to security. There's been an accident!"

"A what?" he asked.

"The bulkhead near the sky bridge has been damaged or something," she said.

The two were off and running again.

Margaret was in the security room monitoring the accident status when Will and Libby burst inside. Video monitors were locked onto level five near the sky bridge entry. She was barking orders through a headset to Gerhardt and the rest of the search parties, ordering them to the upper levels. Through the stroboscopic light, Margaret saw that the door was covered in frost along with the surrounding floor.

"Gerhardt, I'm sealing off everything below deck twelve," she said, punching away at a control panel. "Get everyone into the freight elevator now! The atmosphere's been compromised."

Her order caused a mad scramble through the icy chill. The elevator was up to level sixteen in seconds. Gerhardt was the first off and headed to security.

"Margaret," Gerhardt cried. "It's a real mess down there."

"What in the hell happened?" she shouted.

"I'm not exactly sure," he replied. "I was up on seven when I heard the main airlock opening. We heard Brown shouting Early's name when we got to the staircase. Then the emergency flashers went off, and a cold blast of air blew through the bulkhead and it closed shut. We were fifty meters away, and it knocked us to the ground."

"What about the search team?" Margaret asked.

"I don't think they made it out."

This wasn't supposed to happen. No one had even considered the possibility of a fellow crew member dying.

"Gerhardt," she said. "Get Kirby and Miller to suit up in environmental gear right away. We need to find those men and assess the structural damage."

"We're on it," he replied.

"And Gerhardt," Margaret said.

He was already to the door but stopped short.

"I know they're your friends but be careful."

"Richard," she turned to him. "We need an environmental assessment from command as soon as you can get it. We can't afford to have any methane gas floating around here. I know none of this equipment is supposed to generate a spark, but we found out today that we don't have a perfect design yet."

"Got it," Markham said.

"John?" she asked. "Can you help him?"

"I'm on my way."

Markham and Avery headed for command.

Will sat next to Margaret, watching security monitors with anticipation. Libby wasn't dealing well with the accident or the thought of her friends dying.

"Does this mean they're dead?" she asked.

"Libby," Margaret responded. "I don't know what this means. But we're not going to find out until Gerhardt gets down there. If you don't feel up to watching, you don't have to."

"I'll go to command and help Richard," she replied.

"Thanks, anything is helpful," Margaret said.

Libby turned to leave.

"By the way, an accurate assessment should cover all areas of the facility, not just the blast area. I want to know if anything migrates here or to the Living."

Within minutes, Gerhardt and Miller were visible by monitor near the frozen entry door, dressed in full environmental gear. Miller examined the frozen airlock and pecked at the frosty windows with a scraper while Gerhardt policed the area.

"Gerhardt," Margaret's voice came through his helmet. "Let's secure the area first. We'll work on damage control inside if you can't stabilize the sky bridge."

"Agreed," Gerhardt responded. "There's about one centimeter of ice on the power panel. It's going to take a few minutes to expose it."

"That could be trouble," Margaret said. "There must not be a thermal break between you and the outside. Water vapor will continue to build up until we increase the temperature in the sky bridge. You have to get the hangar end sealed off, so we can get heat in there."

"*Ja*," Gerhardt said. "But we can't do it fast, or the tube walls will fracture. On the other hand, we can't wait too long, or this door will grow into a glacier."

"Your choice," Margaret said. "You guys should have ninety minutes of oxygen to work with, but that's it. Let's not breathe the air down there until Richard gets the air cycles under control."

When the emergency chain was pulled, it released hydraulic control and engaged a backup spring and pulley system. Power was automatically cut off at the main panel, but the doors would automatically close if power was restored.

Gerhardt flipped the breaker switch to close the secondary airlocks at the hangar end of the sky bridge. Next, he uncovered the control panel and restored heat and a breathable environment to the sky bridge. Air pumps rattled and whined for thirty minutes before the bulkhead board flashed green.

"Okay now, step back, *ja*," Gerhardt ordered. "I'll handle this."

There was something very sobering about that statement; Miller didn't argue.

The airlock slowly opened as the ice cracked, spalled, and crashed to the floor. The entire inside surface of the sky bridge was frozen. Gerhardt had opened the door hundreds of times, but this didn't seem real.

Jackson's body was frozen upright against the door, the fabric of his clothes and hair glued to the steel surface. But the door rolled back into its jamb with hydraulic force and dislodged the stone-hard body that fell to the floor. It impacted the steel surface with an explosive sound and burst into pieces. Gerhardt almost jumped out of his environmental suit.

Brown and Phillips lay in a stiff, blue, rigor mortis sleep. Their skin had frozen so quickly and entirely that it appeared powdery. Gerhardt fell to his knees and wept, his breath fogging the facemask at the gruesome scene.

"Gerhardt, I'm sorry," Margaret whispered.

"Mother," Will said. "The monitors show only three bodies, but there should be four."

"You're right."

"Gerhardt," Margaret said. "You need to get a hold of yourself. Now listen, we can only see three men from here. Where is the fourth?"

By the time Gerhardt acknowledged the question, Miller was on his way toward the hangar. He scraped away at the porthole window and shone a flashlight in all directions. Then he stepped aside and cleared the frost off the control panel. He pressed away at buttons as Gerhardt walked up and peered into the hangar.

"What in the hell?" he asked.

"What?" Margaret shouted. "What is it, Gerhardt?"

"You're not gonna believe this," Gerhardt said, "but the hover-shuttle is gone."

Margaret was stunned. She turned to Will. "Get to command and try to contact that shuttle."

Chapter 12
BAD DREAMS

The shuttle raced across the barren ice world. John Early was completely mad; the pressure and pain in his eyes was unbearable. The whites of his eyes had turned blood red, his skin burned and blistered, patches of hair dropped from his scalp and stuck to his face shield. He had no plan. He just had to escape the pain and anger that had driven him to kill his friends.

The brightness quickly turned into a whiteout, but it disappeared as soon as it came on him. The sensation was a brief comfort, and then he was blind.

John released the controls and scratched wildly at the sides of his helmet to get it off. The tiny shuttle careened out of control and dove toward a methane sea. It skipped on first contact, slammed into the liquid methane, and sank into darkness.

***

Margaret blew the dust off a glass bottle that said something about Kentucky's finest. It had been a while. She paused before the first sip, sniffed it, and took a drink. Her eyes watered, but that didn't stop her from taking another sip. *Just when we got a break something else happened. How do we decontaminate the Dead Hemisphere? Hopefully, we'll get better news when diagnostics are complete.*

Margaret sat down, took another sip, and her troubles floated away. She decided to take a nap but was interrupted when the doorbell rang.

***

She hated being disturbed during the last week of the semester until she saw John Avery peering through the sidelight.

Avery was an established Biology professor when he suggested the concept of Ecotechnics, and Margaret grasped it with a passion. Their relationship went beyond the classroom but not into the bedroom.

"I'm coming!" *she shouted and hurried to the door. Avery rang again to annoy her.*

"Hello, Margaret," *Avery said, then leaned over to kiss her.*

She was surprised and pulled back. "I wasn't expecting you," *she said.* "What's up?"

"Would you like to go for a walk?" *Avery asked.* "It's a beautiful day."

"Well, I… I have work."

"That can wait. Besides, the fresh air will do you good."

"Let me get a sweater."

It was a bright afternoon, and the ocean breeze was unusually warm as they walked the white sands. Avery wasn't himself. She noticed something different, a lax attitude that didn't fit him, and wondered if he'd been drinking.

"This was a good idea," *Margaret said.* "I needed to get out of that apartment."

"I know. That's why I stopped by." *Avery slowed.*

"You knew?" she questioned.

"Margaret, I've been thinking," Avery said. "You and I have never discussed our plans after leaving this place. We take it a semester at a time, and we're always so busy with school."

"Look at it!" Margaret shouted. "It's beautiful! Where did it come from?"

A giant arching rainbow appeared in the sky that came from nowhere. She ran to the shoreline.

"Why is it so bright?" Avery grouched as if it irritated him. "And why are there only two or three yellowish colors?"

"Don't be such a grump," she said. "But you know, I could swear I've seen this image somewhere before. Isn't this a planet?"

"A planet?" Avery laughed. "And you wondered if I'd been drinking?"

"No, seriously, I really think it is." She sounded confused. "I can't remember, but these are planetary rings. We have to be orbiting a planet for this close view. How could this be? What's happening?"

The sky changed from blue to an orange haze, and the waves changed to red-orange. She suddenly appeared on Titan in her dream world, wearing an environmental suit near a cryonic ocean, but Avery was nowhere to be found.

She walked the shoreline, searching for remnants of the Gaia 3 mission, and saw something washed up on the beach. It buoyed in the water as waves gently pushed it farther up the beachhead. It appeared to be driftwood or a chunk of ice.

Margaret soon realized it was a dead body frozen in an icy shell. The rock hard body lay face down in the surf. She recognized the clothing, knelt, and rolled it over. It was Avery, but his monstrous face was hardly recognizable. What could have caused the ghastly blood-red color in his eyes? There was no iris, and the pupils were dilated entirely black.

Margaret woke up in a cold sweat, trying to catch her breath, and began to cry. Things were getting worse, and she didn't know why. It could have had something to do with those rings, after all.

She lay in bed for a while and thought about it. Finally, it was time to turn on the lights and drink coffee.

***

"This is getting worse by the minute," Markham growled. "Sensor readings for radiation exposure in the lower levels are about four times higher than normal safety limits. I don't know what's happening outside, but it had better slow down soon."

"Can you filter out radiation and methane gas at the same time?" Robert asked.

"That's not going to be easy, especially with low backups," Markham replied. "We're just not equipped to deal with that type of problem. Hostile gasses are one thing, but radiation is another."

"Wait a minute," Robert said. "If the surrounding atmosphere is saturated with radiation, why isn't it leaking inside?"

"The Cerametallic shell covering Gaia is a very dense material," Markham replied matter-of-factly while punching away at the computer. "It was developed to handle extreme temperature differentials. It also shields against most types of radiation, except the real nasty ones down in the gamma range. But still, traces of it are filtering in; we didn't expect this much. By the way, how will this affect the exposed search teams?"

"They haven't taken a lethal dose, if that's your question," Robert replied. "Radiation sickness is dependent on two things: intensity and time of exposure. You need to absorb about one hundred rads before it's lethal."

Will was seated on the other side of the room, wearing a headset. He'd picked up a faint signal. "Richard," he said, dropping his earphones. "I've found a signal that could be the hover-shuttle. You need to take a look at this."

Markham jumped at the chance to talk about something else. Just then, Margaret entered the room, rubbing the dark circles under her eyes.

"I hope we have some positive news to report today," she said.

"The signal's clean and pulses in regular intervals," Will said, hardly noticing Margaret's entrance.

Markham leaned over next to Will, pointing to the view screen. "Does that show five hundred kilometers inland?"

Margaret moved in behind the two.

"Yes, he really covered some ground," he said.

"Why in the hell would he go inland?" Robert asked.

"Why in the hell would he go anywhere?" Markham retorted.

"I just mean," Robert said, "we have a small weather monitoring post near the ocean, right? It's the only other habitable place on Titan."

"You've found the shuttle?" Margaret asked.

"I believe so," Will replied. "But had a hard time locating it at this frequency. Distress calls are supposed to be sent at 501 MHz, so I started my search in that range. But instead, I found this old-style SOS signal. See here—it repeats in intervals of three."

"And it's coming from five hundred kilometers inland?" Margaret asked.

"That's right."

"Could he have gotten that far so quickly?" she asked.

"It's been nearly twenty-four hours," Will said. "And visibility is at an all-time high."

"I guess you're right," Margaret said. "How much oxygen would he have for life support?"

"It's hard to say," Markham said. "But the hover-shuttle is set up for round-trip missions to the ocean. That's normally ten or twelve hours for two technicians. So, one man should have at least twenty-four hours' worth of oxygen."

"Then he could still be alive," she said.

No one seemed too excited about that statement, and they knew the following line. Early had been their friend, but he was also responsible for the deaths of three men. Sick or not, the idea of a rescue, at the risk of endangering more lives, didn't seem right.

"Richard, have Gerhardt stabilize the sky bridge and prep the shuttle," Margaret said. "We leave in one hour. Robert, I assume he'll need medical attention, so you and Gerhardt will fly out with me to attempt a rescue."

"Margaret," Markham piped in. "I should go instead. They need your leadership here."

Markham considered himself an expendable man. Since he'd lost his wife, his life had never really gotten back on course. He was just an old engineer with nothing left but his work.

"I appreciate your concern, Richard," she replied. "But I need you to stabilize and decontaminate the lower hemisphere."

"Mother, I should go, too," Will added.

"I disagree," she said. She didn't want to put her son in danger, but the response came across as condescending. She could have tried to explain the value of monitoring the communications terminal but hoped he would buy her quick response without question.

"Early was the only pilot qualified to fly the hover-shuttle, other than Gerhardt," he said. "So, if it isn't damaged, I'm the only person qualified to fly it back here."

She really had no argument. Margaret's blank expression was all the confirmation he needed.

Chapter 13
TIN CAN

An hour later, they stepped through the airlock. At its threshold, the imprints of a man's legs lay frozen in the ice that crystallized him. The sky bridge's frozen walls had started to melt, and outside light cut through from all directions. The world that lived in eternal dusk and darkness was completely illuminated.

The radiation issue had sunk in when Margaret stepped into the E-suit. She hadn't worn one for a while, but the suffocating feeling was still the same. No one liked wearing E-suits for the entire flight.

***

She seated herself in the co-pilot's chair and buckled the cross-strapped safety belt. Will and Robert did the same.

"Gerhardt, let's not waste any time," Margaret said through the headset. "We find the hover-shuttle, assess the damage, and get back here ASAP."

"Got it," Gerhardt said, engaging the lift thrusters.

"We have the coordinates, right?" Margaret asked.

"Already logged in to autopilot," Gerhardt replied.

"Let's do it," she ordered.

The trip was similar to flight training over the Antarctic. Water ice in any world, even one buried in methane snow, did the same thing. Peaks cutting through rifts in the landscape were crystal white compared to the reddish terrain below. Numerous crevices and ravines showed the ravages of an ice world ripped and torn by the gravitational pull from Saturn.

"I don't believe the shuttle got this far out," Gerhardt said.

"I was just thinking the same thing," Will said. "This isn't the kind of terrain the shuttle negotiates very well."

"Are you sure about these readings?" Gerhardt asked. "Because we're only halfway to the pre-plotted coordinates, and farther ahead, it just gets worse. The hover-shuttle can't fly over these mountains; it needs relatively smooth surfaces to cross."

Margaret panned the horizon. "I have to agree, Gerhardt. This might as well be the lower Rockies. The hover-shuttle can't navigate this terrain."

"I hear what you're saying," Will said. "But the signal originated about two hundred kilometers from our current location."

"Maybe it's a remote transmitter from an old weather tracking station," Gerhardt said.

"No," Margaret said. "Humans quit dropping junk in space fifty years ago—leave only your footprints."

"How much longer before we reach the signal?"

"About ten minutes flight time," Gerhardt responded.

"You mean we've only been in these damned armored suits for twenty minutes?" Robert piped in. "It seems like twenty hours."

"Just relax," Margaret said. "E-suits take a bit of getting used to, but it beats the alternative."

Minutes later, a circular object appeared on the screen with a diameter of ten kilometers, clearly an ancient impact crater. Its caldera was more than a hundred meters high with a flat central plain and a small central peak. Their destination was off to one side of the mountain.

Gerhardt pulled up as they cleared the rim, then settled back down and started for the central peak. They saw something glisten in the bright light just beyond the mountain.

Gerhardt engaged reverse thrusters as he made a slow circle around the mountain as they approached their destination. The cloud of snow and ice created by their landing lowered visibility, but this was not the hover-shuttle.

"I guess this explains the transmission," Margaret said.

"Is there any sign of the hover-shuttle?" Robert asked.

"Don't count on it," Will said.

"What in god's name are we looking at?" Gerhardt asked.

Margaret's knowledge of space flight, manned or robotic, was as good as anyone's. But she had no explanation for this. It was a small outpost, a construct of cargo hulls pieced together in an X-shape with a circular hub section in its center. It appeared occupied since it was not buried under snow, but it wasn't sanctioned by the World Space Council.

"Once again, we're confronted with a situation we're unprepared for," Margaret said and took a deep breath. "But they must need our help, or they wouldn't have sent an SOS. Has anyone responded to your hails?"

"No," Will said. "The signal seems automated. They're sending but not receiving."

"Surely they heard our landing," Robert said.

"That's a good point," she replied. "Gerhardt, why don't you ensure the decompression chamber is working. We're either bringing people on board or going out to find a way into that station."

"I'm on it," he said, walking to the shuttle's rear.

Will grabbed the pilot's chair.

"It appears to be modeled after old-style scientific research stations in Antarctica," Margaret said. "If that's the case, the spokes are for living quarters, supplies, and power generation. The center hub would have laboratories for research and other things. This design works well on Earth with supply planes only a few hours away, but here's another story. It's temporary housing at best, a big tin can."

"I don't see any identification markings," Will said. "At least from our vantage."

"There's a possibility," Margaret added, "it's an old station. The distress could've been set decades ago."

"That might explain why we don't see their landing craft," Will said.

"Whatever the case," Robert said, "how do we get in?"

"There should be a roof hatch near the center," Margaret said. "Where that ladder runs up the side, near the hub." She turned to Will and Robert. "Chances are, we'll have to board her. I think we should all go. Robert could be sick or injured, people, so pack your bags. I need you for backup. We might need some help there. Gerhardt can stay here and watch the shuttle."

"I wouldn't let you go in there alone," Will said. "Commander or not."

Margaret smiled, then started to the shuttle's rear. "We'd better check the charge on our E-suits and get a full load of O2."

"The decompression chamber is functioning normally," Gerhardt called out from the shuttle's rear.

Margaret instructed Gerhardt on everything but honking the horn during their absence while Will rummaged through the supply closet.

"I know they're in here somewhere," he said. "Gerhardt, have you seen the flashlights?"

"I already grabbed them," Gerhardt said. "They're back by decompression, along with a bag of tools and a first aid kit."

Margaret tapped the top of her helmet. "Why do you want flashlights when we have these?" she asked, as lights around her face mask lit up.

"Not bright enough," Will said. "But it's a good backup, just in case."

Robert didn't chime in but pointed to his medical bag.

Gerhardt shrugged his shoulders. "Just in case, *ja?*"

They'd waited long enough. Nearly half an hour had passed since they'd landed, but no one from the strange base attempted contact. The group stepped into the decompression chamber and descended in the cylindrical elevator to the surface.

The intrigue of discovery faded during the five-minute march through the frigid air. E-suits could be torn or damaged on the ladder or hatchway. And flesh was just millimeters away from instant death if the E-suit were compromised.

They expected to see more detail on the mysterious facility—a logo, a unique architectural feature, or telltale structural pieces. The circular hub was about twenty meters in diameter, with each spoke running about thirty meters.

Simple cargo bays rested flat on the icy crater bed. If there were landing feet, they were buried under drifted snow. The ladder scaling the hub was a good ten-meter climb.

Robert's eyes searched for other things and caught something that appeared to be a tree root from a distance. He moved away from the ladder toward a snow drift at the base of the white metal siding. He knelt and brushed away the dusting of snow.

"Margaret, you'd better take a look at this!" Robert shouted.

When the message came through her headset, Margaret was two steps up the ladder. She turned to see Robert bent over a frozen body. Its bent-up elbow protruded from the snow drift. Otherwise, it would have gone unnoticed. Robert brushed the snow away from the corpse.

"My god," he said. "This man is dressed in street clothes. He didn't make it this far outside the escape hatch."

Margaret kicked through the dusty snow nearby when her foot hit something hard.

"Over here," she said, pushing snow away from the legs of another body. "They must've been thrown out after they died."

"I don't think so," Robert said, examining the corpse. "This man was stabbed to death. He has multiple puncture wounds in the chest and abdomen."

She gazed at the frozen wounds, then turned and stared at the facility as if it were haunted.

"What in the hell is this place?" she said. "We're completely defenseless; we just came to help. But if we're going to need weapons…"

"Even then, none of us are trained soldiers," Will added.

"Margaret." Gerhardt's voice crackled. "I think you should return to the shuttle. I'll go inside the station."

"Since when does chivalry affect me?" she asked.

"I had to try." Gerhardt sighed.

Robert continued uncovering the corpse. "I don't think we have to worry about that," he said, wiping his hands. "These men were probably killed in self-defense."

"Then how do you explain the stab wound?" Margaret stopped, startled.

"It's the same thing that happened to Early," Robert finished for her. "Don't turn away, Margaret. Take a good look at his eyes if you can. This man was probably blind in the end, the poor bastard. This is what I predicted would happen to Early, a secondary form of glaucoma."

The corpse's face was monstrous; its skin was burned and blistered while its bloodshot eyes bulged from the sockets. Their white globes were blood-red and expanded to the point of bursting, and the pupils were completely dilated. His blue-black hair and olive-colored skin were shrouded under a grotesque and bloody veil.

"It apparently causes insanity, too," Robert added. "We saw that when Early flew off to nowhere. At any rate, I think it's safe to say these fellows have died very recently. So, we know it's not a decades-old signal."

Margaret shaded her eyes and squinted at the sky. "So, the light from the rings is lethal," she said. "If these men were afflicted with the same sickness Early had, then there's no telling what we'll find inside."

The shock of finding the dead bodies and the correlation between their apparent demise and that of John Early's captured the moment. Margaret considered going back, but they'd come this far.

"There could be survivors, Margaret," Robert said.

She paused. "Okay, let's proceed with caution," she said. "But be careful and stay alert."

Will already had enough and was concerned about his mother's safety. But Margaret called the shots, and despite his objections, they proceeded. Will felt a bit of *déjà vu* on top of the strange moon base. He turned to take in the panoramic view of the crater walls and caldera and thought of the rock at Gaia.

"See this? It's not sealed," Margaret said, examining the roof hatch. "And it's propped open from the inside."

Will crouched down beside the lid and peered inside with his flashlight. He expected to see gears and a crank wheel, but instead, saw two hydraulic arms on either side of the cover.

"This is good," he said and went to one knee. "The lid is operated by hydraulics. All I have to do is pop out cotter pins on either side, and the hatch is free. We'd never get in if it were held down by crank bars."

"And if the decompression chamber is in the same condition," she added, "then the inside environment has been compromised."

"Won't affect us." Will grunted, reached inside, and played with the pump arm. "It's not iced over. I might be able to pull the pins." He pulled a small screwdriver from his belt pack and worked the pins.

He lifted the hatch and shined his flashlight down inside. The cylindrical decompression chamber, with an access ladder scaling up one side. It was covered with a light frosty film, an ominous sign since frost meant extreme temperature change. Then he craned his neck further down and saw the entrance door was ajar.

"Doesn't look good," Will said and fumbled with his belt pack. "The door at the base is half open, and there's no light inside the facility."

Margaret started down the ladder without saying a word.

Chapter 14
THE ROCK

Libby paused to wipe her brow; the heat was unbelievable. She put up a hand to shade the brightness and locate the sun. The sun was on the opposite side of the sky, but the new path made a difference. The biosphere was coming back to life—she could feel it.

She climbed as high as the treetops, tapped a tie-off clasp, and jiggled her safety belt. Both were secure. The waterfall was only a few meters away, and the idea of swinging into it was tempting, but she had work to do.

The air shaft Will had found open was supposed to be fixed, and she wanted to check it out. When she reached the vent, there were plenty of scratch marks on the newly painted surface, and the grated cover was loose. She lifted it up and aimed a flashlight inside.

Inside the duct was a mess—the tiny monkeys were at it again. Libby crawled inside on hands and knees. Her first move caused the thin sheet metal to make an oil canning sound, and she stopped instantly. She didn't want to alert the primates, so she pushed her knees against the corners of the duct to ensure a stealthy approach.

It was still knocked out when she found the panel Will had talked about.

She decided to wrap a climbing rope around the duct and repel down inside the faux mountain. Flashlight in hand as she descended, she saw a maze of ducts, pipes, and the rough plastered shells of formed caves. There were leaves, vines, and branches sprinkled on the ducts and cave tops.

She kicked back and forth while descending until momentum finally swung her over to a cave top. She landed on a concrete surface after about a ten-meter drop. This area was the same as the caves she'd inspected, but a foul odor overpowered the animal droppings. She dropped farther to investigate.

As she descended, the smell grew worse and sent a chill through her. She spun about the rope and held the flashlight tight to her hip. The lighthouse effect gave her a fairly good layout of the floor underneath. She stopped on a cold concrete floor and panned the light for bearings.

Then her light locked on the half-eaten carcass of a capuchin monkey near her feet. It wasn't skinned or gutted—this had to be the work of other primates. Massive tissue loss near the hind quarters and rib cage meant it was a large predator.

The further she walked, the more frightened she became. Mechanical equipment noise drowned out everything else, so her sense of hearing as a defensive advantage was gone. And her flashlight was the only light source inside the giant, pitch-black concrete shell. The blanket cast over her senses was unnerving.

Then she saw the unmistakable mark of the predator. A rack of sheet metal ductwork turned up and out of sight, but hung from it by crude strings were two monkey hides. Her spine tingled. She felt trapped. She had to get out.

Out of the corner of her eye, or maybe just from heightened senses, she felt something else. She shifted the light slightly to a pair of eyes that turned and squinted as a shadowy figure charged at her. Libby turned and ran but was caught from behind and tackled. Her flashlight fell against the concrete floor, casting a footlight as it rolled. She was pinned facedown beneath her attacker.

"I guess I developed a taste for fresh meat," a voice whispered in her ear.

She recognized the voice but gave no response. She rolled and elbowed her attacker in the face. He let out a cry, grasping his head as Libby wriggled free.

"What are you doing down here?" she demanded, holding the light to his face. "And why did you try to hurt me?"

The man turned quickly, but she recognized his clothing. It was Jeff Kirby. His clothes were ragged and filthy, and his hair was a matted mess. Even though he turned his face, she saw his skin was discolored and blotchy. She hadn't seen him since before the blast, and it was apparent why he wasn't with the rescue party. It was also obvious why the primates were no longer inside the mountain.

"Shut that damn thing off!" he shouted, reaching blindly toward her. "You're just like the others. I can't let you tell them about me!"

Libby backed up a step for each of his. She had to think of some way to escape. Then she realized his eyes were sensitive to the light.

"Kirby, you're just sick and need help," she said. "You need to get to the med lab and see Doctor Lewis. You were exposed to radiation when the sky bridge opened."

He tried to face her, but Libby kept the light straight on him. She wasn't sure if he was bleeding or injured, but the whites of his eyes were gruesome red. Libby slowly reached for the metal climbing clasp at her side and worked her fingers through it like a set of brass knuckles.

"Need help?" he gasped out. "There's no hope for any of us. This whole goddamn place is melting down."

He lunged at her, but she struck him across the face with her makeshift knuckles. As Kirby grimaced in pain, she shut off the flashlight and ran for the repelling rope, still visible by light from the damaged vent above.

She hurried through the darkness, seeing only ghostly images of metal obstacles in her path. Then she saw the dangling rope and leapt for it. She wrapped her legs and pulled as she swung pendulum-style through the dark cave. The flashlight fell from her grip and hit the floor. She was a few meters above the floor and out of Kirby's reach in seconds.

The scream of a raging madman came from below. Kirby grabbed the flashlight and threw it wildly Libby ducked and heard it crash against a concrete wall. She continued her climb but heard footsteps and grunting below. The opening in the duct was within arm's length when she was pulled away from it, not by force on her own body, but by the movement of the rope itself. From a limp cord that tensed under her body weight, it suddenly seemed as rigid as a board. Kirby found his way to the cave top, where Libby stopped on her way down and jumped out onto the rope just below her. The rope swayed away from the duct above. Libby knew she had to get out quickly, or they'd both fall. As the rope swung, she managed to prop her elbows inside the duct. By that time, Kirby was pulling at her feet.

Terrified, she let out a scream and kicked at his hands. She finally got through, but a leathery hand slapped over the edge of the opening. Again, she let out a yell and backed away. In the illuminated air duct, she saw his monstrous red eyes that seemed to bulge from their sockets.

"Don't you want to come back down and play with my pets?" he teased.

Libby instinctively kicked at his head. In the tight confines, it was her only choice. She struck him across the jaw, and he recoiled in anger, pulling farther up through the opening. Then she kicked again and hit him directly in the eye above the cheek. His expanded eyeball was as ripe as an August tomato and burst with the impact. Intraocular fluid and blood sprayed the inside of the duct. Kirby's grip slipped as he burst out an agonizing cry that didn't sound human. Libby pushed with all fours to escape the dreadful sight as Kirby's hold gave way.

She heard banging and scratching before one final *thud*, then silence. Crying, Libby made her way out of the dented and dirty duct. She gathered her strength and descended to the rock's bottom.

She wound her way around the mountain's base, through the jungle, toward the elevator. Jim Miller walked up and met her at the edge of the beach.

"Are you all right?" he asked, noticing her cuts and bruises. "I thought I heard shouting." His suspicious gaze caught her attention—there was something peculiar about his eyes.

Chapter 15
BLAST FROM THE PAST

Margaret stepped through a half-open door leading to the interior of the strange moon base. It was pitch black, except for a handful of computer panels that twinkled in the frozen darkness. Her helmet lights only cast a few feet, so she reached for a floodlight.

The room was circular and appeared to be the same diameter as the outside shell. There were concentrically located doors leading to the tributary wings, but all were closed. The circular walls were lined with electrical equipment except for one blank wall. The ceiling was a simple, exposed structure. Oddly enough, all the lights were smashed out, and shards of glass and metal lamp covers lay scattered on the floor.

There was a conference table in the center of the room with a frozen body in a mannequin pose at one end. The table was centrally located; this was obviously the command center.

The walls and floor were frosted over with a glaze similar to the sky bridge at Gaia. It appeared that all the damage was caused by internal overpressure when the decompression chamber was compromised. It also appeared they were too late.

"Will, Robert, come on down," Margaret called out. "The entire base has been sacked."

Within minutes, they stood next to her in the frozen command center. A web of flashlight beams crisscrossed the room's walls, taking in the damage.

"Let's search this place for clues about why it's here and what happened," she continued, her voice muffled through the headsets and distorted by her breathing. "We need to check the lower decks for survivors. Robert, check that body. Will, your headset has a video camera. I want it to record everything we see here. And also, see if you can reactivate their computer system."

"Marg—you're break—" Gerhardt shouted. "I can't hear y—"

"Gerhardt! Gerhardt!" she said.

No response.

"I guess communication with the shuttle is lost inside this facility."

Gerhardt unlatched his helmet and set it aside. Besides being frustrated with the communication link, he was tired of the uncomfortable E-suit.

Robert leaned over the frozen body; it bore the same monstrous features as the other's outside, except its throat was slit. The skin was soft, powdery and had a light frost coating. The grisly neck wound and bloodstained clothing distracted Robert. He didn't notice the symbol embroidered on the man's shirt pocket. Judging by the amount of blood on the table and floor, the man must have been killed there. And a trail of frozen bloody footprints led to the decompression chamber.

"Margaret," he called, pointing to the frozen, bloody tracks. "Apparently, this man was killed by whoever last walked out of here."

"That's possible," she said, examining the footprints. "These prints were left by wide boots, probably an environmental suit. That would explain why the man didn't bother to close the decompression chamber, and maybe there's no landing craft."

Will was on his way to investigate the nearest closed door when he stopped short. His flashlight passed a familiar sight, then jerked back onto it. A large print was neatly preserved under glass and bounded by an ornate golden frame. It was the inspirational centerpiece of the room, the facility, and probably the project itself. Somehow this madness had come full circle and made sense to him.

Margaret noticed her son staring at the wall-sized photograph. "What is that?"

No response.

Margaret and Robert approached, but Will did not acknowledge their presence. He gently rubbed the thumb of his free hand over his ruby ring as if there were no heavy glove covering it.

"Will!" Margaret shook him. "What is that? What does TIgrIS mean?"

There was a photograph of Doctor Ahmad Shastri kneeling in front of an ancient stone temple that Will did not recognize. Shastri had a prized find propped up in front of him—the stela that Will found at Kos Island eleven years ago. Next to it were paragraphs of text in Arabic and English, deciphering the three forms of writing on the tablet. And a map showing Saturn, the object's path, and its passage date over the past four millennia. The cosmic connection made sense to Will without explaining the details, but the setting was all wrong.

Shastri was not kneeling at Kos Island. And beside the photograph was an explanation of the find and how it had been uncovered in a previously unknown burial site in the lower Tigris-Euphrates River Valley.

The description said that heathen Europeans supposedly buried the secret of the tablets there to appease a god they feared. The

Roman army had pillaged the ancient burial site during a military campaign, and its spoils were brought back to their emperor. But a deadly plague soon followed, so the emperor ordered them to return to their original burial site.

"This is bullshit!" Will barked, while Robert and Margaret curiously listened. "It couldn't have happened that way. They wouldn't be fighting Persians a thousand miles from their border when Bar-

barians knocked on their front door. I wonder if TIgrIS presented this interpretation of their findings to the worldwide archaeological community?"

"What are you talking about?" Margaret asked. "How do you know so much about this?"

"Mother, I know this sounds hard to believe, but *I* found this, not *them*!" Will snorted, pointing a finger at the stela. "The summer I was in Europe, eleven years ago."

"Excuse me?" she said again.

Robert shined a pen light in his eyes, but Will pushed it away.

"I'm not going crazy," he said. "This ring of mine is a stolen artifact. I didn't steal it, but the person who did sent it to me. The ruby was a part of that stela. I didn't think there was any significance since the find was never reported in published journals."

"So, I take it this isn't art," Margaret said.

"No, Mother, it's prophecy," he responded. "This whole facility was probably funded by TIgrIS—the people I interned with that summer. I knew they had deep pockets, but this is hard to believe."

"This entire place violates all established international rules of interplanetary preservation, safety, and political conquest," Margaret added.

"Mother," Will interrupted, "the creation of this facility results from deeply rooted religious beliefs. In their view, it had nothing to do with politics or ecology. Look here. They're talking about two Dark Ages."

The decipherment of the three inscriptions told of chaos and destruction raining down on Earth from the heavens. Both occurrences had a passing comet and Saturn shining brightly in the sky. The effect on the civilized world was so profound that it disrupted all religious philosophies and led to mass hysteria.

The second of the two passages translated the stela. Will had loosely translated the Latin piece years ago but had yet to conceive its meaning.

Description of the pictograph:

The Assyrian King Shalmaneser I pleaded with the god of the third planet, Saturn (The Star of the Sun), for mercy. The other four planets known to the ancients, Jupiter, Venus (the star Ishtar), Mercury, and Mars, are all shown behind. The ring-nose serpents and arching light emanating from Saturn's comet bring death to the people as Nergal, the lion-headed God of Death, looks on. Behind the king is the crescent moon (Nanna Sin). Its position indicates that it is blocked from view or not as bright as Saturn. The king's soldiers are hiding behind the shadow of the king, helpless and pleading for mercy.

The Assyrian inscription reads:

"*The star shone as bright as the sun for thirty days, then winds blew the desert as dark as night. The king's army cowered behind city walls, while out in the countryside, women were raped and murdered. The red-eyed daevas pillaged the kingdom as all men ran mad.*"

The Latin inscription reads:

"*Those whom a god wishes to destroy he first drives mad. Eternal Rome. May god forgive me, Theodosius.*"

1149

The Senate and the Roman people

"There's something else that doesn't make sense," Will said after the reading. "The cuneiform writing is Assyrian, not the early style that would've been used at Uruk."

"So, you're saying these TIgrIS people predicted this strange phenomenon in the rings based on past occurrences," Margaret said.

"Yes, look here," he said, pointing to a map of the Saturnian system. "They're showing our planetoid with the 1,682 period. I'm sure that corresponds to the dates of the Roman and Assyrian passages. This ring of mine has 1 6 8 2 engraved on the inside, but I never made the connection."

Will paused for a second, remembering his dream. "But Ben knew. He found out years ago. Maybe that's why he's not here anymore."

"The man who sent you the ring?"

"Yes."

"So, the effects of this radiation have reached Earth!" Robert interjected.

"Yes, in the past and could very well be again soon," Will replied. "Or maybe the planetoid's tail when it passes."

"They must have known what to look for," Margaret said. "We didn't see the object until it got close enough, but if they knew where it was?"

"Yeah, they'd have found it all right," Will said.

Ancient history and superstition had never been Margaret's cup of tea. Although unbelievable and undoubtedly an exciting tie to the ancient forefathers, she had always been more concerned about completing the mission.

"Okay, this explains why they're here," she said, looking about. "So, what happened to them?"

"I think it's obvious, isn't it?" Robert said.

"Is it? Then why hasn't the same thing happened to us?" she asked.

"It *is* happening to us," Robert replied. "Just at a slower rate. Our people weren't exposed at the same rate these people were. That thick surface shell on Gaia shields us from most of the radiation. These poor devils are in a tin can like our sky bridge that doesn't deflect anything. Our technicians will all end up this way."

"We need to access the rest of this facility," Margaret said. "There could still be survivors in the lower decks if there's a breathable atmosphere. Will, you need to download all the information you can from their computer system. Robert, come with me."

"Shouldn't we go back and get some weapons?" he asked.

"We didn't bring any; this is a rescue mission," Margaret said. "Besides, whoever killed that guy left already."

"Mother," Will interrupted. "This could be the most significant archaeological find in recorded history. Its effect back on Earth could be devastating. Shouldn't we get the hell out of here and contact Earth?"

"Sorry, we take care of business here first."

***

The first airlock led to a frozen storage room. The air was breathable, but the temperature was -150 degrees. The second led them into the living quarters, where the air was warm and breathable. Glass was scattered on the floor, lights were all bashed out, and the damage appeared to be deliberate. Next to the airlock, a staircase led down to the next level.

Two flashlights shone down the corridor separating stacks of bunk beds. Margaret did a quick head count and found at least six people should be on board, not counting the three bodies they'd seen. They passed the lofts and came to a dining area with two hardtop tables surrounded by chairs and dirty dishes. Across the hall was a bank of laundry machines. When the mound suddenly burst toward him, Robert had fixed his light on a large pile of soiled clothing.

Margaret turned to see Robert's glass facemask covered with dirty linen as he swatted frantically and was pushed to the floor. As a frightened, naked man lunged for the kitchen sink, grabbing a knife, Margaret stepped aside. He sweated and breathed heavily as he turned to face her with a knife in his shaking hand. Covered in third-degree burns, his red eyes bulged from his dark Middle Eastern appearance. Robert jumped to his feet and backed away from the man.

Margaret motioned down in a nonviolent gesture. The man fearfully stood his ground, his eyes shifting between Margaret and Robert.

Will's attention shifted from the frozen computer consoles to the commotion beyond the airlock. He started across the room to get a glimpse inside.

"He's in shock," Robert said through the headset. "If he doesn't get medical attention soon, he'll die."

"I wish I could take this helmet off," Margaret said. "To try and talk with him."

"It won't do any good," Robert said. "He can't be reasoned with."

Robert aimed his flashlight at the man's face. He turned and screamed in pain and ran toward the sleeping area. Margaret and Robert both followed the man with their lights. The man darted away from the beams of light as if being sprayed by a cold garden hose.

"Now I see why all the lights are broken out," Robert said. "I guess we won't need weapons as long as we can keep him at bay with flashlights."

"I don't think he means us any harm," she said.

"Okay then, how do you propose to disarm him?"

Just then, another person wearing an environmental suit appeared at the end of the corridor. The shadowy figure emerged from the stairwell holding a gun. For a second, Margaret thought it was

Will. But when her flashlight hit the dark silhouette, it revealed a uniform she didn't recognize. The gun raised instantly and pointed directly at her.

There was a brief stand-off. Margaret and Robert stood still. The man's gun switched back and forth between the motionless adversaries.

"What was I just saying about these flashlights?" Robert whispered through the headset. All he heard was Margaret's heavy breathing.

The gunman moved to the airlock controls while holding everyone at bay. He reached for the open lever and pulled it down. The naked man desperately scrambled for the pile of clothes and burrowed under them. Will darted away from the airlock.

Margaret stepped up, "No!!!"

A tremendous wave of frozen air rushed through the compartment and knocked Margaret off her feet. The armed man hung to the door handles as the air blew past him and filled the Living area.

The control room shook as the heavy frozen atmosphere blasted through the airlock. Will turned as the pressure differential balanced. The armed man crossed the threshold of the airlock door. His facemask frosted over as he stumbled into the conference room.

Will wondered if he had been seen, so he stayed in the shadows. Then he remembered his emergency beacon for the shuttle. He pushed a button on the side of his helmet to alert Gerhardt. Will watched as the armed man crossed the room toward the decompression chamber.

Robert was tangled between a table and two or three chairs, struggling to get back up. Margaret scraped the frost from her facemask and got to her feet. She quickly checked her E-suit for tears or leaks, then turned toward the end of the corridor, but the armed man was gone.

"Will!" she cried and rushed for the airlock.

"Don't worry, Mother, I'm all right," he softly replied. "An armed man just climbed out of the decompression chamber. Are you and Doctor Lewis, okay?"

"Yes, I think so," she said.

Robert stopped to sift through the frozen laundry pile. He knew the naked man's fate but still had to check. He found the man frozen, glued to the previously wet pile of clothes, eyes wide open, and skin hard as a rock.

"At least it was quick." He sighed. "No more pain."

The onboard navigation system had plotted flight path and fuel consumption for review when the comm panel flashed *Emergency*. It was a loud pulsing alarm, so Gerhardt hit the cancel switch and reattached his helmet. He headed to the shuttle's rear to activate the decompression chamber, fumbling with the headset as he ran.

He lowered the decompression chamber to the soft powdery surface, and the cylindrical outer shell rotated open. Gerhardt could see from the fuzzy under-hull camera someone had stepped into the chamber. He punched *Close*, *Lift*, *Decontaminate*, and *Repressurize*. Then a voice came over his headset.

"Gerhardt!" Margaret cried. "Do you copy?"

"*Ja*, Margaret," he said, adjusting the headset's fit. "Did anyone get into the chamber? I couldn't see, but it looked like just one."

"No, don't open the chamber!" she shouted. "We have a problem down here."

"Problem? I don't understand."

Air pumps rumbled in the chamber as it made a slow ascent. A sweating and shaking man nervously checked the count on his weapon. The reading was near zero, so he unzipped a pouch on his thigh. No ammunition. He patted his chest and found a hard spot that had to be the extra clip of bullets. The atmosphere quality sensor went green, so he quickly unzipped the front of his E-suit, exposing the clip.

"You have an armed intruder!" she shouted.

The all-clear light flashed in front of Gerhardt.

His heart pounded as the cylindrical chamber rotated open. He frantically entered commands to close and lower the chamber when a hand reached through the opening door. A loud *pop* echoed through the shuttle. Gerhardt's left side went numb as he saw the decompression chamber close. A bullet had penetrated his back near the upper rib cage. He saw blood flowing from his chest and felt a brief chill. The room went dark.

The chamber began its descent. The already crazed man beat at the control panel, but the chamber kept moving. In the split second that the doors moved open, he remembered his unzipped E-suit. The pressure and cold hit instantly as he tried to press a hand against the open seam. But his hand didn't respond and locked in place just centimeters from his chest.

All the cold needed was the small surface area near his neck for access. The near-absolute-zero temperatures rushed through him like an anesthetic. No pain. No movement.

"Quickly," Margaret shouted, pulling on Robert's arm.

Will followed close behind.

"I can see the cylinder; it's lowered and open."

"I don't see the TIgrIS man anywhere," Will said, panning in all directions. "He's either behind us or already on the shuttle."

"The cylinder wouldn't be down if he were on board," she said.

"But why haven't we heard from Gerhardt?" Will asked.

"Good god!" Robert cried. He raced into the chamber where the TIgrIS man lay on the floor. "Help me get him to his feet." Robert pulled the gun from the man's icy grip.

He and Will propped the unconscious man up against the wall. Margaret tried contacting Gerhardt, but no response. She activated the control panel, the door rotated shut, and the chamber began to move.

When it opened, they found Gerhardt lying on the floor in a blood-soaked uniform.

"Gerhardt!" she shouted.

There was no movement.

Margaret stumbled across the room, tossing her helmet and gloves. She knelt on the bloodstained floor and rolled him onto his back. She unlatched his helmet and gently pulled it off. His eyes were glassy and fixed, and he had no pulse. Margaret closed her eyes, clenched her fists, and wept.

Will and Robert dragged the half-frozen body out of the decompression chamber. They pulled it through the rear mechanical room and laid it on the floor in the passenger compartment.

They returned to the mechanical room where Gerhardt lay dead on the floor. Margaret was still bent over his body, crying. Robert placed a hand under Gerhardt's chin and pressed against the jugular, hoping for a faint thump. But there was none, so he gently pushed Gerhardt's eyes shut. Will helped Margaret to her feet and got her over to a chair.

"I'm sorry, Mother," he said softly. "I know he was your friend."

"This never should've happened," she whispered. "How did this happen?"

Will held her close. "This isn't your fault."

She shook her head. That old cliche worked for spilled milk, but here it went unnoticed.

"We're all lucky to be alive right now," he continued. "If you hadn't pushed as hard as you did, we'd be in big trouble. And now we're going to need you to get through this."

The distance between them, the gap that slowly narrowed, had finally disappeared there on the shuttle floor with Gerhardt lying at their feet.

"We have to get out of here, Mother," he said. "And I have to fly us."

Margaret slowly regained her composure. "I know." She sighed, then turned to Robert. "Can you take care of the bodies? Will and I must get up front and figure out how to fly this thing."

"Don't worry about it. Just get up front," Robert replied. "By the way, you'd better get your helmet and gloves back on. No chances on radiation exposure, right?"

Will strapped himself into the pilot's seat. The preset navigational routine was something he'd not even played with before. But he'd seen Gerhardt initiate the onboard computer from the pilot's station.

"First, we have to set the computer to routine status checks of standard system functions," he said. He was a one-man audience but didn't know it.

Margaret sat next to him, still upset and stunned. With Gerhardt dead, she'd suddenly lost interest in the mission; maybe it was finally getting to her. Besides, if there was one thing in life she had no knowledge of, it was piloting any flying machine. She calmly watched her son attack the navigational controls and felt an eerie comfort, as if Gerhardt's spirit were still with them.

"I'm not sure about the navigational controls," Will said. "That was one of Gerhardt's specialties. He told me that flying the shuttle was easy once it knew where to take you. I'm hoping the flight path is already calculated and logged in."

"Great, there it is," he continued, pointing to the view screen. "The destination is preset at Gaia. The loop closes, and there's plenty of fuel and O2. Hang on!"

Will initiated vertical thrust to the high-pitched sound of jet engines as the shuttle craft lifted off the frozen crater bed. The hull creaked and vibrated as thrusters rotated to a forward position, accelerating the craft. He switched control to autopilot, then sat back as the ship pitched and rolled into its preset flight path.

Within minutes, the shuttle streaked over the Huygens ice plateau toward Gaia 3. The sky was as bright as ever and dominated the view from the cockpit. Will hadn't thought about it until then, but the brightness never seemed to end. Since Huygens was on the bright side of the moon, it would stay illuminated as long as the rings remained excited.

"Good job," Margaret said and patted his shoulder and kissed his cheek. She leaned back, relaxed, and closed her eyes.

PART V

Chapter 16
SATURNALIA

A cold, dry gust blew past, cutting through the seams of his insulated body suit. John Avery squinted and turned away while a flock of penguins stood motionless at his feet, as if a mild summer breeze had passed. Avery was in awe of any species able to adapt to the ice world of Antarctica. Was this really his home planet?

The penguin, whale, and seal were all warm-blooded creatures that lived in sub-zero environments. But could this world be transplanted to another, even colder, world if suitably modified? The first step would be to adapt simple life forms to the base elements of the new world. Methane was that element for Titan.

Another stiff breeze pushed in larger waves. Penguins scurried up the beach as a primitive wooden sailing ship lumbered toward the shoreline. Made from heavy crude timber with no mast, sails, or side oars, the ship was enormous, nearly five hundred meters from stern to bow as it crashed ashore.

A wooden gangway dropped with a splash onto the icy-hard shore. A slow procession of animals marched down the gangway and crowded the frozen beach. There were farm animals, wild cats, *and crocodiles. They gathered around Avery and stood as if waiting for him to speak.*

A robed and bearded man wielding a shepherd's staff appeared at the top of the gangway.

***

Inspired by his dream, Avery tracked down Richard Markham in systems command.

"I'm telling you, it's our only hope!" Avery shouted.

"John, you might as well be talking to the wall," Markham said, punching away at his terminal. "Radiation is spreading, and I have work to do. Margaret has the final say on whatever decision is made. She'd have to get approval from the Space Council for a wild idea like that, and it's not my concern right now. I'm still trying to contain a leak."

"She can't even talk to Earth right now," Avery said.

"And she's not going to," Markham said. "If that's the best we can come up with."

"Don't be so damn narrow-minded!" Avery continued, pushing his point. "Haven't you been listening to me? The oxygen levels are not the problem anymore. We can't fight the radiation. We must cryo-freeze the entire facility until this disturbance passes."

"Entire facility." Markham scoffed. "And who stays around to monitor the life cycles while the animals and people are playing Noah's Ark?"

"You idiot!" Avery shouted. "Nothing can survive radiation exposure, plant or animal life. We have to freeze the Living, too."

"If things progress the way you predict."

"*When* things progress the way I've predicted."

"Just how do you propose to freeze the Living?" Markham asked. "Make a big cryo-freezer to put it in?"

"In a manner of speaking," Avery said. "We initiate a series of controlled temperature drops to limit thermal damage to the structure. Then open the thermal exhaust vents and channel them directly through supply air ducts. The Living would be contaminated with methane and radiation, but at least it would be neutralized."

"And how do you expect to bring *that* back online?"

"You don't!" Avery shouted. "It's dead. We set a distress signal before cryo-freeze and wait for a rescue."

"I doubt if anyone," Markham said, "especially Margaret, would ever approve of abandoning and destroying this base."

"If you don't freeze the Living, it'll be the death of us all," Avery argued. "We can hardly keep the thing balanced with full-time maintenance, and if we're all in cryo-freeze, the whole thing could turn into a giant green mold. Besides, leaving the sun active while we're in cryo-freeze is like going on vacation with the oven left on."

Markham's response was cut short by a knocking sound.

"Help! Richard! Help!" Libby beat at the entry door and fidgeted with the keypad while watching both ends of the corridor nervously. "C'mon!"

Markham hurried across the room, reached the door, and pulled her through. She wrapped her arms around him and buried her head in his shoulder. He could feel her heart pounding while she tried to force out words.

"I was up inside the rock," she bawled. "It was Kirby. He was eating the… He's dead."

"What?" Avery crossed the room. "You see, it's already happening!"

"Shut up!" Markham shouted while Libby shook in an adrenaline rush. "Calm down, it's all right. It's all right. Now, explain what happened."

She paused and took a deep breath.

"I was investigating the upper caves," she said, "when I saw that the upper supply air grill was damaged again."

"The one that Kirby and Miller repaired?"

"Right," she continued. "I crawled inside and roped down to the floor of the mountain. I found half-eaten carcasses everywhere. Then I saw Miller. His eyes were—"

"His eyes were what?"

"Like a monster's," she said.

Markham turned to Avery and saw a distant, grim expression.

"Then he attacked me. I barely got out. But he fell inside the rock. I think he's dead."

"I've got to find Miller," Markham said. "We have to check this out."

"He's on his way now," she said. "But there's something else. He didn't seem right. Miller was a bit jerky, and his eyes looked funny."

"That's it," Avery said. "It's started. We have to prepare."

"For what, Noah's Ark?" Markham scoffed. "I don't think so. We wait 'till Margaret gets back before we do anything."

"If we wait for Margaret, we'll all be dead," Avery said and stormed out of the room.

"Libby, I'm going to check on Kirby," Markham said. "Do you want to come with me or wait here?"

"I need some rest," she replied. "I'm going back to my room."

Markham hurried down the corridor and rode the elevator up to the Living. "Come on, come on," he grunted nervously as the air compressors rumbled.

"You may proceed," Sys finally said.

Markham stumbled out onto the white sand. "Miller! Miller!" he shouted.

No response.

Markham made his way through the jungle underbrush and around the mountain's base. Through the foliage and steam he could make out the supply air grills on the mountainside. One grill was propped open, and a climbing rope hung down to the ground nearby, but still no sign of Miller.

He rummaged through the maintenance room and found an old flashlight with a charge in the battery. In minutes, he'd crawled inside the dented air duct and saw the broken side panel. A cold stench blew up from below as he shined the flashlight down inside.

The light panned through the maze of metal hangers and pipes. Markham soon found the floor far below and saw Kirby's body suspended in twisted wire and ductwork. It was difficult to make out, but scattered carcasses of dead animals were lying everywhere. Then out of the corner of his eye, he noticed a light.

"Miller," he shouted as a hatch in the concrete floor lowered. It was an access hatch to the Dead Hemisphere. The silhouette of a man ducked down inside, and the hatch dropped shut.

Chapter 17
A TALL TALE

The shuttle streaked toward Gaia and bounced through a turbulent pocket of air. The rumble woke Margaret from a deep sleep as the shuttle passed through a cloud bank with zero visibility.

"You feel all right?" Will asked and patted her hand.

"What's the flight status?" she asked.

"No problems," he replied as they passed through the cloud. "We're cruising on autopilot, about thirty minutes from base."

"What was that we just passed through?" she asked. "I've never seen a low cloud on Titan."

"This moon doesn't get much light," he said. "It's a greenhouse effect of some kind. The methane oceans must be vaporizing."

"Marvelous." Margaret moaned. "Will, do you suppose there could be some connection between the ring phenomena and these dreams we've been having?"

"Robert already told us about the combination of low O2 and radiation," he replied.

"I understand," Margaret said. "But maybe there's more to it than just the medical explanation. Every dream I've had in the past few weeks involves the rings. There's some psychic connection."

"Or maybe it's because it's always on your mind," Will said.

"Could be," she said. "But I need to know more about TIgrIS and that picture on the wall. What more can you tell me?"

"I've been going over it in my mind since we left," he said. "What I found all those years ago must have been one of the best-kept secrets of the ancient world. The Romans stumbled across an ancient archive of Assyrian clay tablets, translated their secret, and decided to hide them away forever.

"It's one of the best-kept secrets of *modern times,* too. TIgrIS suspected they were getting close, so they hired cheap help to do the dirty work, then brushed it under the carpet like it was no big deal.

"I can still picture Shastri, all smiles, boarding the transport with the headstone. I knew he was lying to me, but I could not find out what it was. A man tracked me down after Ben died, and I've had this ring ever since."

"But what did they expect to find out here?" Margaret asked.

"Maybe we should ask them," a voice came from behind. Robert stepped into the cockpit in full E-suit gear.

"What are you talking about?"

"I've been listening to your conversation," Robert continued. "I've revived our guest."

"What?" she shouted.

"I don't think he's going to make it," Robert said. "But he's able to talk."

Will unstrapped and moved past Robert while the doctor and Margaret continued their discussion.

"I thought he was dead," she said.

"Close and in shock," Robert said. "I doubt we can bring his body temperature down quickly enough to save him. There's just too much frozen tissue. Before they thaw, his internal organs will quit functioning. If you want to talk to him, you'd better get back there fast."

Robert had removed his icy environmental suit and helmet. His dark hair glistened as a light coating of frost melted away from his face. The man's frozen legs and arms were locked in a stone-like stillness while steamy vapor rolled away. But his upper chest and face appeared undamaged by the freeze. He was showing the first signs of madness; his dilated pupils and bloodshot eyes faded in and out. Robert gave him a mild sedative to relieve the pain.

"Can you hear me?" Will asked. "Do you understand me?"

"Yes," the man whispered. He swallowed and winced; the air released from his lungs was painful. "Are you from the living ship?"

"We are," Will replied.

Margaret and Robert knelt next to him.

"I am a scientist," the man whispered. "I was sent on this mission to study ring dynamics. Specifically, the modified motion that would occur as the comet passed."

"We answered your distress call. We just came to help," Will said. "But we need to know why this base is here."

The man gasped for air, then seemed to relax. "Don't you know already?" he asked. "As in the time of the great flood, or the dark ages that follow every two thousand years, this is the end of things. I believe you Christians call it the Apocalypse."

"If you knew this was going to happen," Will said, "then why didn't you warn the rest of the world?"

"What good would it do?"

"If the prophecy of the tablets said there was no hope," Will said, "then why come out here at all?"

The man paused. "To touch the hand of Allah."

Will turned to Margaret. These cryptic statements were getting nowhere. She pulled him aside while Robert attended to the patient.

"Will," she said. "He has a nine-year head start on us. Maybe he knows more about why it's happening or how long it'll last."

He approached the man again. "Listen," he said calmly. "We don't have much time. We need to know more about what's happening. How long will the rings remain excited? Do you know?"

The man sighed. "Only what the ancient ones recorded," he whispered. "The star shone as bright as the sun for thirty days, and the comet rained madness across the land."

"So bad things do happen on Earth?" Will asked.

The man nodded.

Will pulled the ring from his finger and held it out.

"So, you're the one," the man said. "You have known for all these years, yet you did not alert the world."

"Alert them to what?" Will barked. "Everything was taken from me before I even had time to study it."

The man took a long painful breath.

"I understand," he said. "The secrecy surrounding the Cenotaph resembled your Manhattan project."

The man's eyes shifted to his side, concentrating on the arm that could still move. He managed to lift it and raise an open palm toward Will, then raised and lowered his hand again and again.

"Just as a shutter opens and closes," he said, "this planet faces our planet with its rings broad-faced or on edge in a regular cycle. Twice during its orbit, the rings disappear from view, and twice they lean toward us. And the comet's period is synchronized perfectly with that cycle. Its period is exactly fifty-four Saturnian years. So, each time the comet passes Saturn, the rings are at their widest face to

Earth. And it always passes in early summer when Saturn is at opposition from Earth's perspective, so it is at its brightest in the sky."

The man's hand dropped to the floor, his head rolled to the side, and his dilated eyes locked in a fixed glassy gaze. Robert pressed a hand to his neck.

"You two had better get back up front," Robert said. "I'll see if I can do anything else for him."

"This is unbelievable," Margaret murmured, staring at the frozen man. "These effects could be felt on Earth, and they didn't warn us."

"Maybe TIgrIS didn't believe it themselves," Will said. "Babylonians were excellent record keepers, but mythology can't be taken too seriously. I can tell you this, though, no modern history book has ever recorded such a phenomenon. When we get back, I'll have Sys look into it."

"They were curious enough to fund the construction of that facility," she said. "And secretly, I might add. I have to find some way to warn Earth."

"In the meantime," Will said. "We have to hold out inside Gaia 'till this thing passes. And that could be weeks or even months."

"That's it." Robert sighed. "He's gone."

"Here." Robert handed plastic packets to Margaret. "I want you to keep these with you from now on."

"What is it?"

"Something to fight the symptoms of this sickness," he answered. "Sedatives for sleeping and pilocarpine if your eyes get irritated or dilated."

"Thanks."

They all moved upfront. Margaret took a deep breath and pondered their hopeless situation as the shuttle thundered over a bright frigid landscape. Visibility was worse. They flew through fog bank after fog bank between blinding patches of a white landscape. And past the horizon, where hills leveled off to flat coastal terrain, a cloud engulfed the entire inland ice mass, including Gaia.

"Let me see that ring of yours?" Margaret asked.

Will handed it over.

"So, your friend carved this out of that ancient headpiece and made a ring just for you? That doesn't make any sense."

"Well, that's not exactly how it happened," he said. "He sent it to me a few years later, obviously after he discovered its secret. He must've hoped I'd investigate it, but the numbers inside didn't mean anything to me."

She turned the ring to examine the inside. "Two, one, six, eight."

Will chuckled., "That's what I said when I first read them. The correct order is one, six, eight, and two. 1,682 years is the orbital period of the planetoid. I guess someone else discovered it first."

"Yes, but if notoriety is what you're after," Margaret said, "then you don't have to worry. This ring will be worth a fortune when you return to Earth."

Chapter 18
SABOTAGE

Lights in the cryo-lab flickered over the cryo-freezer control panel. A cloud of cold, dry vapor blasted from pressure relief vents on either side of the freezer. The clear glass chamber frosted over to a translucent white, and the status board flashed green.

John Avery cautiously keyed in a command sequence monitoring vital signs. Metabolism had all but stopped, and the pulse was almost nonexistent, but a small monkey had survived cryo-freeze. Avery slowly unlatched the cover and lifted it back.

He unhooked the mesh of monitor wires and gently lifted the primate from the chamber. Its soft, chilly body was as limp as meat in a butcher's window. Its eyes were closed in a deep comatose sleep as John carried it over to a storage locker.

Avery took it upon himself to round up as many inhabitants of the Living as possible. If the station went into deep freeze, as he planned, there'd be no time to waste. Anything not placed in cryo-freeze would die.

The faint glow of light from the equipment irritated his eyes. Avery knew the first symptoms of radiation sickness were affecting him. He struggled with the fact that, in a few hours, he might lose track of his senses. His focus on the task at hand was all that kept him going. It didn't matter what Markham thought, but Margaret would understand if she made it back.

"That'll do for now," he murmured and stepped out of the storage room. He nervously panned the cryo-lab for unwanted visitors, then pulled up a chair in front of his terminal and summoned Sys.

"Sys," Avery said. "I would like to review recent modifications to the daytime sky simulation."

"Acknowledged," Sys said. "Would you like a complete readout of the change in energy output and luminosity levels?"

"No, thank you," Avery responded, cautiously looking around. "Actually, I would like to discuss the limits of such modifications and if further changes can be made."

"Please proceed."

"Please cancel the audio portion of this discussion," Avery said. "It's late, and I have a bit of a headache."

"Acknowledged."

"Question," Avery continued. "Can the daytime simulation be canceled?"

"Processing… Cancellation would require a voice authorized command from the base administrator before the complete evacuation of the facility."

"Understood," he said. "Can the daytime simulation be restored to its original path?"

"Damaged screen material prevents the use of that portion of the screen until repairs can be made," Sys said.

"Understood," Avery said. "Can the daytime simulation be accelerated to provide more nighttime hours?"

"Processing... Minimum daylight hours set at twelve to accommodate life cycle requirements. Temperature control through stored energy would be reduced, requiring additional mechanical heat."

"I'm sorry," he said. "Stored energy?"

"Please be more specific," Sys said.

"Please define how energy is stored."

"Heat energy from the artificial sun is absorbed by the solid components of the Living Hemisphere," Sys said. "Soil and biomass account for twenty percent, and rock structures account for the remaining eighty percent. The concrete mountain releases sixty percent of the total, while the terraces and desert rock releases another twenty. Reduction of daylight hours by thirty minutes would require an additional mechanical load of—"

"Stop," Avery interrupted. "So, the rock is a giant thermostat. In the same way, the desert acts as a humidifier."

"Please be more specific."

"Please hold!"

"Sys," he said, letting out a deep nasal sigh. "What criteria were used to alter the sun's path to its current position?"

"Processing... The ground base was relocated from Tucson, Arizona, to Buenos Aires, Argentina."

"I don't understand," he said. "How did that alter the path of the sun?"

"The celestial path across the sky in the southern hemisphere is opposite that in the northern hemisphere," Sys said. "Its path tilts northward in the southern hemisphere and southward in the northern hemisphere. The choice of cities was irrelevant, provided the city was located in the southern hemisphere."

"Understood."

Then it hit him, the sun's angle in the sky. If he set the daytime sequence to winter when Earth tilted away from the sun, that put it low in the sky.

"Sys?" he asked. "Can the daytime simulation be set to match seasons?"

"Processing... The celestial path is preferred to vary between the vernal equinox and the summer solstice. This provides maximum solar intensity and prevents damage to the view screen."

"Understood," he said. But then, summer in Canada differed from summer in Panama.

"Sys," he said. "Can the daytime simulation be altered again to a new ground base in the southern hemisphere?"

"There are three hundred forty-three usable coordinate references in the southern hemisphere," Sys said.

"Sys," Avery said cautiously. "Please reset daytime simulation to a ground base reference of the South Pole."

He didn't think Sys would allow such a move. The Antarctic sun hardly moved across the sky from late September to late March, the highest the sun ever rose above the horizon was about twenty degrees. The sun's low passage was merely a warm glow on the horizon.

"Please note," Sys said, "this setting was only used during the start-up phase for testing the range and intensity of solar passages. I do not recommend its use since it will require supplemental heating and artificial lighting. Shall I calculate the power usage requirements?"

"No," Avery said abruptly. "That won't be necessary. We'll just be using it for a few days. Please continue."

"Processing... Complete."

THE KUIPER ROGUE

He was shocked. That was too easy. First, he'd verify the change, then go down to the lower levels and sabotage the heaters.

Chapter 19
RETURN

Markham patrolled the corridors of the upper decks. He hadn't seen Avery or Libby since he'd left command. His boots clanged against the steel grating and blocked out other sounds, so he paused to listen. He leaned over a guardrail at an open area of the catwalks near the med lab. The drop-down was fifty meters through sheet metal and guy wires.

"Libby! Avery!" he shouted.

No response.

Where in the hell are they? He moved on.

Libby was asleep when the doorbell rang, she swatted her alarm clock. Then the noise changed to a pounding.

"Libby!" Markham pounded at the door. "Are you in there?"

The door slid open. Libby stood with bloodshot eyes and an irritated expression.

"Sorry to wake you," Markham said, stepping into her room. "How are you feeling?"

"Tired."

"I went down inside the rock," Markham said.

She perked up.

"I found him just where you said he was."

"Was he alive?"

"I don't think so," Markham continued. "I didn't get to the bottom, but I saw the body lying there. I saw Miller, too, but he crawled away through a floor hatch. I'm not sure what's going on. I can't find Avery either."

"Wait a minute," she said. "What time is it?"

"It's almost sunset, I believe," he replied.

"Then the shuttle should be returning soon," she said, splashing water on her face. "Let's get to command and try to contact Margaret. We can do an all call for Avery and Miller from there."

"I don't know," Markham said. "This is getting pretty weird."

"Don't get so wound up," she said. "Avery's probably in the cryo-lab playing with his pets or something, and Miller's just chasing down a stray monkey."

"Are you sure you want to go down there?" Markham asked. "We'll have to suit up."

"Given the option of sitting up here for an hour," she said. "Or going there in an E-suit would normally be an easy choice."

***

Libby was anxious as she and Markham waited for the sky bridge airlock to open. Repeated hails to the shuttle got static, and their comrades on Gaia ignored the all call. Markham assured Libby the issues were due to ring interference, but the pause in his voice wasn't convincing.

Markham panned the airlock with his flashlight. Repressurization was nearly complete, and the thick layer of frost had almost melted. Air quality and pressure remained poor in the Dead and worse in the sky bridge. Sys compensated; the green light flashed for them to cross the sky bridge. Their wait wasn't long, and soon they heard shuttle thrusters whining.

"Where the hell is it?" Markham panned around. "I can't see anything through this damn fog."

"I've never seen this much fog before on Titan," Libby worried.

"It must be heating up or something," Markham said. "I just hope Gerhardt has enough sense to land with autopilot."

Dust and fog whirled like a thunderstorm was blowing in. They couldn't see it, but the shuttle danced outside the hangar bay.

***

"Are you sure about this?" Margaret asked.

"Of course, Mother," Will tossed back. "The problem is I can't see anything."

He got that look.

A rectangular shadow appeared while the shuttle slowly steadied itself, and the outline of the hangar formed in front of them.

"There it is," Will said, adjusting controls. "Now, just a little forward thrust, altitude adjustment, and we'll be inside."

"You're actually enjoying this, aren't you?" she poked.

"I don't want to have all the fun," he said. "Do you want to taxi us inside?"

"No thanks," Margaret said. "Never tried it."

"Me neither." He smirked at her motherly scorn.

Markham and Libby couldn't believe it when the shuttle maneuvered inside the hangar for a soft landing. The tired shuttle crew greeted the tired team from Gaia in E-suits and helmets.

"Let's regroup in the cafeteria in thirty minutes," Margaret said. "I have to get out of this damn E-suit."

"Where's Gerhardt?" Libby asked.

Margaret kept walking.

"Let's get some coffee," Will re-directed, smiling at Libby. "I need to re-group."

"But -"

"I could really use it," Will said. "Especially before the entire group shows up."

"OK."

The cafeteria was empty when they arrived. Will walked over to the coffee machine and pressed a few buttons while Libby grabbed a seat.

"So," Will said. "How are things going here?"

Libby looked away, then back.

"It's getting worse," she replied. "Avery and Miller have gone AWOL. We can't find them anywhere, and they don't respond to all calls."

"I don't understand?"

"Join the party."

Will sipped his coffee.

"And that's not the worst of it," she sighed. "But let's not talk about that now."

"Not sure I want to talk about our trip either," Will said. "But we couldn't find Early; he's presumed dead."

"We did find something else, but I think Mother wants to update everyone on shortly."

"Are you OK?"

"Not really," Will placed his hand on Libby's. "We can talk about some other time."

Libby studied his drifting eyes.

C.P. SCHAEFER

"Things are getting worse," he said. "I'm not sure where all this goes."

"Join the party."

PART VI

Chapter 20
CONFERENCE

Margaret entered the cafeteria to a table of tired faces and half-empty plates.

"Libby, what's going on here?" she asked. "There's barely enough food for two people, let alone eight. Were you and Kirby sleeping while we were away? And where is everyone?"

"Margaret, I'm sorry but—"

"Kirby's dead," Robert interrupted. "Avery and Miller are missing."

Margaret paused, sat down, and went over the losses in her head. Six of her crew were dead, two missing, and one entire base was wiped out. The others were talking among themselves, so Margaret had to find something positive.

"Robert," she said. "I want you to administer medications to the entire crew. This problem is getting worse, and we need to contain it."

"I'm on it," he said.

"Good," she murmured.

"So, what the hell happened out there, Margaret?" Markham asked.

"We'll talk about that later," she said. "First, tell me about Kirby and how you're doing with decontaminating the Dead Hemisphere."

"Libby was attacked by Kirby down inside the mountain," he said. "Attacked!"

"Yes," he continued. "She just got a few cuts and bruises. But Kirby fell to his death, chasing her out of the mountain. I went down to investigate and found him. I also saw Miller, but he ducked down a hatchway into the Dead area, and we haven't seen him since."

"Avery's not responding to all calls," Libby added.

"As far as decontamination is concerned," Markham said. "It's as good as it's gonna get. I advise E-suits in the Dead Hemisphere for a while."

The most concerned face in the crowd belonged to Robert Lewis. He knew that in time, the sickness would take them all down. Sleeping pills and eye drops wouldn't last long if the base remained contaminated.

"Unfortunately, our news isn't much better," Margaret said. "We could not locate Early, so we assume he's dead. The distress signal led us to a previously unknown research station tucked away in an ancient crater. Most of the crew were dead, all suffered from radiation sickness, and it appeared they killed each other. Two were still alive when we arrived, one died on the base, and the other made it to the shuttle before he died."

She dropped her head and sighed. "Gerhardt didn't make it."

"Gerhardt!" Libby moaned. "I just thought he was on the shuttle closing it down. Oh, my god."

"Wait a minute," Markham cut in. "Someone put a space station up here without the Space Council knowing about it? I find that hard to believe."

"I know it's hard to believe," she said. "But I'm exhausted right now, and I need time to put this whole thing together before we go any further. There's much more to talk about, but it can wait 'till morning. Why don't we call it a night and reconvene at eight?"

"What do you mean, there's a lot more?" Markham scoffed. "I think we should talk about this right now."

"She *said*," Will stated firmly, "it can wait till morning."

Markham held his tongue. Margaret didn't speak. She hoped that was enough to break the discussion and get some sleep.

"But without Gerhardt," Libby said, breaking the silence, "we couldn't leave even if we wanted to."

"I'm sorry, Margaret," Markham gestured. "You look like you could use some rest."

"Will, are you up to a little more discussion?"

"Sure."

"Good night, everyone," Margaret patted Will on the shoulder and left the room.

Markham watched her walk down the hall and turned to Will.

"So, what else happened up there?" Markham asked.

"It was a tin can base sent up by a middle eastern contingent," Will replied. "Sent to study the comet when it arrived. Only, they did not anticipate the side effects from its radiation."

"When we entered the base, it was ram-shackled, lights broke out, and bodies everywhere. Sound familiar?"

"Wait," Markham interrupted. "Did you say they sent the base to *study* the comet? The comet just discovered?"

"That's right," Will said and flashed his ring. "It's a long story."

"How about just the highlights," Markham said.

"OK," Will sighed. "I worked a job one summer with an Archaeological team on an island in the Mediterranean."

"And what's that have to do with anything?"

"We found something," Will said, uploading files to Sys. "An ancient tablet and crypt full of clay bricks with cuneiform writing."

"It was taken away in secrecy, and I've not heard a word about it since. Or at least until we visited that mysterious base."

Photos of the ancient Stella from KOS Island appeared on the view screen to raise eyebrows. Will pulled the ring from his finger and handed it to Markham.

"This stone was originally set in the eye of the stone king," Will said. "My partner took it and, years later, sent me this ring."

Will stood and approached the view screen.

"The Stella," Will pointed out. "Is a portent of my comet's passing. And it's written in three different languages. But I didn't expect it would be confiscated, so I had no record of it for research."

"An alliance of middle eastern nations studied it in secrecy. They determined Saturn was the key object mentioned in all three passing Apocalypses. And decided placing a scientific outpost on Titan would be the best way to obtain first-hand information about the phenomenon."

"You're not making this up," Markham asked. "are you?"

"No," Will sighed. "You can't make this shit up."

Chapter 21
PROPHECY

Will couldn't clear his mind of the TIgrIS base discovery. Despite Robert's warnings, he was determined to avoid sedatives. He wanted to stay awake, research the TIgrIS issue, and know exactly where to start. He could work uninterrupted with Sys all night from his living quarters.

He needed the translation of the Kos Island cuneiform tablets but hadn't gotten it downloaded from the TIgrIS computer. Hopefully, there was a written record of the comet's last two passages, but clues about Saturn were hidden in the cuneiform crypt.

"Sys, I'd like to initiate a data search to help investigate the disturbance in the rings," he said. "Please access the astronomical reference library. Display all information from the two previous passages of comet 2092312 in 396 AD and 1286 BCE."

"Accessing… Complete," Sys said. "No information available."

"All right then," he said. "Please access the historical reference library. Display all natural catastrophes associated with the same years."

"Accessing… Complete," Sys said. "No information available."

"Nothing?" Will paused. "Sys, I'm trying to find records of any unusual activity associated with the planet Saturn. Any suggestions?"

"Perhaps a search of the political or mythological source material would yield better results," Sys replied.

"Yes, you're right," he said. "Please access references to classical mythology but limit the search to European and Middle Eastern civilizations."

"Would you like a display of all available information?" Sys asked.

"No, I don't think so," he replied. "That could get too cumbersome. For now, let's discuss the main references from the database and see what comes up."

"Processing… Complete," Sys said. "Where would you like to begin?"

"The late Roman era," he stated. "What significance did the planet Saturn have, and was it associated with the underworld or other dark powers?"

"Accessing… Saturn was considered the harvest god, protecting fields and flowering the vines," Sys said. "The festival of Saturnalia was celebrated in the fall of every year and marked by feast and drink. It was a time of lascivious behavior, orgy, and animal sacrifice that lasted one week. The festival originated in the early Roman era and continued in the western Empire until the late fifth century.

"As the Empire expanded in the early years, the seat of power shifted between the Greeks and Romans. The Roman armies suffered a series of defeats at the hands of the Greeks in the mid-third century BCE This led to a renewed religious fervor that initiated the Saturnalia.

"Other associated divinities such as Tellus Mater are represented—"

"Stop," Will interrupted. "That implies there was an eastern influence. What about the Greek equivalent?"

A pause, "Kronos (representing Saturn) was much feared and hated. He was one of the original Titans who murdered his father, Uranus. Driven by prophetic fear of the same happening to himself, he devoured his newborn children one at a time. All but Zeus, who would later defeat Kronos and expel him to the underworld, fulfilling the prophecy."

"Stop," he interrupted. "That's dark enough. So, we have the Roman festival of Saturnalia and the Greek god Kronos, a deceitful murderer. Please list comparisons in other ancient cultures."

"Please specify."

Will loaded the film disk from his helmet into an access drive. "Please access the video file, time frame 21:31:00, and read the translations shown. The stela, shown here, was the doorway to a hidden vault that contained tens of thousands of clay tablets with cuneiform writing on them. I discovered the vault years ago, but its contents and meaning have been kept secret. I believe there is a relationship between the events described and the strange phenomenon in the rings of Saturn."

"Processing… Complete," Sys said.

The view screen flashed the picture of the stela and its description as seen at TIgrIS.

"Sys, please cite references you have in related files."

"Processing… The Assyrian King Shalmaneser I ruled Mesopotamia from 1289 BCE to 1250 BCE. After his reign, celestial record-keeping disappeared for approximately one thousand years. Comet 2092312 would have reached the inner solar system during his reign."

"Question?" Will asked. "I'm curious about the rings through the serpent's nose. Is anything in there related to Saturn's rings?"

"Processing... When Galileo discovered Saturn's rings, they appeared as handles through his primitive telescope. But later observations occurred when the rings were edge-on and not visible. His journal noted: *Has Saturn devoured his own children?*"

He chuckled. "I don't remember reading that." He pondered the ring on his finger. "What about rings in general from a religious and mythological perspective."

"Processing... Finger rings first became popular in western societies during the Roman era as a sign of matrimony. From a broader perspective, rings have always been a symbol of unity, bondage, ownership, and closure."

"So, the rings in the pictograph are most likely the translator's imagination," he said. "And not some kind of universally shared vision."

"When Emperor Constantine chose the cross as the symbol of Christianity," Sys said, "he did so because the crucifixion of Jesus Christ was known throughout the ancient world. But if the ring's use in religious ceremonies resulted from a comet's passage, then it is something not known in the historical record."

"Good point," Will said. "Let's proceed with the Assyrian inscription."

"Processing... The translation references thirty days. If this is accurate, we can expect two more weeks of heightened activity in the ring system. The passage referring to the *red-eyed daevas* would seem to parallel a medical condition recently recorded in Doctor Lewis' medical logs."

"Agreed," he said. "But consider that Mimas exploded and contributed to the ring disturbance. Our situation could be far worse than the previous passages of the comet."

"That is possible," Sys said. "However, there have been no recorded observations of an object that size breaking up. Its reformation could be quicker than expected. The orbital periods of the comet and the moon are directly proportional. So, their paths probably cross with each cometary orbit."

"And the madness that affected John Early caused some form of glaucoma," he said. "So, we have to assume Earth will also be affected. Okay then, what about the Latin inscription?"

"Processing... The Roman calendar year 1149 is equivalent to 396 AD, the last year of the reign of Emperor Theodosius. This brings the dates written on the stela full circle. They correspond exactly to the two previous perihelion passages of the comet."

"Holy shit," Will said softly. "Sys, so why was it hidden away?"

"Processing... From a political perspective, in the latter decades of the fourth century, Christianity threw off the chains of four hundred years of persecution. The Empire was fragmented and collapsing, half holding to the old ways and half to Christian orthodoxy. An illuminated Saturn could have been viewed as the work of pagan gods and helped fuel the fires of the Christian following.

"But perhaps it was a sign from god, a warning to the pagans. Theodosius was a Christian emperor and the last emperor to control the eastern and western halves of the Roman Empire. He led an attack on Rome in the same year, shown on the stela. Fifteen years later, the western Empire fell to Barbarian hordes."

"So, civil unrest caused by this catastrophe," Will extrapolated, "could have triggered widespread chaos and revolt. The beginning of the end."

"A definite possibility," Sys said. "The Dark Ages in Europe began with the sacking of Rome in 410 AD. And apparently, a similar dark age began in Mesopotamia shortly after the previous passage of the comet."

"Now it's back," he said. "TIgrIS knew, and they didn't even warn us. What in the hell were they thinking? Civilization has fallen to chaos twice already because of this thing and whatever it does to people."

"Question," Will said. "Could it happen again?"

"Insufficient data to confirm," Sys said. "But it's a definite possibility."

There was nothing left to discuss. He paused for a moment. He knew what to tell the others in the morning, but he wasn't sure if they'd believe him. His exhausted mind drifted, and he stared at his prophetic ring and thought of his cometary research. Searching the heavens for unknown balls of ice used to mean everything to him. Now, he'd almost forgotten about them.

"Sys," he said. "Please save all files outlining this cometary research. Continue all tracking commands with Shoemaker and save the unchecked data for future reference. Also, save the minutes of this discussion to file.

"I would like a comparative spectral analysis of outgassing from Planetoid 2092312 and that emitted from recent ring system disturbances.

"This concludes our session."

"Processing… Complete."

Will went over it repeatedly, but there wasn't much more he came up with except guilt. Suddenly, his crusading efforts to discover new comets and asteroids seemed trivial and selfish. The key to understanding and preventing this catastrophe was literally at his fingertips. He'd had the ring for all these years and never tried to uncover its secret. He'd let Ben Murphy down. He'd let the whole world down.

His deep thoughts were broken by a sound. He heard it again. It was the entry buzzer, someone at the door.

"Oh, Libby," he said, pushing his brown hair aside. "Why are you still up?"

"Probably the same reason you are," she said, holding out her Lewis-issued package of sleeping pills and eye drops. "I don't want to be forced to sleep. These dreams are bad enough already."

Will gestured for her to enter, then walked back to his desk and propped an arm up under his chin. Libby took that as an invitation and followed him across the room.

"You're making me feel better already," she joked. "At least I still have a sense of humor."

"Oh, I'm sorry," he said. "I've been sitting here thinking about things. And by the way, I was sorry to hear about Jeff, and I hope you're all right."

"Thanks," she replied. "I've hardly slept since then."

"Too much on my mind right now," he said.

"Aren't you afraid of ending up like Kirby or Early?" she asked.

"All we can do now is take our medicine and monitor air quality," he said. "But right now, that's the least of my concerns. This whole thing is just unbelievable."

Will tossed a couple of pills in his mouth and chased them down with water. He held the glass her way, and Libby reluctantly did the same.

"What happened out there?" she asked, then swallowed her pills. "Nobody wants to talk about it."

"We'll be talking in the morning," he said. "You can count on that."

"Hey, I felt like talking. Maybe you're just not up to it," she said. "You just don't seem yourself. Maybe you should see Robert."

"I don't need to see anyone," he replied.

"Then maybe you should get some rest."

"I just finished a library search with Sys," he said. "These effects are going to reach Earth, and it's happened before."

Libby paused and gazed at Will with a confused and anxious expression. "How do you know that?" she asked.

Will held up his hand and twisted his ring. "Remember this?" he asked. "It's a souvenir from a place I used to work and turns out to be a key to what's happening out there. And the base we found was established to see if it would happen." Will focused on the ruby. "Or maybe just to get a front-row seat."

"What are you talking about?" she said. "How could anyone know that this was going to happen?"

"Prophecy," he said in a bewildered whisper. "Or something like that."

"So, people on Earth are having the same problems that we are up here?" she asked.

"If we could talk to them, maybe we could find out," he replied. "But most likely not 'till the planetoid reaches the inner planets."

"But it's late, and I need some rest." Will stood. "We can talk about this in the morning."

He walked to the door, but Libby held back.

"What's wrong?" he asked. "Are you feeling all right?"

"I'm afraid to fall asleep," she said. "I can't take these dreams anymore, and I saw those red eyes. What if I wake up like that?"

"If you don't get any sleep," he said, "it'll just get worse."

"I know," she said softly. "Do you mind if I stay here tonight?"

Will felt a rush. "Uh, sure," he fumbled. "I'll sleep on the couch."

"No, you don't have to do that," she said.

She'd caught him off-guard. He couldn't help it; he was a guy. But it was a good feeling, something he hadn't experienced for a while, so he went with it.

"Would you just hold me tonight?" she softly offered and took his hand. They curled up under the blankets and were asleep in minutes.

***

Will found himself on a rocky hilltop overlooking a vast desert.

"Will Vandolah!" *a familiar voice shouted from a distance.* "Over here!"

Winds blew up over the hillside, raising swirls of dust. He saw a figure waving a hand a few hundred meters away. The man looked familiar, but he couldn't be sure. It seemed to take forever, but Will slowly got closer. A thousand pinpricks stung his hands and face as sand whipped past. His heart hung low in his chest; he nearly dropped from the anxiety but finally made it and stood before Ben Murphy.

"Ben, what are you doing here?" Will shouted. He was excited to see his old friend dressed in a loose white robe and turban. He didn't understand the attire and thought it must be the spirit of the real man.

"It's good to see you again," Ben said. "We have much to talk about. But first, I need your ring."

The twilight sky was turning a deep shade of blue, and the evening air cooled. In the valley below, a legion of red and gold-clad soldiers flanked a team of chariots. The soldiers marched two abreast on either side of a line of chariots guarding a golden caravan. A group of strong-armed enslaved people shouldered a shining carriage to the sound of cracking whips.

A centurion barked orders, bringing the procession to a stop just below Will and Ben. Then the soldiers turned to the eastern sky and knelt on one knee. They slowly lowered the glittering carriage to the ground.

"What are they doing?" Will asked.

"Praying to the star," Ben replied. "They're not far from the school now. It won't be long before they burn it to the ground. Everything will be lost. We must hurry."

Will didn't know whether it was a dream or his knowledge of the skies. "It's Saturn, isn't it?" he asked.

"I see you finally figured it out," Ben said, reaching for Will's hand. "You should have paid attention years ago, but you didn't. It's too late for you, just as it was too late for me."

"I don't understand," Will said.

"There's no time to discuss," Ben said, pulling at his hand. "Give me the ring. They need it down there."

Will held back briefly as the two struggled, then Ben lost his footing. He tumbled down the gravelly slope end over end, banging against rocks and underbrush as he went. A slow-growing wave of stones and debris followed him down the hill in a dust cloud.

Will stood frozen as he watched Ben tumble to his death. Was this how it really happened to Ben? All he could remember was what the man on the bus had told him years ago. But that had been relayed as an excavation accident. He was too tired but had to get down there and help.

Will stumbled down the hillside and stood beside his injured friend. Ben was nearly covered with rocks and dust. He knelt to brush the material away when foot soldiers approached. They stared curiously at the oddly dressed man, then drew swords when they saw the ring. Will motioned for them to stop as he attended to his wounded friend.

"Ben! Ben!" he shouted, shaking his shoulder.

"Why didn't you listen?" Ben whispered as his eyes rolled back and went glassy.

Will turned to see the centurion dismount his chariot and approach. He stood over them, staring down as if they were nothing *more than a couple of unwanted rodents. Then he saw the ring and took it from Will's trembling hand. The centurion raised the ring to the eastern sky. A priest emerged from the golden carriage and studied the ring curiously.*

"Audentes Fortuna juvat," (Fortune favors the bold) the centurion said and walked away.

Then a soldier drew down on Will and thrust a dagger into his chest.

***

Libby stood in the front yard of her parents' house, overlooking the great city in the valley. Smoke and flames rose from the skeletal remains of buildings for miles in all directions. Sirens from emergency equipment and the thumping of helicopters echoed throughout the hills. A faint popping of gunfire crackled through the city.

Who knew how many had died. She couldn't bear to think about it. But standing high on the hill, far from the rioting crowds, made her feel safe.

She hoped it would end soon, but no one knew how long the comet's biblical tail would last. It was all over the news that scientists and astronomers scrambled to determine when the effects would end.

It was sunset, and the bright comet would soon light up the eastern sky. A chill came rolling down the hillside and brought the echoes of voices, violence, and vehicles. The sudden noise distracted her hypnotic gaze. She quickly pulled her sweater together and ran toward the house.

She pulled open a rickety gate that slammed behind her as she raced across the lawn toward the front door. Her father was inside the door near the gun cabinet, checking his supply of twelve-gauge rounds.

Before she could even say hello, there was a loud explosion outside, lights flickered, and the house went dark and quiet. She ran to the windows and saw the entire neighborhood had lost power.

"They blew out a transformer," Mr. Owens said as he fumbled through the dark.

Libby's heart stopped when her father dropped his ammunition boxes on the floor. When she turned to face the window, a swarm of street people had jumped from a truck and dispersed into the darkness. Her arms and legs tingled; she stepped back from the window in anticipation. She heard glass breaking, followed by screams and gunshots.

"That's about enough," Mr. Owens said boldly, then started out the front door.

"Daddy!" *Libby shouted. She ran for the door but stopped short. Two men had dragged her neighbors out of their house and held them at gunpoint. One man held them at bay with an automatic weapon while another circled them like a hungry vulture.*

"Let 'em go," *Mr. Owens said, his twelve-gauge aimed and ready.*

"What are you gonna do?" *The man laughed.* "This?"

He shot his hostage in the back of the head, then turned quickly toward Mr. Owens, his gun raised and pointed. The rage inside him revealed itself in his shaking hand and glowing red eyes that pierced the darkness.

"Or maybe this?" *The man swung around and shot the woman, who dropped to the ground.*

Owens blasted at the man as a powder flash blew out of the barrel. But before he could fire again, the other man turned quickly and shot Owens dead.

"You bastard!" *Libby screamed.*

The men sprang toward the house, kicked open the door, and slowly walked up to her. Their bulging red eyes were ready to burst. Libby tried to run, but her feet were frozen, and the harder she tried, the weaker she became.

This has to be a dream. She was horrified had to get away. Her conscious self tried to work its way through the subconscious paranoia and take control. If she couldn't move, she could try to wake up.

"What did you call me?" the madman cynically asked and put the gun to her temple.

***

"Are you all right?" Will woke her up, wiping sweat from Libby's face with his T-shirt.

"Yeah, just another bad dream," she whispered. "Thank god."

She sat up to catch her breath and reached for a glass of water while Will wiped down her neckline. She gulped the water and looked at the clock.

"It's only four AM," she softly said. "How many more hours of suffering can I take?"

"Hey," Will consoled. "We're all going through this, just hang in there. We'll get up in a few hours and go for breakfast, with coffee, lots of coffee. Everything's going to work out."

Chapter 22
TIgrIS AND BABYLON

"What I'm saying," Robert reiterated, "is that the forces of good and evil are inherent in all of us. This might be a mechanism that throws them out of balance."

"Oh, Jesus," Markham scoffed.

"Gentlemen," a pale and tired Margaret interrupted. "We really need to get this meeting started. By the way, where are Avery and Miller?"

Markham quickly acknowledged, like he knew where they were, so she continued.

"First, I want to fill everyone in on our rescue mission," she said. "And then find out just what in the hell is going on around here.

"By now, I believe everyone knows that we could not locate John Early in the hover-shuttle. He is presumed dead. We found a previously unknown base placed here by a group of Asian countries to observe this ring phenomenon.

"When we arrived, we found two dead crewmembers on the ice. We proceeded inside, and the place was wrecked, but two remaining crew members were still alive, one armed and one not. There was an accident that killed the unarmed man. The other man escaped to the shuttle, where there must have been a confrontation. When we arrived, the armed man was lying in the decompression chamber with a compromised E-suit, and Gerhardt had been shot dead."

"Let's back up a second," Markham said. "Someone actually knew that all this was going to happen?"

"Apparently so," Margret replied. "But as far as we can tell, no one inside the Space Council was aware. I'll have Will fill you in shortly. I've been going over this all night, and we are grossly understaffed now. It'll be impossible to operate this base for a prolonged period. So, we should send a distress signal to Earth and make a backup plan for a shuttle escape."

"And who's going to fly us out of here?" Markham asked.

"Will got us back from the inland mountains," Margaret started.

"Margaret, that's hardly the same as achieving orbit!" Markham interrupted. "And plotting a course back to Earth."

"I understand," she said. "That's why it's a backup plan. Will's going to discuss just what we found out there and why. You'll find this interesting."

"Well, half this group already knows the story," he said. "But last night's discussion with Sys revealed even more information."

**

Will described the find at Kos and his involvement, although his ring story raised a few eyebrows. He discussed the TIgrIS base and why it was kept a secret. It all seemed far-fetched and led to some heated discussion.

"Okay," Robert said. "Let's suppose this happened two or three thousand years ago, and some ancient mythology was formed or transformed. But you suggest someone put a base up here to test that theory?"

"That's exactly right," Will finished. "And funded entirely by the TIgrIS bloc of countries. News of the Kos Island finds must've sent a shockwave through that region. To western thinking, religious customs of ancient civilizations are just superstition. But to these guys, it's real. Traditions handed down for countless centuries have not lost their meaning.

"Sumerians studied the heavens and clearly understood the movement of stars and planets. These heavenly bodies were viewed as godlike and coexisted with our world. So, if one piece fell out of sync, it was likely to have some biblical connotation. This was nothing more than a curse. So, a king ruling a land in disarray would fix it quickly and bury the evidence.

"The tablets from Kos speak of red-eyed devils in a time of madness and recorded something extraordinary with dates that match this planetoid's passage exactly. Now we're seeing the same effects on people directly exposed to that light."

"I still can't believe something this important was lost from all historical records," Robert said. "And now, when it is finally rediscovered?"

"Excuse me," Markham cut in. "Have you ever heard of a government cover-up?"

"I remember," Margaret said, "that a few Middle Eastern countries opposed funding this station. They disagreed with any permanent facility in the Saturnian system and gave only vague explanations."

"All right, then," Markham huffed. "Back to our immediate problems—where do we go from here?"

"The first thing we do," Margaret regrouped, "is make sure the life cycles on Gaia are functioning normally again. Richard, where are Avery and Miller?"

"I don't know," Markham sighed.

"What do you mean?" Margaret said. "You don't know where they are now, or you don't know, period?"

"We haven't seen either of them since the Jeff Kirby accident," Markham said. "And they don't respond to station-wide calls."

Margaret panned a cynical gaze from one person to the next but saw only blank faces.

"Okay then," she said. "We're going to find them both within the hour. Richard, I want you to seal off all the lower decks. If we have to search there again, we'll be in full E-suits—too many accidents can happen there. But we'll comb the upper decks and the Living first."

"Margaret," Robert added, "at this point, I'm going to insist regular use of sedatives at night be enforced. And if anyone develops vision problems *of any kind*, see me immediately."

"Robert!" She stopped him, then regrouped. "Perhaps you're right."

The words had hardly left her lips when emergency alarms sounded. Standard lighting changed to emergency strobes in the hallway. Margaret headed for the door.

"Everyone follow!" she said.

They hustled down the flashing corridor, listening to a distorted message from Sys. It wasn't the same as before, something about *Thermal Limits*. All Margaret could think of was another sky bridge breach.

At command, they found manual entry was locked out. The system only accepted Margaret's voice authorization. The last emergency had no control measure, but what could be worse than a sky bridge breach? Once inside, Markham hurried to the central control station and punched in a status check.

"Oh, Jesus," Markham cried. "The goddamn heaters have been shut down."

"That can't be," Margaret shouted above the alarms. "The gauge readings are just off."

"No, they're not," Markham said. "And it wasn't shut off at the board either. The board has no power; the lines have been cut or something."

"Will!" she shouted. "Check the temperature in the Living."

"Got it," he replied. "We're at… ten degrees Celsius… and falling."

"That's impossible," Margaret said, checking the time. "It's almost eight o'clock in the morning; the sun has been up for two hours."

"I know," he said. "The coldest it normally gets at night is the mid-teens. But we're at ten degrees Celsius in there right now."

"A few more degrees," Libby cautioned, "and there'll be irreparable damage."

"Mother, at this rate, we'll reach freezing in two hours," he said, shouting.

"Will, you and Libby get up top and check this out," Margaret said. "Richard, have Sys shut off these damned flashers!"

"Margaret," Markham said, pushing fingers through his hair. "We can't just go down there and flip a switch. These heating coils are overly sensitive and take time to warm up. Refiring the system from scratch could take forty-eight hours."

"Then let's suit up," Margaret said. "I want to see just what in the hell's going on down there."

Chapter 23
THE BIG CHILL

Will and Libby nervously rode the elevator up to the Living Hemisphere. Will had a lump in his throat the size of a golf ball; the station's fate lay in the balance. The ride seemed longer than usual but just as steady. At least the elevator was working. The car slowed while air pumps rumbled away.

The sound grew closer, and soon Sys signaled to proceed. The elevator doors whisked open, revealing the secondary chamber. Its windows were steam-covered, they had never seen that before—the thermal problem was real.

"Oh, my god," Libby whispered.

The door slid open, and chilly air rushed past their faces. They stepped into a murky, wilted world. A blanket of steam rose from the moat and covered the entire Living Hemisphere. The sky was too dark, almost dusk.

There was no sun, just an orange glow welling on the horizon. Libby hurried across the sands to the edge of the jungle where underbrush showed signs of fatigue and lofty palm fronds drooped.

"Will." She turned decisively. "If we don't do something fast, we'll lose all the vegetation."

They stood dazed, contemplating the sky.

"The system must be locked up or something," he pondered. "But I don't understand why Sys hasn't reported this."

"Maybe the alarm had a combination of messages," she said. "After all, we left as soon as we heard about the heaters."

"Yeah, maybe you're right," he said. "Let's get back to command."

They started across the cool sands but stopped short.

"Leaving so soon?" a voice shouted from above. "Don't you like the way I've redecorated up here?"

Jim Miller stood naked at the edge of the desert terraces. He'd draped a dead snake over his shoulders and hung animal pelts from a rope tied around his waist. He'd cocked a wooden arrow tight against the string of a simple bow and aimed it at Will. The prehistorically garbed huntsman gazed down at them with his blood-red eyes.

"It's much nicer up here in the dark," Miller said. "Don't you think so?"

Will gently pulled Libby behind him.

"Protecting the fair maiden?" He laughed.

"Jim, you need to get down to the med lab," Libby said. "Dr. Lewis can help you. He knows what's going on now."

"Look around you!" Miller shouted. "The sun is dying. Unless we're strong enough, we'll all be dead in a few days. This is just a test, you know, just another survival situation in the biosphere. Survival of the fittest, and I don't intend to lose."

Will knew the elevator would take time to change air, so his options were limited. The underbrush was just a few meters away, but the waterfall was closer. He wasn't sure if Miller would shoot at them, but behind a rock was a better negotiating place.

He pulled Libby's arm and stumbled through the sands to the foot of the waterfall. As they ducked behind the rocks, Will felt a sharp pain in the back of his leg. He made a painful cry, which was muffled by water crashing against the rocks. He instinctively clutched his thigh to rub out the pain and felt an arrow sticking out the back of his leg. He watched in horror while the spray of splattering water washed away a steady stream of blood.

But there was no time to waste. They turned to see Miller making chase, hopping down the desert terraces. Libby tugged Will around the mountain's base and into the jungle underbrush. Miller screamed wildly as they struggled through the misty foliage. He was more than a match for them with his outdoorsman skills and knew every nook and cranny of the Living Hemisphere. All Will could hope for was to hide or sneak back to the elevator. There was no other way out.

"Over here," she said softly.

They stopped for a second and ducked near the base of a tree.

"I think our best bet is to get to the moat or the wetlands. He'll never see us in the fog."

"Wait a minute." Will grunted. "Didn't you say Miller disappeared down a hatch inside the rock?"

She nodded.

"Let's go," he said.

They crouched down and quietly moved to the concrete mountain's backside. Will saw the maintenance room at the base from a clearing ahead. He cautiously panned the area for any sign of Miller and spotted him crouched near the moat's edge.

Will motioned for Libby to stay where she was, then hobbled over to the maintenance doors. The handles moved quickly, so he signaled for her to follow. She hurried over while Miller's back was still turned. Will pulled the doors ajar with a grinding *creak*, then hit the ground as an arrow banged into the door beside them. When he and Libby crawled inside, Miller was clawing at the door. Will quickly found the lights and pressed his back against the door.

"Quick!" Will shouted. "Find something to prop up against this door. Anything! Grab that table end and swing it over here."

After wedging the table against the door, he grabbed a pickax hanging by a fire extinguisher.

"What are you doing with that?" she asked.

"Stand back," he said, steadying himself on his good leg. Then he started bashing away at the side wall of the room. Chunks of concrete crumbled away with every blow.

"What good is that going to do?" Libby asked, anxiously.

"Just wait," he responded. Within minutes he broke through the thin concrete liner panel and into the darkness.

"Now, we should be inside the mountain," he said. "With any luck, we'll find that access hatch Markham talked about and get down to medical. But we need to move fast before Miller gets wind of what we're up to."

Libby smiled with an admiring grin. She peered into the bowels of the concrete mountain and saw a light on the floor cast down from the broken vent above. A stench rolled in from the darkness. Libby hesitated, thinking of Kirby, then helped Will through the hole, tugging at his shirt.

***

"Level five, please," Margaret said through her E-suit headset. They'd had no luck reactivating the central heater from command. Markham's prediction that power was cut to the lower levels was apparently correct. Sabotage was the only explanation.

He fidgeted with his helmet and checked the seals of his E-suit. Margaret could only ponder their desperate situation. In a few minutes, she'd know if the base was lost.

"Level five," Sys said.

They stepped into a dark corridor. Their helmet lights filtered through the hollow steel grating and illuminated other levels as they walked.

"Why are lights out down here?" Markham grumbled through the headset. He quickly found a circuit panel and flipped it open, but nothing was turned off.

Margaret noticed an overhead light broken out and checked other nearby lights. "This is what happened at the TIgrIS base," she whispered.

"What are you talking about?" Markham asked.

"All the lights are broken out," she said. "Robert said people affected become overly sensitive to light. There wasn't a single working light in that entire base."

"Looks like Miller is up to the same thing," Markham said.

"Or Avery," Margaret added. Her voice muffled through the headset, and a chill rushed through her. She tingled from head to toe and looked in the darkness for hidden shadows. Her peripheral vision, limited by the helmet, made every step cautious.

"Let's just find out what's going on with the heater," she said, "and get back up to command."

Markham headed straight down the narrow steel corridor.; Margaret slowly followed behind. The lights from their helmets flashed like fireflies in a dark forest. Markham soon reached the control panel and opened the cabinet underneath.

"Jesus," Markham said nervously. "Margaret, they've cut the main lines. Why in the hell would they do that?"

"Where does that leave us?" she asked, examining the severed wiring.

"Will and I could repair this in a few hours," Markham replied. "But without the control board, we cannot determine the temperature of the main coils. They'd blow out if we flipped the switch while they were cold. If we assume it's cold and do a cold start, it'll take forty-eight hours to bring it back online. Either way, you'll have to count on the sun in the Living to heat everything for a while."

"Let's get up there and find Will," she said. "I hope he has better news."

They headed back toward the elevator, clanking their way along the steel grating. A figure in the shadows gazed down through the framework and smiled as they entered the elevator. Soon, it would be Avery's turn to explain their only option.

***

Will moved cautiously toward the beam of light that shone down on the floor of the concrete mountain. Libby covered her nose and mouth to mask the stench.

"It's got to be in here somewhere," he said. "Markham said he could see the hatch from up there. But I doubt he could have seen through all those pumps and piping. Let's try over this way."

"Good," Libby followed. "Kirby skinned animals over by the pumps. I don't want to go that way."

They moved into the darkness. The farther they walked away from the light, the harder it was to see. Finally, Will waved blindly and tapped the floor with his feet to avoid hitting anything. Libby was beside him doing the same when her foot stepped into something cold that oozed around her foot.

"AAAHHH!" she screamed.

Will's heart skipped a beat. "What?" he said sternly, clenching her wrist.

"I just stepped in something."

"Get a hold of yourself," he said. "We just need to find this access hatch."

A few minutes later, they reached the wall, but the hatch was nowhere to be found. They'd passed all the way across the base of the mountain to the concrete wall.

"Damn," Will said softly. "We're never going to find it this way."

"Hey, something's not right," she whispered. "Feel the wall; it's cold."

"Yeah, so what?" he answered. "We're at the bottom of a dark cave. I'd expect some concrete to be cold."

"Not this concrete," she said. "It's impregnated with a fibrous heat-absorbing material. It takes in heat during the daytime hours, then releases it at night to help maintain temperature balance in the Living. We're in big trouble if something doesn't get fixed soon."

"That's what we're working on," he said. "But first, we have to get out of here."

Will knelt and put his face to the ground. "Maybe we can see the hatch silhouette against that light."

All he could make out was the carcass of an animal a few meters away. His stomach turned when Libby stepped in it. Then he moved along the perimeter of the mountain a few meters and saw something, a rectangular-shaped object low to the ground.

"There it is, this way," he said, hobbling toward the shadow, pulling Libby along.

"This is it," he said. There was excitement in his soft voice as he felt all around for the handles. But there were none. He worked his hands all around the top and sides again, but nothing.

"Damn, this must open from the underside only," he said.

"Now, what are we going to do?" she asked.

"We can go back out the way we came and take our chances with Miller," he murmured. "Or I can try hitting this lid with the pickax, but it's made of plate steel, and I doubt if that would do any good."

"What about the opening in the duct?" she asked.

"Wait." Will gasped and sat down. "I think we're going to have to pull this arrow out of my leg before we do anything else."

Libby put a hand to his head. "You're feeling flushed," she said. "Let's get back to the maintenance room and lay you on the table."

She pulled him to his feet and helped him along. They stumbled through the broken-out hole, pushed boxes and tools to the floor, and Libby managed to get him up on a workbench.

"Now roll over," she said, tearing back the seam in the leg of his purple outfit. "This isn't too bad; there's not as much blood as I expected. We don't need a tourniquet. The arrow didn't go all the way through. I can probably pull it out."

"Here," she continued. She rolled a torn piece of his uniform into a cigar. "Bite on this while I… pull… this… out."

Her arm jerked back. Will recoiled and groaned, but the arrow came out in one piece. Libby tore off more material from his pants.

"I'm going to wrap this," she said, feeling his forehead again. "Your color is not too good. Why don't you lie there for a few minutes."

Will needed medical attention; he wasn't up to any more chasing. And they still had to warn Margaret about the sky simulation. She had to think of something and decided to leave him on the table. At least he'd be safe. She'd climbed up and out that vent once before. Hopefully, Miller wouldn't be expecting it.

"Will, I'm going to go check out that broken vent," she said. "Maybe I can sneak out and get down to command."

He nodded and drifted off.

***

"This isn't real. I've been here with you before. Is this what it does, drives you crazy? Is that what the ring's all about?" Will asked.

Murphy went about his business without acknowledging him. Will choked and fanned the dust cloud that filled the cave. Murphy just worked away, pulling out stone after stone until he revealed the stela.

"Stop!" Will shouted. It seemed real, like when it happened years ago. But he was somehow aware he was dreaming. As he appeared long ago, he was himself but felt contained in that younger man's shell. "Would you listen to me? We need to leave this place. Now!"

"Look at it!" Murphy shouted, not listening to his disoriented colleague. "This is what we've been looking for. What does it say?"

"Listen to me," Will pleaded. "You don't want to know. Let's cover it back up and leave."

"What are you talking about?" Murphy asked. 'This has to be what they sent us here to find."

"No," Will sobbed. "No, it's not. It's not what anyone's been looking for. That's why it's hidden away. Let's leave here and say we never saw it."

"What's wrong with you?" Ben shouted.

"Nothing," Will replied. "Wait, I'll prove it to you. See this ring?"

He lifted his hand, but the ring wasn't there. He checked both hands but found nothing. Murphy stared at him like he was crazy. Then Will noticed the ruby was still in the king's eye. He thought it must be the dream; that was the only explanation.

"Prove what?"

"Forget it," Will said, brushing a hand over the face of the stela. "See this gemstone? It can never be removed from the stela, or terrible things will happen."

"Terrible things, what kind of terrible things?" Murphy asked and scratched at the ruby.

"I'm no prophet," Will said. "And I don't want to sound paranoid, preaching ancient religion. But we need to leave this thing and go."

Murphy knocked the gemstone loose. As it fell to the dust, the tiny shaft started to rumble. Men out in the main tunnel ran for their lives. Will turned to see rocks and dust shower down, but he and Murphy were wedged in tight and too far from the main shaft. Murphy's flashlight flickered and died, leaving the small tunnel dark. The dust and debris were overwhelming; all he could do was close his eyes and cover his head.

Then the stela started to move, pushing them down the tunnel. The leading edge of the stone piled debris as it slowly moved along. That's when it hit him, the king's eye! Will frantically fished through the dusty floor near the base of the stela. He felt cold dust and rounded pebbles. Maybe the gemstone was caught under the moving stone.

Finally, he grasped something with jagged edges, yet smooth. He grabbed the gemstone and desperately reached for the stela. Then worked his fingertips across the surface and made out a crescent moon in the upper left-hand corner. In seconds, he felt his way to the king's head and pushed the gemstone back into the king's eye.

The rumbling slowed, and the grinding of stone against stone stopped. Murphy fumbled for the flashlight and managed to shine it at the face of the stela.

"What in god's name is going on here?" Murphy shouted, spitting dust and wiping his face.

"If you've seen enough, old friend," Will said, "let's go back to the tent. I'll tell you all about it."

***

Libby went through every box and drawer and found a flashlight, an extra climbing rope, and a belt with a dozen support clasps.

She fashioned a piece of Will's pants into a mask to block the smell of decaying bodies. Flashlight in hand, she stepped back through the hole inside the mountain.

She knew Kirby would be lying dead just around the corner. With any luck, her climbing rope would still be hanging nearby. Flashlight or not, she was terrified, able to see only what the flashlight revealed. If Miller had managed to sneak in, he could drop out of the darkness without warning.

She saw the light beaming down from the damaged duct above the maintenance room. It was only a few meters away, but she couldn't see Kirby's body where it should be. Her rope was still hanging from the opening above, but it was draped over the top of the maintenance room's concrete shell.

She jumped up and pulled, but the rope was caught. When she tugged with both hands, the rope slipped, and she fell to the ground. As she untangled the rope, she heard something shift above her. But she was knocked to the ground before she could react and move. Libby cried out, reached for her flashlight, and kicked frantically at the dead weight on her legs. When she finally found the light, it shone right in the dead, bloated face of Jeff Kirby.

She started to scream again, but it was quickly cut off by a swelling deep in her throat. There was no controlling it; she rolled aside and vomited. She kicked away at Kirby's body and wiped her mouth, backing away from the gruesome sight. His legs were still tied in the tangled ropes and hung above his torso. Despite the way he'd died, Libby couldn't leave him there. So, she climbed the maintenance shack and cut him down. From there, she could climb the rest of the way up to the open duct.

On top of the maintenance shack, she panned the flashlight around. There was a bloody spot where Kirby lay and dusty footprints from primates scattered around. Then she noticed an access ladder running up the inside of the concrete mountain. It started from the top of the maintenance room and ran into the darkness.

Flashlight in hand, she walked over to investigate. A caged ladder ran straight up to the top of the mountain and died out in a small mechanical room. Protruding from the back of the room were a group of heavy pipes that turned downward and tied into the pump system at the mountain's base. It could only be one thing, the waterfall.

***

Margaret wondered what she'd find at the top when the elevator doors opened. Indeed, there was no problem up there; the readings from command had to be off. She also wanted to find her son so he could help Markham with repair work or stand guard while he worked.

The elevator came to a stop, Sys signaled to proceed, but Margaret stopped dead in her tracks. The windows of the secondary chamber were frosted over. She slowly stepped inside, and the doors to the Living were whisked open and revealed a dark blue sky with wilted flora. She crossed the threshold and could see her breath. Her heart raced.

The temperature dropped faster than expected, and most of the biomass had died. The sun was on the horizon, and the only sound was the splash of the icy waterfall. The usual commotion from animal life and insect trilling was gone. It was over just like that. The project of a lifetime, the crowning achievement of Ecotechnics, was destroyed.

For those first few moments in the cold sand, Margaret felt nothing but guilt. The safety of the crew was all that mattered now.

"This is all my fault," she whimpered.

"A bit nippy, don't you think?" a voice came from behind.

Margaret turned to face the red-eyed madman. His hideously swollen eyes were dilated entirely now. His naked body was nearly blue from exposure, but he moved and spoke as if nothing was wrong. He jerked his head from side to side to keep track of things since his field of vision was tunneling. Margaret was still shocked by seeing the failed ecosphere, so she took this in stride.

"Miller," she ordered. "You need to go see Robert immediately."

"Oh." He sighed. "I don't think that'll do any good at this point. Won't help young Will or Libby either, or you for that matter."

"What do you mean?" she asked. "What's happened to them?"

"Nothing really," Miller chuckled, stroking his wooden bow. "The last time I saw them was over there by the waterfall. They'd been struck by Cupid's arrow."

When Margaret turned to look, Miller lunged at her, tackling her into the sand. She struggled to her knees against his weight.

Her elbow swung around and hit him across the face. Miller released his grip as pain shot through his swollen eyes. She managed to break free and crawl away, but Miller dove for her feet.

Margaret darted into the jungle underbrush. Miller rolled to his back in pain, wiping sand from his eyes. By the time he was up, she was out of sight. He strained with his failing vision to see any sign of her, then hurried in the most likely direction.

She ran through the limp, damp foliage, gasping for air. She was running in circles, and Miller would find her before long. And the drooping leaves were not much cover against her purple uniform. The rock wasn't much help unless she could get to the upper caves and hide. A new wave rushed out into the moat, and she got an idea.

Margaret unzipped her purple uniform and stripped down to her underclothes. Ice had formed at the water's edge, but crossing the wetlands was the best camouflage left. If Miller took the time to cross, she could make a dash for the elevator. The perimeter river circled around to the elevator, so she slowly dipped into the water and disappeared into the high grass.

Miller huffed along, screaming as he cut through the forest to the moat's edge, but Margaret was already hiding in the high grass. Miller's limited vision frustrated him, so he ran back into the trees.

She waited a few minutes before crawling through the marsh. She stopped momentarily to warm her hands, but Miller was nowhere to be seen, so she circled back to the elevator.

***

Libby clinched the flashlight between her teeth and started up the caged ladder. At nearly forty meters, she wasn't thrilled about the climb and decided to use tie-off clasps and rope.

At the top, she reached a steel landing tied to the side of the waterfall room. There was a small black hatchway that led inside the room. She leaned a shoulder into it, and the door gave way.

Before she could react, Libby was facedown in a pool of water. She'd fallen into a basin of water that flowed out the mouth of the cave.

She'd also accidentally found the primate's secret hiding place. A dozen capuchins splashed around the room, shrieking and cackling as they retreated to the corners. They usually ran when confronted. Instead, they grouped like frightened kittens in corners. Libby was so surprised by their reaction that she hardly noticed the near-freezing water she was sitting in.

"Oh," she said softly, reaching out an open hand. "I've been looking all over for you guys. You must be scared to death up here. And starving—your coats look awful."

Their defensive cries slowed to passive whimpers. They didn't seem affected by the radiation, so Libby pulled a food bar from her sleeve pocket and broke it into pieces. After she calmed them down and made a few friends, she returned to the business at hand. Will was still alone in the maintenance room and needed help.

Libby crawled to the mouth of the cave where icicles almost caged in the opening. She hoped for a stealthy descent to the beach under cover of the waterfall, just a stone's throw from the elevator. But the rocky slope below was ice covered, making the climb even more dangerous.

She had enough rope to drop straight down the side if only she could find a good tie-off point. All she had to do was reach through the door, latch onto the steel landing, and heave the rope down the side of the falls. It reached the first set of steps just a few meters from the sands.

***

The waterfall dropped down the mountain's north side, covering the surface with algae and moss. Libby grasped the rope and carefully backstepped out of the cave. She'd never tried scaling the slippery north side before, but she had to try. She'd be meters from the elevator with a quick drop down the side.

The tiny monkeys scrambled back inside their refuge and watched her slowly drop away. She pushed out with her feet to maintain balance and control the descent. That system worked fine for the first few jumps… until she slipped.

Her footing gave way on an ice patch and rolled her sideways into the falls. But she felt something else pushing her—at least, it seemed that way. Before she could react or stabilize herself, she'd swung into the waterfall. The icy water pounded on her head, and it felt like her body weight had doubled. She fought against its power, but her hands lost the battle. She started slipping down. At the same time, she was freezing under the cold blanket of water and kicked wildly to get out from under it.

She finally pushed herself to the other side of the falls and stopped to breathe. She had dropped almost ten meters while navigating across the falls. Then something caught her attention.

"Refreshing, isn't it?" Jim Miller asked from above. The madman was about ten meters above and descending fast on a rope. Fortunately for Libby, he'd pushed her to the other side of the falls. Unfortunately for Libby, it was a long way to the bottom, and she was slower than Miller.

In a panic, she tried dropping straight down, but her rope was crossed over the fall and pulled her back to the other side. Her rope banged into Miller just meters above.

"Look out, girlie," he said with a sly grin while pulling a knife to her rope. "It's a long way down."

She thought for a moment. If she tried jumping into the trees, she might die or break bones, but another option was available.

This was the dark side of the mountain, and the primates hated their master and tormentor. She could see them above, descending the rope and closing on Miller, whose vision was limited. They might have been curious, but Libby sensed the primates were coming to help. When they were just about on him, she pulled out the flashlight and shone it in Miller's eyes.

He turned away from the light and saw the troop of monkeys. They were on him with the ferocity of angry hornets, scratching and clawing at his face. They swarmed over him, biting away at his exposed flesh. He managed to knock a couple to their deaths before finally slipping himself.

Libby swung back into the falls, where screeching death cries were muffled under the roar of falling water, then the figure of a man fell past her. When she swung back out of the falls, she saw two dead primates lying on the rocks below, and Jim Miller twisted up in the rocks with them.

Libby was freezing cold and out of strength, but she managed the rest of the descent. At the base, she found Miller. His head was crushed, and those hideous red eyes appeared to have exploded on impact. With those dark, dilated pupils, she wondered how he could see and turned away in disgust.

Then a light chatter echoed from above. The troop of monkeys called out from their icy cave. It was hard to say, but they appeared happy, or maybe they were saying thank you.

"Are you all right?" Margaret approached, shivering in her underclothes. "That was fairly good work up there. I would have helped, but it was all over by the time I knew what was going on."

"A friendly face." Libby sighed. "I'm fine, thanks. It all happened so fast. I just… What happened to you?"

"The same thing that happened to you, I suppose," Margaret said.

"Margaret," she said, "we have to find Will and get back down to command."

"Will!" Margaret cried. "He's up here? Is he all right?"

"I think so."

"What do you mean, you *think* so?"

"I left him in the maintenance room," she responded. "He got shot in the leg. It was all we could do."

Margaret ran off into the woods with Libby close behind. A pounding noise suddenly drew Will away from the collapsing cave dream. His head throbbed from the sound until the sensation finally woke him.

"Yeah, right," he muttered and sat on the table. "If only it were that easy."

Maybe his subconscious was just out of options, with no logical explanation for these strange happenings. All the bits and pieces of the puzzle were caught up in a confusing whirlwind inside his head. The best his dreaming mind could do was to go back to square one and pretend nothing had ever happened. Returning the ruby to the stela was the same as forfeiting the game and starting over. Or was the dream telling him to not feel guilty?

The pounding startled him again. This time he realized it was the doors behind him, and those were voices.

"Will! Will! Are you in there?" Margaret shouted.

It all suddenly came back to him—the sky at dusk, the chase with Miller and the arrow. He eased off the table onto the floor. It sounded like Libby, but there was more than one voice. Miller was either nearby or at the door. Whatever the case, he reached for the pickax and hobbled over to the double doors.

Margaret and Libby waited patiently, to the sound of moving furniture behind barricaded doors. When the deadbolts finally turned, he pulled open the door to see two very wet, tired, relieved women.

"And I thought I looked bad," Will joked.

"Oh, my god," Margaret cried. "Let me see your leg."

"Never mind about that," he replied, stepping outside the doorway and eyeing the nearby rocks. "Where in the hell is Miller?"

"There was an accident near the falls." Libby sighed. "He's dead."

As he listened, Will couldn't believe he could see her breath. He'd hardly heard a word she said except to note the relieved expression on her face and the calm tone to her voice.

"Mother," he said, "I think I know what's going on with the sky simulation. But we have to get down to command and fast."

"No sense in talking about it here," Margaret said, propping a shoulder under his arm. "We're all in need of medical attention."

Will threw his other arm over Libby's shoulder and hopped along the best he could. They slowly worked their way around to the elevator.

Chapter 24
THE MIDNIGHT SUN

Markham didn't wait around for Will. He grabbed a cable splicer from storage and headed down to the lower levels. There was no time to waste—it had been nearly an hour since the alarm sounded. Hopefully, it was only a heating unit shutdown. If so, he still had sixty minutes before the coils cooled down, before a complete unit restart was required. He was determined to make the necessary repairs, even if it meant running into Avery or Miller.

During a forty-eight-hour restart, the Living Hemisphere's delicate balance would suffer significantly without nighttime heat. Even though there were portable heaters in storage, they were for supplemental use only and had a fraction of the capacity of the primary heat source.

"Level five, please," Markham ordered.

He watched the display count down from sixteen, but it stopped at eight, and the doors opened into a dark corridor.

"Sys," he said at the doorway, "I said level five, not level eight."

Markham was yet to hear a response when a canister of liquid nitrogen hit him in the chest. It crackled, popped, and released a condensation cloud that filled the elevator. Markham instinctively turned away, wiping at his face mask, but there was nothing he could do. A second later, he felt a sting in the shoulder.

***

"Glad to see you're finally coming around," Avery said, wearing a soiled technician's coat and dark sunglasses. His hands and face were burned red. "We normally catch the small primates with those darts. I thought it would take two or three to bring you down."

Markham's first concern was the status of the heating unit, but he was distracted by Avery's behavior. He couldn't make out where he was at first—maybe it was a dream. But the lighting was turned down, and he soon realized he was strapped to a prep table in the cryo-lab.

"Avery, what in the hell's going on here?" Markham demanded as he flexed his arms against the restraints. "Was I in an accident or something?"

"You never were brilliant." Avery chuckled.

"You pompous airbag," Markham shouted. "Cut me loose from these belts. I must reconnect power."

"Richard, Richard," Avery confidently interrupted. "If you're worried about the mechanical unit, it's all taken care of."

"So, it's back online?" Markham asked.

"Always so direct," Avery said. "You never could see the big picture. It's that engineering thing in you, I suppose. The real issue here transcends the simple question, *Do we have heat?* The question should be, *Do we need heat?*"

"Would you please just cut me loose?" Markham grumbled. "I don't have time for this."

"Look," Avery said, pointing across the room to the freezers where scores of animals lay in frozen incarceration. "They don't need heat. They can't have heat, or they die.

"Don't you understand what's going on around you? We're orbiting a poisoned world. And another one poisoning our entire solar system. This isn't some chance happening. It's a natural cleansing mechanism, survival of the fittest, and that sort of thing. There is no more life, at least not in the way we're accustomed. Our only chance for survival is cryo-freezing."

"I think Margaret should make that decision," Markham said, straining against the bed straps. "Besides, I have no intention of returning to those freezers."

"Oh, but Richard," Avery politely said. "You're going to be the first to try it."

"So, *you* sabotaged the heaters," Markham redirected, "to limit Margaret's options: leave this place or hibernate."

"And what else would we have done?" Avery asked. "Sit around in environmental suits while you and Tinker Boy try to find perfect eco-balance?

"I know! We could all hold our breath every other minute to conserve oxygen. And while we're at it, we could tell the rings of Saturn to dim it down a notch. Then there wouldn't be any problems at all.

"Or better yet!" Avery shouted. "Why don't we all just kill ourselves and get it over with?"

Markham knew reasoning with him was pointless in his disoriented condition. He couldn't stand reasoning with Avery when he wasn't sick. He'd just about worked one of his hands-free from the bed straps.

"Okay," Markham said. "So, you think we must go into cryo-freeze and ride this thing out?"

"We have no other realistic chance for survival," Avery replied.

"Then why don't we go up to command?" Markham said. His hand noticeably slipped free. "Discuss this with Margaret?"

"I have a better idea," Avery said. "You've been naughty, haven't you?" Avery pulled a remote-control device from his pocket and aimed it at the prep table.

"No!" Markham shouted. But an instant later, he was engulfed in an icy vapor cloud. A heavy, numbing pain shot through him, then darkness.

***

Will grimaced in pain as he eased to a sitting position on the elevator floor. Margaret ordered Sys to call for Robert and have him meet them in command ASAP. He waited with a bag of medical supplies when his wounded comrades hobbled into systems command.

"What in god's name?" Robert gasped. "Get him up on the table. Libby, run down the hall and get a change of clothes for you and Margaret."

Margaret went to the systems console to call up the sky simulation.

"What is this?" Robert asked. "Did you fall through a tree and catch a branch?"

"That would've been nice," Will replied. "A bit less dramatic that way."

"It's an arrow, Robert," Margaret said. "But we don't have time to discuss that right now."

"Will, what is it we need to do?"

"Damn, it's freezing in here!" he shouted. "I was hoping we'd get a little relief from the elements here."

"Will," Margaret continued. "The sky simulation."

"Oh, sorry. The first thing is to call up the sky simulation," he said. "We have to check the current status of the daytime sky before anything else."

"Sys," Margaret said. "I'd like to review the current status of the daytime sky simulation."

"Acknowledged," Sys said. "Would you like a complete readout of energy output and luminosity levels."

"Yes, thank you."

"Acknowledged."

"Processing... Complete," Sys said.

"This display is Greek to me," Margaret turned to Will.

But Robert thought it would be a good time to cut in. "Infection has already set in," he said. "I'm going to give you something to ease the pain."

"Can you see a moving time clock?" Will asked. "I suspect the system is just locked up. If that's true, then the clock won't be moving."

Robert didn't want to interrupt and thrust a needle into Will's thigh.

"Wait a minute," Margaret said. "Okay, here it is. Time of day, daylight hours remaining, and both clocks are moving in the seconds' column."

"Damn," Will said softly, then shouted across the room. "Sys, please explain why the sun is not moving across the sky and why we were not made aware of the problem."

"Acknowledged," Sys said. "Celestial movement continues as scheduled under the currently modified ground base. No simulation warnings were issued."

"Understood," he said.

"Understood?" Margaret asked. "We made these changes days ago, and everything was working fine."

"Something went wrong," Will said. "Something to do with the original programming... I don't know. Let's recheck the control settings."

"Will?" she asked. "There's something that looks odd here. Under daylight hours remaining, the number reads 4,308 hours, 32 minutes, 24 seconds, and counting. Does that make any sense?"

"No, it doesn't." He lifted up and swung his feet over the side of the table. "Excuse me, Doc, I have to check this out."

Sure enough, when he saw the monitor, it read just as Margaret said. But scanning the rest of the screen, his eyes caught another piece of information: the South Pole. Then it hit him.

"Sys," Will commanded. "Please cancel the current simulation immediately. Reset ground base to Buenos Aires, Argentina."

"Processing... Cancellation is not possible at this time. However, the ground base can be reestablished for the following day."

"Question." he said. "Who reset the ground to the South Pole?"

"The change was authorized by John Avery," Sys responded.

"We're in trouble," he said. "I hope Markham's got the main heating unit back online."

"What do you mean?" Margaret asked. "Let's just change it back."

Will shook his head. "It doesn't work that way. Changes can only be made during nighttime hours. The important safety rule built into the system is no alterations to sky simulation are allowed during the day to promote the life cycles. They didn't want us to mess with the time exposure to light."

"So..." she said. "What?"

"So, Avery broke into the system and reset the simulation to the South Pole," Will said. "Days last six months down there. The only problem is the sun barely gets above the horizon, and there's no direct sunlight. We're not seeing a sunrise. We're seeing an average day, and we have nearly six months until sunset."

"I can't believe the system would accept such a change," Margaret said.

"Me neither," Will said. "He found something in there I don't know about."

"Damnit." She grunted and hit her fist to the table. "Robert, I'm freezing, and I've probably been exposed to more radiation than I care to think about. We need warm clothes now!"

"Libby will be back soon," he replied. "Sit down and take a break."

"And take one of those eye exams," she followed. "By the way, has anyone seen Richard?"

"No, I'm *not* concerned about him right now," Robert said. "Now, the both of you, I need to examine that leg."

"Is it going to be all right?" Will asked and lifted his feet back on the table.

"I'm getting it under control," Robert replied, then redirected. "So, I take it Jim Miller's dead."

"How'd you guess?" Will asked.

"For one thing, he's the only person I know who can hunt with a bow," Robert said, wrapping the wound. "Can you feel this?"

"No," Will replied. "And?"

"The other is he'd be here by now if he were still alive," Robert finished.

Libby ran through the door with a pile of clothing. "Take your pick," she offered to Margaret.

"Doesn't matter to me." Margaret focused on the computer screen. "Why aren't the emergency flashers shut off in here?"

"Markham killed audio before he went down to the lower levels,"

Robert said. "He needed to remember the flashers."

"I thought you said you hadn't seen him?" Margaret asked.

"I guess it slipped my mind," Robert replied.

"Slipped your mind!" she shouted. "Markham went down there alone?"

"You were up in the Living," Robert said. "Markham decided it was more important to take the risk than wait for you to come back."

"Oh, Jesus!" Margaret said.

Will sat back up and rubbed his fingers through his hair. "And there's something that slipped *my* mind," he interjected. "With everything else going on, I just forgot."

"Forgot what?" Margaret demanded.

"Sys completed a comparative spectral analysis of the planetoid and the rings," he said. "And they're identical. The ices in the rings have the same chemical signature as the object *and* emit the same unusual radiation."

"So, the *planetoid* is either a rogue that does all these strange things to the rings every sixteen hundred years, or it's from here, a Saturnian moon that got ejected somehow into an elongated orbit."

"Either way, when it reaches the inner solar system, it'll form a radioactive tail that could easily sweep through Earth's atmosphere. It's more of a moon than a comet because only a compressed, rocky core could create radioactivity, and comets are just dirty ice balls.

Margaret nodded. "We have to contact the Space Council."

"Mother, the planetoid won't reach Earth for another four and a half years," he said. "We'll contact them well before that, assuming this ring disturbance dies."

Blank faces.

Libby zipped up a new dry outfit and tossed one to Margaret. The red light finally quit, but a new message was flashing:

OUTER SHELL PRESSURE LIMIT CRITICAL

"Oh, my god," Margaret called out.

Chapter 25
ABSOLUTE ZERO

"Margaret," Libby said. "It sounds like you and Will need to stay here and devise a plan of action. I'll run up top now that I've warmed up a bit."

"Wait a minute," she said. "Why are you doing that? We could use you down here."

"We have to salvage everything we can from the Living before it freezes any further," she replied. "The livestock and agriculture will all be lost in a few hours, assuming we can't restore heat. Also, the wildlife in the rock won't last long without heat. Most of the reptilian population is dead already. And I found primates hiding in the waterfall cave. It's not too late to start bringing some of them down."

"I suppose we've been reduced to a survival situation," Margaret said.

"Okay, where do you plan to take them?"

"I can stock agriculture on the floor with the storage bins," she replied. "The wildlife and livestock are another story. But we must develop something until it warms up in the Living."

"Go ahead then," Margaret said. "But be careful. Avery has been affected like the others and could be dangerous."

"Margaret." Libby stopped at the doorway. "I've taken on Kirby and Miller and survived them both. Believe me, I'm not afraid of that wimp Avery."

"Just the same, be careful up there," Will added. "It's getting cold really quick."

"Tell me about it," Libby muttered and walked out.

"Margaret," Robert said, "I'm leaving for a few minutes to gather supplies for that wound."

"Why don't you bring back some heat packs?" Margaret said. "I'm still chilled to the bone."

"Got it."

Margaret went on with checks and balances—there had to be an alternative. Her son lay seriously injured, but that was the least of her worries.

"Okay, let's go over this again," she said. "So, you're convinced we can't reprogram the simulation, right?"

"Right."

"What if we simply cut the power in the facility," she continued. "Then restart everything with its original setup?"

"Don't you think that's a little risky?" Will asked.

"Just hear me out," Margaret said. "The sky simulation is run from the main power converter and supplemented with backup generators. If we shut the generators down, too, then it should work. All we need is just a few seconds of downtime. It'll work."

"Wait a minute," Will said. "In that few seconds, lots of other things could happen. For one thing, the freezers in the cryo-lab will be interrupted. We could lose everything in there. Another thing is the heating unit. If Markham's had any success, then we're back online. Cutting the power guarantees us no heat for another forty-eight hours."

"Then we just have to track him down," Margaret said, "and check the status."

"Mother, I think you must face the fact that the living space station is lost. We need to start an evacuation plan."

"Of course, I realize the extent of the damage," Margaret said. "But that doesn't mean we have to pack up and leave. We have to assess our current situation. Libby has the right idea. What do we have to work with? What can we salvage? We have to assume we can hold up here until help arrives."

"What if all this prophecy is true?" Will asked. "That life on Earth is being affected. Will they even send a rescue ship? I doubt it. In fact, we're probably the least of their concerns."

"That's a distinct possibility," Margaret said. "But wouldn't you rather stabilize our position here until we get a signal to Earth? The least attractive option is to panic and jump on the shuttle. Especially without an experienced pilot at the helm."

"We're better off staying put and regrouping if we can. Although I admit, I've never liked the *Tin Can* method of life support. But it looks like our only option right now."

***

When Robert walked in and reached for the lights, the med lab was dark.

"Looking for something?" a voice came from the shadows.

He stopped momentarily. "John, is that you?"

"Well, of course, it is," Avery replied and stepped out from behind the door. His red face was grotesquely pocked with seeping blisters, and oozing bloody fluid ran down his face. He wore a medical cap to cover the hair falling off his head in bunches. "And please, take your hand away from the lights."

"John, you've been affected and—"

"I need help," Avery finished for him. "How kind of you to be so concerned about my health. I know the first sign is sensitivity to light, then the patient gets delirious. I've read your files on the crew; they were beautifully written. I'll ensure that your scout leader learns about your good deeds."

"John, you need medication. It's not too late."

"I'm afraid Margaret's tied up at the moment," Avery continued. "She's having trouble with the winter sun upstairs."

"I don't know why you felt it necessary to sabotage the system."

"It all came to me in a dream," Avery preached. "A dream of rather biblical proportions, I might add. You see, we can't live here anymore. Our only hope is to hibernate until the storm passes."

"Don't you think we should work as a team?" Robert asked.

"Let me give you a hypothetical situation, Robert," Avery said. "We're already down to half the original crew, and the rest are slowly being affected. The oxygen situation appeared to be under control, but radiation levels were growing throughout the facility. The microcity and macrocity of the Living Hemisphere are in critical condition. This means our food, water, and oxygen are nothing more than question marks. The storm might last for months, and we don't have a pilot to safely fly us out of here.

"So, if you're missing something, our only option is to cryofreeze for a while. The problem is Margaret will screw around with every possible alternative until we all kill each other."

"John," Robert said, "you're being totally irrational. Do you hear what you're saying?"

Avery sighed. "You know, you and Markham are a lot alike. He didn't understand either. Now, have a seat over here at your desk," Avery commanded, pointing a tranquilizer gun at Robert. "I need you to write a new entry into your personnel file."

"This is crazy," Robert said. "I'm not going to—"

Avery raised his weapon to Robert's head. "I think you should."

Robert reluctantly moved over to the desk and sat down.

"Now then," Avery said. "One at a time, we'll pull up all current personnel files. All living personnel, so we can update them."

"What are you talking about?" Robert asked.

"You said it yourself, Robert," Avery replied, "all personnel have been affected in some way by the current radiation problem—true?"

"I don't recall making that comment," Robert said.

"Well, I do!" Avery shouted. "And it's time we made it official before everyone is put on ice."

"You want me to falsify medical records?" Roberts asked. "Is that what you're asking?"

"Why don't we start with an easy one?" Avery waved the gun forcefully. "Let's update the deceased files, shall we? How about Jeff Kirby or Jim Miller, maybe? The list keeps growing, you know."

Robert didn't respond but grudgingly pulled up the menu of all personnel.

"There, that wasn't so hard," Avery said and moved behind the table to avoid the light of the view screen. "We should begin with a cryptic opening statement. How about this, *Though the brave crew fought valiantly against seemingly insurmountable odds—*"

The room suddenly rocked with a seismic-like tremor. The rattle was accompanied by the grinding of steel framing, followed by flickering lights. Robert's computer screen flickered and went dark.

That was his chance. He hit the floor and scampered in the direction of the door. Avery heard the frantic sounds of chairs rolling and feet shuffling as Robert did a reptilian crawl across the floor. His poorly adjusted eyes couldn't make out just where Robert was off to.

"Goddammit, Robert," he shouted, tripping over a rolling chair as he gave pursuit. "I'm gonna freeze-dry you the same as Markham! Then pack you on ice like a med-school cadaver!"

He fired tranquilizer darts blindly toward the door, but Robert was already down the hallway.

"We'll serve you up as daily dinner," Avery shouted. "While we wait for your goddamned transport ship to arrive!"

Robert found his way through the darkness to the back stairs and quickly started down to the lower levels.

"What was that?" Will shouted.

"I don't know." Margaret's ears perked.

"It felt like a tremor," he said. "All we need now is seismic activity on Titan."

"I'm going out to look around," Margaret said. "You stay here for a minute."

"Sorry, I'm coming with you." He got to his feet.

The corridor was dimly lit by emergency lighting, and the hissing of pressurized gas filled the air. Will hobbled alongside Margaret, who was determined in her direction. Her pace was quicker, but he tried to keep up.

"Mother, shouldn't we just run a system-wide diagnostic?" he asked.

"We probably will," she responded. "But first, I want to check out the lower levels. From level fourteen, we'll have a clear view of the entire Dead Hemisphere."

Soon the elevator dropped them on the fourteenth floor. Margaret walked out to the edge of the catwalks overlooking nearly one million cubic meters of steel, pipes, and mechanical equipment.

"Nothing looks unusual, no fire or smoke," she said. "Except for that hissing sound—it seems louder down here than above. Don't you think so?"

"That's not surprising," Will replied. "It's probably just a cracked steam line. The sound echoes off the metal down here."

"I'll agree with the echo," Margaret said. "But this doesn't sound like a gas leak. It's more like an egg frying."

They concentrated on the noise that seemed to grow in intensity. Soon, it was coming from all directions, above and below. Then he caught a glimpse of something smoke near the end of the catwalk.

"Over here!" he said, holding his bum leg as he hopped along the steel grating.

Margaret followed him past the elevators toward the end of the catwalk. They stopped a few meters from the outer shell, where a sizzling vapor cloud expanded.

"This isn't part of any mechanical system I'm aware of," Will said.

"Oh, my god," Margaret whispered. "This is part of the superstructure shell. It's freezing."

"How can that be?" Will asked.

"The outer hull must be compromised," she said.

"So, we did have a seismic event," he said.

"Possibly," she said. "But why is this the only evidence? The floor didn't shake enough to cause this kind of damage. We'd have been knocked to the ground along with bookshelves and anything else that wasn't tied down. No, this is something else."

"The Living must be freezing," she said. "When water freezes, it expands and creates tremendous outward pressure. It must have ruptured the intermediate layer of the Cerametallic shell."

Margaret studied the framework in all directions.

"Look,." She pointed. "The longitudinal steel framework encircling the station is turning white. The absolute zero temperatures are working their way inside."

A sizzling sound of vaporizing water raced around the outside hull as frigid temperatures conducted through the steel gridwork. The white-crusted steel stood against the dark background like a giant spider web.

***

Libby was surprised to find the ground frozen. Even the beach had a crusty sandpaper film, and the moat had a coating of ice thick enough to walk on. Miller's body lay frozen under a mass of ice at the waterfall's base. One arm hung free from his icy cocoon with tiny icicles hanging from his fingers.

Two things were apparent to her. The first, the vegetation was frozen but would keep here better than down in storage, and the second, all aquatic life in the wetlands was lost.

She found grim news in the livestock area, where Miller had killed most of the goats and chickens. They lay beheaded in and around their cages. Smaller animals spared the slaughter had succumbed to the extreme cold.

Libby's fear turned to determination when she called for the primates in a gibberish capuchin monkey language. But they silently watched from nearby underbrush and kept their distance.

Then it hit—the *pop* was deafening and knocked her off her feet, and she screamed.

The ice sheet covering the moat buckled at its center as ice and water bowled up and rocked back and forth. Then another pop followed a grinding sound, as if an enormous rusty hinge had been pried open. Seconds later, a white jet stream shot across the sky, then another. Then suddenly, the sky went black.

Once hot, damp, and full of life, the Living Hemisphere was now dark, bitter cold, and silent as the dead of winter. Libby fell to her knees and wept. There was no hope.

***

Will and Margaret slowly backed away from the freezing steel superstructure.

"That's it," she said. "We can't stay here much longer. Will, get up to the Living and find Libby. You two get supplies and prep the shuttle. I'm going to find Markham and shut this place down properly. Hopefully, we can talk some sense into Avery."

"Mother," he said, "are we talking about interplanetary space travel?"

"Don't get cold feet on me now," Margaret replied. "You trained for this sort of thing. You're the only one who can fly us out of here."

"But achieving orbit is an entirely different thing."

"We can't stay here any longer," Margaret interrupted. "We just saw that this place will be sub-zero in a few hours. Now, go find Libby. Everyone's in E-suits from now on. I'll meet you in the sky bridge within the hour."

"But—"

"No buts, we take this one step at a time," she ordered. "First, find Libby."

"But—"

"Don't worry," Margaret cut in again. "You can fly that shuttle. We achieve orbit, get telemetry from Sys, and go to sleep. Right?"

"Right." Will sighed.

"Besides," she said, "there's no longer a shortage of freezer spaces on the shuttle."

"Margaret!" a voice shouted from below.

"Robert, is that you?"

"Down here!" Robert replied. He turned like someone was behind him. "I'll come up to you! We have to talk about Avery!"

Another shock wave rattled the Dead Hemisphere, nearly throwing Margaret off the catwalk. An explosive sound followed that echoed through the bowels of Gaia 3.

Seconds later, the trough of the moat gave way, and a wave of water burst through cracks directly above system command. Robert leaned out to see what had happened and was hit with the full power of the passing wave. Margaret and Will were spared the crushing blow but were still smashed down against hard steel grating.

"Robert! Robert!" She pulled herself to her feet and shouted. There was no sign of him where he'd stood before.

Water still dripped from every piece of steel and piping in the area. A good spring rain wouldn't have soaked the place any worse. But Robert Lewis was nowhere to be found. The tidal wave of water had knocked him over the side of the rail and into the darkness below.

Then another incredible explosion rocked the facility. This time it came from below with a firework of flashes and sparks. The methane power converter had blown when the falling water dropped through its venting system. As yellow and blue electrical flashes danced fifty meters below their feet, facility-wide lighting went out. At the center of the tentacles of crackling light was a bright white fireball. A smoke plume swiftly rose and engulfed the upper catwalks. Margaret and Will quickly made their way to a stair shaft where the air was breathable. Shortly after that, emergency lighting was activated.

"At least we still have emergency power," she said, catching her breath.

"More thermal movement," he said and lowered to the floor to massage his leg. "We don't have time now."

"I can't believe what just happened." She grimaced.

"Neither can I," he added. "But we're not getting out of here if we dwell on it."

"I know," she said. "We have to get to work. Let's get to supply and suit up first. Can you make it?"

"I still have good feeling in my feet," he said. "But I don't know how long I can hold out on this leg. We've got to find Libby and Markham."

"Will, be careful," she said. "And watch out for Avery."

***

With no response to all calls, Libby and Markham were assumed dead or unable to respond. Will soon found himself anxiously riding the elevator up to the Living Hemisphere. The explosion left the lower levels filled with smoke, so he brought an extra E-suit along just in case he found Libby.

His heart dropped when he stepped into the frozen ecosphere. He hadn't prepared himself for the changes; it was dark and silent. He'd never seen the Living Hemisphere without a sky before. But there it was, dark as pitch and dead quiet. Only the light from his headset filled the cave-like surroundings. His feet crunched across the frozen beachhead. He panned the light of his helmet side to side, sweeping as much ground as possible. If she were injured, he'd have to find her since cries for help wouldn't be heard through a sealed helmet.

He walked to the moat's edge and saw heavy sheets of ice splintered and spiking in the air. Then something jumped on his back. Will screamed and tried to swat it away, but it clung to him. Then it scurried around his side and up his chest.

"Oh, Jesus." He sighed, staring a wide-eyed monkey square in the face. "Hey, what are you doing down here?"

Will felt the monkey's arms and legs cling to him in a maternal embrace as he stroked its furry back. Just then, he caught a glimpse of a human figure stepping out of the woods, illuminated by his beacon light. It was Libby and the rest of the troop of primates. They clung to her shoulders and waist, followed alongside, and darted around her. He was elated to see her unharmed.

"Libby!" Will shouted, limping over to see her. "Oh, you probably can't hear me, can you?"

But hand motion was all they needed as they embraced and made eye contact.

She pointed to the troop of primates and mouthed *I'm taking them with us* as she pointed to the elevator.

"We're stopping by storage," Will said on the elevator. His voice was muffled through the headset while she pulled on her E-suit. "Then down to the sky bridge. We have to evacuate."

"I guessed that much already," she replied. "How is it going down there? Is everything in one piece?"

"It's getting worse by the minute," he answered. "There was an accident when the power converter exploded. Robert didn't make it."

Libby closed her eyes.

"We're down to four now, assuming mother can locate Markham," he said, petting one of the little monkeys. "I don't know about Avery or if there's room for these little guys on the shuttle, but we'll see what we can do."

***

Margaret had not seen Avery or Markham for a while. They were probably in one of two places: the cryonics lab or near the heaters. But there was no sense in checking mechanical since it probably had been destroyed in the blast.

She quietly opened the staircase door at level ten. She made a stealthy approach to the lab—soft steps, no headlights—and watched her backside. Only emergency flashers lit the corridor as she crept closer to the cryo-lab. The room was dark, its sliding door propped open by a chair jammed in the threshold.

She crept down the corridor, watching for sinister shadows. More jittery than confident—she was, after all, a scientist, not a soldier. And even though the walk seemed to last an eternity, no spirits or madmen materialized. She carefully stepped over the chair lodged in the doorway and walked in to investigate.

The only sources of illumination were panel lights from active cryo-freezers. There was little doubt Avery had sabotaged the sky simulation and the heaters.

The last thing Margaret remembered from cryo-command was that the freezers were only twenty percent full. But the stack in front of her now was an active, programmed wall full of hibernating animals. It must have taken days of constant work to fill, let alone capture, the animals. Their vital signs were good, but without primary power, the chambers would shut down soon.

A slight movement on the opposite side of the room caught Margaret's attention. She was startled at the moving apparition but soon realized it was a cloud, a misty kind of dry ice cloud. The vapor emanated from a prep table and draped down to the floor.

She drew closer and saw a red light flashing on its side panel. Something was lying in the mist, something frozen, something dead. She reached out and fanned the mist with her hand. The thin cloud layer dispersed and eddied with each stroke of her hand and revealed a blue human face—it was Markham! His strained expression showed the pain of an instant, freezing death. His curled fingers were clenched in fists, pulled tight against leather arm restraints.

Margaret pulled back and felt her stomach flex as she stumbled through tables and chairs and fell to the floor. Her stomach flexed again and filled the inside of her helmet with vomit. She scratched at the head straps to release the helmet and threw it aside. Seconds later, she tripped out of the room, crying and wiping her mouth.

She had to leave, but there were still details to take care of, essential closeout items. At first, it seemed impossible, but it was the only choice. Everything else disappeared as she headed for command.

"Think! Think!" she forcefully grumbled.

She hadn't considered evacuation procedures since she'd penned them, but all options assumed the main power converter would be operating. Without it, nothing would work, and nothing could be shut down. And she needed the power to open the hangar doors for the shuttle.

On the other hand, she didn't have to control-freeze the Living; the shell breach took care of that. Everything in the Living was as dead as the Dead Hemisphere. The cryo-lab was doomed but used all the power the backup generator could spare.

That was it! The only way to channel power to the sky bridge and hangar was to shut down the freezers in the cryo-lab. Sys would disagree, so Margaret had to find a way to override standard control.

She finally reached command and pulled up a seat at the main terminal; its screen pulsed with a red light and still flashed the fateful warning:

'OUTER SHELL PRESSURE LIMIT CRITICAL.'

Margaret keyed in commands to try and clear the screen, but each removed item led to another. She finally reached an impasse where Sys stopped to speak.

"These warnings are of a serious nature," Sys said. "System-wide diagnostics confirm the situation and indicate that each problem is real. I cannot recommend the *No action taken* response as an appropriate course of action."

"Sys," she said. "I don't have time to argue with you. I've been trying to clear the board manually to avoid a debate. Please, you have to help me. You are aware that main power is lost, true?"

"Yes, I am aware," Sys replied.

"And that the life cycles aren't functioning in the Living Hemisphere?" Margaret said.

"Sensors in the Living Hemisphere are not functioning," Sys said.

"Without power, there is no heat," Margaret said. "Without heat, there is no life. The only chance for the three remaining crew members' survival is evacuation."

"Another option would be to hibernate and hope that a supply mission is underway," Sys said.

"Auxiliary power will last only a few more days," she said. "And the next supply ship isn't scheduled for six months. We would die."

"Understood... Agreed."

"The shuttle can achieve interplanetary flight," Margaret said. "And its combination of batteries and solar panels can power the freezers for the flight duration. But we can't access the sky bridge or open the hangar doors without power from backup generators. With its current usage, does the backup generator have the power to open the hangar doors?"

"Computing... Complete," Sys said. "No, it does not. Would you like to see the current power distribution?"

"No, thank you," Margaret responded. "If all power to emergency systems, lighting, and the cryo-lab were cut off, would the backup generator be able to transfer enough power to open the hangar doors?"

"Computing... Complete," Sys replied. "Yes, but all in hibernation would die."

"I understand," Margaret said. "I need voice command authorization for this power transfer, effective immediately."

"I'm sorry," a low voice whispered from behind.

Margaret nearly jumped out of her seat.

"But you spoke of only three on the ship." Avery paused. "Am I not invited?"

Avery dropped a box of syringes on the table next to her. "Excuse me," he whispered, more of an exhausted tone than a whisper.

He fumbled through the half-spent box of preloaded hypodermic needles to find a good one. Margaret was no physician but could easily read the inscription on the label. He calmly looked for a convenient spot and jammed the morphine solution into his chest.

"Doesn't really matter where you get it," Avery lightly said. He'd wrapped his face and hands with surgical gauze, but the stains from seeping blisters still soaked through. "Just so you get it."

His illness was advanced, but he fought with his intellect to control the madness. He shook with pain and forced his sentences into slow, controlled fragments. The madness possessed him. His mind was on a one-way train track, and Margaret was headed in the opposite direction. His poorly conceived plan had gone awry and convincing her to salvage it would be difficult. In his deranged state of mind, Avery didn't realize that she wouldn't even consider the option.

"John, thank god you're still alive," she said, reaching for anything. "I've been looking for you everywhere."

Even half-mad, Avery could see the lack of concern in her eyes. He raised his tranquilizer gun. "Please," he said. "Sit still for a minute. We have to talk."

"I don't think we need that weapon to talk," she said. Upchucking in her helmet had been a good thing; it allowed them to talk face-to-face.

"For you, Margaret, okay," he said and dropped his aim.

"For me?" she asked. "What about Markham?"

"I told the poor bastard—" Avery chuckled "—not to tense up. It hurts more that way. Maybe I used too much of the cold stuff on him."

She was stalling. Maybe the hide of her E-suit could stop a dart. If not, she'd end up the same as Markham. Madman or not, it was hard to see the man she admired and had maybe even loved once reduced to this rabid state.

"I had a dream, Margaret," he offered. "More of a revelation, I suppose. Biblically, the only way to save the base was to gather everyone and go into hibernation. If there's one thing we've learned, life in your ecosystem is a delicate balance that can be easily disrupted. I thought the only way to convince you was to freeze the base. We would be forced into hibernation until this cosmic phenomenon passed. The plan was working perfectly, too. I'd killed the entire ecosystem. All microspecies and plant life are dead but can be reintroduced later, just as in the initial start-up phase. I have enough biomass in storage and cryo-lab to regenerate the entire biosphere from scratch."

"So, we're supposed to bury our heads in the sand," she calmly said, "and hope when we wake, everything is back to normal?"

"We can still repair the power converter!" Avery shouted.

"How?" Margaret shouted. "You killed Markham. Gerhardt's gone, and so is everyone else who could have repaired it."

"Margaret, we must stay here," Avery's painfully scratchy voice continued. "I don't know why, but there's some cosmic significance to this affair. We have to wait it out."

"John, by the time we wait it out," she said, "we'll all die in the cryo-lab, just like poor Richard."

"No, it won't be that way."

"It already is," she said. "I've cut power to the cryo-lab."

"What?"

Avery turned to the computer screen and saw the status change. Margaret rolled her chair at him, then reached for her flashlight. Avery was struck in the back of the legs and let out a muffled groan.

He reached for his tranquilizer gun, but Margaret shone the light in his eyes, blinding him for a split second.

She ran for the exit and heard the whisk of darts as she cut through the door and stumbled down the dark corridor.

She found the back stairs and hurried down but felt slight dizziness coming on. She stopped to check her E-suit, and a dart was sticking out of the tough fabric near her hamstring. She reached down to examine it, moving it side to side. The only pain was a slight skin prick; the dart must have lodged in her uniform. But loud metallic footsteps drew closer, so she dropped the dart and went on.

She finally reached level five, where Will was at the sky bridge with a set of mechanical pry bars, trying to open the airlock.

"Will!" Margaret shouted.

He saw by her awkward movement something was wrong. He hurried over to meet her but pulled back when they embraced.

"What's that smell?" he asked. "Where's your helmet?"

"I have a good excuse. Where's yours?" she asked.

Will pointed to a supply cart.

"At least you suited up for the flight," she said. "Anyway, there's no time to discuss it."

She walked past him to the control panel, hobbling the same as he.

"Is this a hereditary thing?" he joked. "It's no use, Mother, I've tried that already. The backup generators don't channel power to the air compressor."

But just then, it kicked on with a rumble. Will stopped short, dumbfounded.

"You just need the administrative touch." She smirked. "But we don't have much time."

"Why not?" Libby asked, walking up to Margaret with a monkey on her shoulder.

"Libby! You're all right!" Margaret shouted.

"Why don't we have much time?" she asked again.

"It's Avery," Margaret said.

Then a *pop* and a whisking sound. Libby fell to the ground as Margaret, and Will scrambled for the shadows. They saw Avery three levels above in the catwalks with an air rifle with enough power, no doubt, to pierce fibrous E-suit material. She glanced at Libby and saw a dart projecting from her back.

Margaret softly tapped Will on the shoulder and motioned with her floodlight toward the big air pumps a few meters away. She aimed the light directly at Avery, who covered up and cowered away from the light. They ran back into the maze of piping near the oxygen tanks. By the time they returned, Avery was nowhere to be found, but they heard nearby footsteps echoing above the rumble of the air pumps.

They were only meters from the airlock, and when the rattle of the pumps stopped, it would be ready for access. It was a waiting game of cat and mouse. If Avery came after them, they would have a fighting chance under cover of the pipes. He was, after all, in a weakened state; his only advantage was the weapon. Hopefully, he'd head back to the cryo-lab and try to override the System Operator. That would keep him occupied long enough to carry Libby onto the shuttle.

But there wasn't any sign of him; it was like he had just disappeared. Margaret looked at both stairs carefully, but the doors didn't open. He was probably waiting for them to come out of hiding, so she continued her quiet vigil. Libby lay at the foot of the airlock, knocked out cold from the tranquilizer, while a frightened troop of monkeys sat patiently by her side.

The motors and pumps soon stopped. Margaret knew it was time to move.

"Will," she whispered. "I'll go first and open the airlock. When I motion to you from the other side, you run, grab Libby, and pull her in with us. Got it?"

He nodded.

They slowly worked their way around the airlock and saw Avery step out of the darkness and bend over Libby, apparently checking for a pulse.

"Get away from her!" Will burst out.

Avery turned to pick up his rifle. "This is the only way, Margaret." Avery gasped and fired.

Will ducked behind an electrical control panel. Margaret tugged on his shoulder, and they disappeared behind conduit and piping.

"We need to split up and circle around," she said. "I'll try and draw his attention with the light."

"But—"

"Just do it, now!"

Will started through the pipes and through the massive oxygen tanks. Margaret took a deep breath and crept along until she reached a misty aisle at the outside wall. The mist in the aisleway blocked the view of the airlock just meters ahead. She bravely moved along until she saw the silhouette of a man standing in the fog about ten meters away, his weapon cocked and ready.

"Margaret." He gasped. She could hardly hear him above the hissing steam. "You should've listened to me. I'm sorry, but it's better this way." He steadied his weapon to fire.

Margaret reached for her flashlight and dropped to the floor. Avery squinted and fired, but Will jumped out from Avery's blind side and swatted the rifle away, knocking Avery aside with his body. Avery fell back into the hissing mist and disappeared.

He landed face-first against the steel superstructure of Gaia's frozen hull. His head and hands instantly froze to the frost-coated steel pipe. In a micro-second, the cold conducted its way through his body, leaving it crystalline and rock-hard.

"Are you all right?" Will cried, running to Margaret's side.

"Yes, I'm fine," she answered softly. "I guess it's over. Let's get the hell out of here."

***

Will punched away at navigational setups while Margaret worked with cryo-containers in the cargo bay. A small primate sat next to him in the co-pilot's chair with its head cocked curiously. Will didn't pay much attention to the little beast but appreciated the company. The rest of the primates kept a quiet vigil at Libby's side as she lay asleep in the passenger compartment.

When the shuttle was readied for take-off, Margaret strapped Libby into a seat behind Will. She'd also managed to herd the primates into cages in the cargo hold. They had to open the hangar bay doors, but the backup power on Gaia was depleted. Their only chance for orbit depended on transferring the remaining power, if any, to the hangar door motor control board.

"Here we go," Will shouted back and pushed the *Hangar Door Open* button.

Margaret looked up to listen. Then she heard the unmistakable rumble of fifteen-meter-high doors rolling on their tracks.

"We did it!" he shouted up front as the doors rolled open to the bright Titan sky.

The tiny monkey next to him ran to the back. Will flipped down his visor and returned to flight status checks. Margaret joined her son in the co-pilot's seat and strapped in for liftoff.

"Have we even thought about hull integrity for such a long flight?" Will asked.

He taxied the shuttle from the hangar and hovered next to the colossal moon base. They didn't say a thing, no fond farewells or exchanged glances.

"Let's get the hell out of here," Margaret ordered.

Will engaged the forward thrusters, and the shuttle lifted to the sky. He hit the heat shield button as the shuttle ascended, calmly watched the altimeter, and readied the ramjet. On the last mission, Gerhardt said three hundred kilometers meant they'd cleared the cloud tops. But atmospheric changes from a greenhouse effect changed all that. This time, the altimeter read almost four hundred kilometers before the onboard computer signaled ready, and the screen flashed *Ramjet Functional*. A red line appeared on the screen, and the counter moved from 0% to 100%, initiate firing system.

"Hang on, here comes escape velocity," Will said, and he was shoved back in his seat.

***

Margaret slowly woke up. "I'm surprised that I passed out," she said. "All the blood from my legs must be back in my head."

"Same thing happened to me," Will offered. "But it was not as bad as the first time with Gerhardt. I must be getting used to it."

Will reached over and patted her hand. Margaret smiled.

"I've been checking our telemetry," he said. "We cleared the atmosphere and are right on course. The modified ion propulsion is online and working properly.

"The Navi-computer calculated a tricky flight path. We'll slingshot around Saturn and hurl in the opposite direction of its orbital path. We must fly backward and fire the thrusters to decelerate enough to get home."

No response.

"How do you feel, Mother?"

"I've been better," she said quietly. "How's Libby?"

"She's not awake yet," he said. "But her breathing is normal."

Margaret smiled and patted his shoulder.

"Now that we're out of the atmosphere," he said. "I'm going to try a communications uplink. There's a chance we can send or receive with Earth. Besides, I have time to kill while autopilot finishes its flight calculations."

"Good idea," she said, unstrapping. "I'll go back and continue with freezer setups."

Will had difficulty communicating with Shoemaker on his last mission, so he verified the orientation of its transmitting dish and boosted the signal. The first message he keyed into the uplink terminal made a connection. He followed with a distress signal to Earth and set the message to repeat in two-minute intervals. He also downloaded all stored information regarding the comet, the TIgrIS base, and all messages sent in the past thirty days.

Libby slowly came out of her deep sleep. "I had a terrible dream," she said. "Did we make it?"

"Glad to see you're up," he said, softly. "Yes, we've made orbit, and our flight path is being calculated."

"The freezers are ready," Margaret's voice cut in from behind. "I had to put two little guys in each compartment, but I think they'll be okay." She knelt next to Will. "Is the flight path confirmed yet?"

"Not quite," he replied.

"Got it," Margaret said. "I want to see the rings. I still haven't seen any of this yet."

"Sure," he replied and hit the heat shield button.

The armored shield slowly rolled open and lit up the cockpit with the glow from the rings. Their brightness was the same as he remembered, but Margaret and Libby were shocked. The rings appeared to have a life of their own compared to the dim yellow planet they encompassed. Margaret gazed in awe at the magnificent glowing halo.

The planetoid had passed but was still visible, with multiple ejecta plumes shooting away from it.

"Look." Will pointed. "There goes our planetoid, and it's even more active now."

"My god," she whispered, taking it all in. "Is this where angels come from, Will Vandolah?"

"No, it's not, Mother," he answered. "I think the other guys come from here."

"What do you think's happening on Earth right now?" Libby asked.

"I don't know," Will replied. "But I hope they get my warning messages to prepare."

"I'll go finish prepping the freezers," Margaret said and kissed her son on the cheek. "I'm proud of you."

Libby moved up to the co-pilot's seat and saw a rare smile on Will's face. She reached for his hand, made eye contact, and gazed at the rings in amazement.

PART VII

Chapter 26
WORLD SPACE COUNCIL

Max Barry sipped on a glass of bourbon and nervously watched a news telecast from his director's chair at the World Space Council. His worst fears had come true; Earth was in total chaos. All nations were under martial law, major cities were burning, and crazies ran madly through the streets.

An African American, Max made his way to the top the old-fashioned way with a hard work ethic. He was well respected and paid that same honor to everyone around him. His fear of this apocalyptic crisis was not for himself, but for humanity, for civilization. Would the world reunite to a common goal or dissolve into eternal chaos.

Worst of all, Max dreaded that all our accumulated scientific knowledge, which took millennia to amass, could be lost forever. Was this the dawn of the next dark age?

Eventually, the ice melted away, and his drink went flat. Max pushed it aside and turned off the news feed. He walked over to the UV-shielded windows of his office and peered out, focusing on the eastern horizon, just above the San Gabriel Mountains. For the first time in months, the ominous white fan was not there. The giant comet was no longer visible during the day. The silent killer had finally faded into darkness, only to be seen at night.

His deep thought was interrupted by a voice from his desktop computer.

"Max," a voice stated. "You'd better get down here."

Max didn't hesitate; he grabbed his coat jacket, pulled it on, adjusted his tie, and stepped out of his office. He was used to daily (even hourly) crises these days, but when a call came from the Comm Center, it was operations critical.

Max burst into the Comm Center with eyes on the view screen.

"What do you have, Jack?" Max asked the controller while staring at the giant overhead viewscreen. "What is this?"

"It's ISS-3," Jack replied. "Some kind of a mutiny."

A female astronaut, fully suited with a helmet shield lifted, saw Max enter the Comm Center. She held one hand to a safety bar while her feet floated behind her.

"Max," she grieved, while punching away at her computer. "I think we've lost it."

"UV shielding in parts of the station didn't hold up to radiation from the comet. Most of the crew were affected, and some went mad. They took half the station and killed two of my officers."

"An explosion disabled the big wheel, so we lost gravity. I've counted 42 bodies in the debris field, and now our orbit is decaying."

"Eleanor," Max nervously replied. "Can't you do a burn to re-establish orbit?"

Eleanor tapped a key, and the image switched to an exterior view.

Max dropped his head.

"Ejecting material from the explosion damaged the Ion propulsion system," Eleanor said. "so, we have no main drive, only thrusters."

"Eleanor!"

"It's okay, Max," she said. "Besides, we still have a couple of hours before re-entry. I have two people prepping the escape pod and calling station-wide for other survivors."

"In the meantime, I'm going EVA to see if I can affect repairs to the Ion drive."

"By yourself?" Max cried.

"I'll set the cameras on a live feed of the exteriors," Eleanor said. "So, you can watch my progress."

She tapped a key, and the screen went to a silent view of the Ion engines.

"I'm so sorry, Max," Jack consoled.

"She's the best we have," Max firmly stated. "I'm not losing her."

Max's head was spinning.

"How soon can we get rescue up there?" he asked.

"Max, all flights have been canceled. No more launches," Jack said, shaking his head.

"How soon!" Max shouted.

"No governmental craft available," another voice cut in while typing away. "And no time for prep anyway, so it has to be something already up there."

Max approached her station.

"Okay," she amazed. "A Swedish research vessel *is scheduled* to arrive at ISS-3 at 1400 hours today."

"Really?" Max asked. "How do we verify that?"

"Evidently, they need medical assistance," Jack added. "And are enroute."

"I guess they figured they'd be safer on the station," Max said. "Can you get me in contact with that vessel?"

"I'm on it."

"Does anybody speak Swedish?" Max teased. "We have to tell these people it's a rescue mission."

No responses.

Eleanor appeared on the main view screen minutes later in an operable EVA suit, drifting toward the Ion engines.

"Eleanor," Max said. "Can you hear me?"

"Loud and clear, Sir," she replied.

"A Swedish ship, the Vanadis," Max said. "Is enroute to ISS-3 and will rendezvous at 1400 hours."

"Vanadis?" she queried. "They sent a distress signal a few hours ago, but command was under attack."

"Have you confirmed their ETA?"

"Yes."

"That gives me ninety minutes to get these engines operational," Eleanor said.

***

Max Barry's mind was a steel trap; he had to rescue the commander of ISS-3. He knew politics and public opinion, and losing Eleanor Collins would be as bad as losing the station.

Eleanor not only commanded the most advanced space station in human history but was a well-respected public figure. Legendary in her own time, she was a submarine commander, piloted one of the first mining missions to the asteroid belt, and was integral in the design of ISS-3. If there were still rock stars, she would carry that status.

Max Barry's place was really not on Earth. As director of the World Space Council, he had to maintain control of expanding humanity's solar system exploration.

But amidst the crisis on Earth, he had other issues to address. ISS-Luna, orbiting the moon, had crash landed into the Sea of Tranquility, all contact was lost with Titan base Gaia 3, Mars base Gaia 2, and now Gaia 1 was reporting an 'uprising of red-eyes.' But all were kept secret from the public. Max's reasoning with Congress was 'wait until the smoke settles'; we have too much to worry about down here.

Worse yet, all intermediate shuttles and cargo ships had gone silent. And no one knew about that except JPL.

Max wondered if the Swedish shuttle would even arrive at ISS-3.

***

"Let's make contact with the Swedes," Max ordered.

"It will take a few minutes to access their communications protocol," Jack said.

"I understand."

Minutes later, the face of the Swedish commander appeared on the main view screen. He seemed to be distraught and spoke broken English.

"Vanadis here," he said. "Commander Olsson speaking."

"Commander," Jack said. "This is JPL. We show you are currently enroute to ISS-3. Is that correct?"

"Correct," Olsson replied, breathing heavily. "That's correct. We have many passengers that suffer from this madness. We need medical attention."

"Commander," Max Barry cut in. "Are your ill passengers secure?"

"Secure?"

"Yes," Max replied. "Secure. Are they restrained or unconscious?"

"Restrained," he said. "Yes, restrained."

"Okay, then," Max said. "Listen carefully. ISS-3 has been severely damaged and only has a few hours left. We need you to rendezvous with it and retrieve passengers."

Olsson looked confused.

"Docking could be difficult," he said. "Or impossible, depending on the extent of damage."

"We will continue to assess that situation," Max said. "And keep you informed."

"In the meantime, we'll contact Edwards Air Force Base and alert them that you'll make an emergency landing there. Keep this channel open until we contact you again."

"Understood," Olsson replied.

**

From the distance and angle of her view, Eleanor could not make out the entirety of the engine damage. But when she arrived, the metal shell of the engine bell was severely bent and partially torn away from its base. Repairing it was out of the question, and firing up the engines would cause an explosion. She was out of options.

"Fuck!" she shouted and kicked the wrecked engine bell. The zero-G effect of action and reaction immediately shot her away. Before she could adjust the thrusters, her head slammed into the engine housing frame. The headset crackled and went silent.

"Max! Max!" she shouted. No reply.

She made her way back to the airlock. She reached command and checked orbital decay. The station was already heating up; it was happening quicker than expected. Then she noticed a monitor with red lights flashing.

ESCAPE POD ACTIVATED
ESCAPE POD JETTISONED

"Oh my god," Eleanor panicked. In disbelief, she looked out the command center windows to verify, but the pod was gone.

"Sys, please verify escape pod activity," she asked. "Who authorized the jettison?"

"Authorization not required," Sys replied.

"Clarify."

"Outer hull temperature activates automatic jettison when occupied," Sys replied. "And current temperatures are more than two times normal limits."

Eleanor considered her options. If ever the phrase *'Going down with the ship'* applied to a captain, it was her. She was more disappointed than afraid; how had it come to this?

About the time she uttered the words *'I refuse to accept checkmate'*, her eyes caught a glimpse of something outside the portside window. It was the Vanadis hovering about one hundred meters away, holding velocity and distance.

Eleanor scrambled for the airlock, fastening her helmet as she went. She entered the airlock, punched depressurize on the console, and stepped out into the void. She flipped on a flashing distress beacon and piloted toward the Vanadis.

As she zeroed in, the main cargo bay doors opened. She maneuvered down inside to the waiting arms of Commander Olsson. He snapped a safety clasp to her EVA suit and tapped the 'close bay doors' button on the arm of his own EVA suit.

With the cargo bay re-pressurized, Eleanor popped off her helmet and breathed a grateful sigh of relief.

"Commander Olsson at your service," he saluted.

"Eleanor Collins," she extended a hand. "Thanks for coming. If you hadn't shown up when you did –"

"Boom, right?" Olsson kidded.

They made their way through the shuttle, where some people were restrained and sedated in their seats, while others tended to them.

Olsson contacted Edwards AFB from the shuttle cockpit to confirm their landing timing and flight path.

Eleanor watched as ISS-3 broke away into fiery pieces. The once majestic space station tumbled, exploded, and split into thousands of shooting stars. She could not help but feel responsible; could she have taken different measures at different times to prevent this?

She dropped her head and covered her face.

"This is not your fault," Olsson consoled. "It is symbolic of civilization down there."

"Let's hope not."

***

Max knew ISS-3 was breaking up in the atmosphere, but he'd lost contact with Eleanor and feared the worst. He sat down and tallied the losses. Congress wouldn't even talk to him now, if ever. It might take a century to put this planet back together. How could he blame them if he were laughed out of the Capitol building?

He tried to focus on the facts, not the possibilities. What was left to work with and repair? He needed an accurate assessment, but like he told Congress, it was a wait-and-see game until the crisis passed. Still, he had to stay in the game and salvage everything he could 'till the end.

His computer screen lit up with a message from Edwards AFB. Max tapped the screen to read it.

'Swedish space shuttle Vanadis successfully lands on runway 05R/23L.'

'Heavy one U.S. Astronaut.'

Max broke into tears of joy, "Thank God."

Just then, a man burst into his office.

"You're not going to believe this!"

"I know, I know," Max happily said. "I just saw the message. The Vanadis made it back safely."

"Vanadis?" the man sounded puzzled. "No, listen. We just received a signal from a Gaia 3 shuttle; it's just cleared the asteroid belt."

Redeemed confidence filled Max from head to toe.

"So, there *are* survivors," Max murmured. "Maybe, I still have two of my best commanders after all."

***

Max poured a drink. He knew this victory was merely a finger in the dike of a catastrophe that would be with humankind for decades, maybe centuries. But for the here and now, it was a happy moment that he could build on. He thought about the possibility of having his two superstars back in the saddle.

He sipped the drink, relaxed, and leaned back in his chair.

***

Max found himself face-to-face with his favorite bartender at his favorite bar on the Luna station orbiting the moon. It didn't have the greatest ambiance, but the views were incredible. Out of this world, you might say. The dark side was bland, but seeing Earthrise as the station cleared the crescent rim of the moon was an awe-inspiring sight.

And the panorama of the unending landscape of craters was so Neil Armstrong. Even for a man born a century after him, it never got old.

In time Margaret and Eleanor greeted him, both passing through on their way to new assignments. They were his favorites, like two daughters; he could not be more proud of them, what they had achieved, and what they represented.

"Let me guess," Max said. "Gaia 3 and ISS-3."

"Close," Margaret said. "I'm Gaia 3. She's ISS-3."

"Well, I've been sitting here longer than you two have," Max chuckled. "So, how long are you here?"

"Four days," Eleanor replied.

"One week," Margaret followed.

"I need you both on top of your game for this one," Max said. "I can't tell you how critical both stations are to the stability of our mission."

"We're well aware of that, Sir," Margaret said.

"We won't let you down, Sir," Eleanor said.

Then they heard a large explosion that rocked the station and took gravity too. At the same time, cries from the corridors rang out as people floated in all directions. Max and Margaret grabbed the countertop as bottles of bourbon and vodka spilled away from their expensive glass casings. Eleanor was tossed over to the outside glass window and rolled up to the ceiling.

More cries followed in the corridor as red-eyed madmen cut their way through the floating mass of people with machetes and knives. People helplessly kicked away at them as blood bubbles and more giant blobs drifted in all directions.

"We have to assess the damage!" Max shouted and was tossed over the bar. "Margaret! Eleanor! You need to access the central hub and get the main thrusters back online!"

They quickly pulled their way to the corridor and kicked past a few red eyes. They passed through more of the floating crowd and finally made it to the first open spoke.

"This spoke should take us there!" Margaret shouted.

Moments later, they were at the entrance door to the central hub. It was pressure-locked and required E-suits for entry. E-suits that hung on a nearby wall where Eleanor was already pulling one on.

They finally got access to the gigantic engine room of the rotating space station. Hearts sank when they entered to see the roof was gone entirely; exploded debris floated and whirled in all directions. What was left of the main turbine crackled and sparked, and its mechanical connections to operating machinery were all blown away. Four of the six spokes connecting the hub to the primary, habitable wheel were utterly detached from the hub. And too many bodies to count drifted out into space.

They turned back to see Max pounding at the entrance door.

"Get out of there!" he shouted. "We have to find the escape pods!"

Then another explosion rocked the space station, and Max was knocked to the ground.

He quickly got to his feet and gazed through the porthole window, but they were gone. The blast destroyed the entire hub, along with any hope of survival.

Max looked on astonished, as the once mighty space station was shredded apart. It tumbled aimlessly through the void, dropping closer to the lunar surface. He looked out to see hundreds of bodies floating helplessly along the same path as the doomed station.

His heart sank as guilt for this disaster throttled him like a noose around his neck. He could not bear the thought of so much loss for which he blamed himself.

The tumbling station moved nearer and more rapidly to the surface. Small craters seemed city size and passed by in a flash. They barely cleared one final ridge to the open plains of the sea of tranquility. And just before the space station impacted the surface, Max woke up screaming.

***

An aide rushed into the room, out of breath.

"Is everything all right, Sir?" he asked, with the door standing open behind him. Max was soaking wet with sweat. He pulled off his glasses, rubbed his eyes, and regrouped.

"Yeah," he replied. "I'm all right, and I'm sorry if I startled you."

He stood and paced the room, rubbing his neck.

"All right, Sir," the Aide said. "Let me know if you need anything."

"Thank you for checking on me."

Max walked over to the bar sink, splashed water on his face, and took a long look in the mirror.

'Just another bad dream,' he murmured. 'That's all.'

***

It took some time, but Max pulled himself together, devised a plan, and called for his Aide. He wanted to stomp out every negative feeling from that dreadful dream.

"Yes, Sir," the Aide asked.

"Get with Comms," Max said. "I want a repeating message sent to the Gaia 3 shuttle ASAP. We need to inform them about what's going on down here and formulate a plan for their safe return."

"And contact Edwards too. Let's get Commander Collins back here to JPL as soon as she is able."

"Yes, Sir."

Chapter 27
WAKE-UP CALL

Margaret awoke to tingly feet and crusty lips that she pried open with her tongue. Her vision was blurred, and moving her head only revealed spotty images, but she could make out flashing lights and a repeating audible message.

"*Urgent, Urgent...*" the voice repeated, louder as the glass cryo-lid lifted away.

It took a few minutes, but Margaret finally sat up and threw her feet over the side of the cryo table.

"Cut that out!" she finally managed to burst out. Her foggy head cleared to see Will and Libby still in hibernation.

"Sys," she said. "Why did you only wake me? What's so urgent?"

"Incoming message from the Space Council," Sys replied. "Designated urgent."

Data streamed across the view screen in binary code, something she recognized but could not decipher. She was still groggy and sighed. "How long was I in cryo-freeze?"

"Three years, two hundred fifty-four days, twelve hours, twenty-four minutes and—"

"Stop!" Margaret shouted. *Christ, still two months away from home.* She tried to focus. "Sys," she said. "Can you interpret this data?"

"Not at this time, download incomplete."

She waited and waited but grew impatient. Her gaze switched between the computer monitor and Will's cryo-chamber. A few minutes later, she was at the cryo-control board, punching in wake-up procedures. She finally hit *Early Wake-up*, then *Enable*.

Will's cryo-chamber flashed and hissed. The computer screen read *Thirty minutes remaining*.

"How much longer 'till the data file download is complete?" she asked.

"Unknown," Sys replied.

"Okay." Margaret sighed. "I'll get cleaned up while Will's chamber finishes thawing procedures."

***

"Man, I hate waking up from cryo-freeze," Will mumbled and yawned, but seeing Margaret's face was a relief.

"How do you feel?" Margaret asked.

"Hmm," he let out. "Okay, I guess."

"We were awakened early," she said.

"What?" He looked up. "Why?"

"I need you to look at something," she said.

***

They pulled up chairs in front of the monitor where streaming data files had finished downloading.

"This message's received file is huge," Will said. "Even larger than my cometary research files. But something's wrong, it's either corrupted, or it's an overrun dump from tracking procedures. There's no broken-down structure, just one giant file that's almost filled its allocated storage space. It's definitely from Earth but not all from the Space Council."

"I don't understand?" she asked. "How can other messages get mixed in with Space Council messages?"

"Not sure, some kind of interference," he replied. "But incoming messages got backed up and intertwined."

"Well," Margaret fumbled, "can you sort them out?"

"It'll take some time," he replied, typing away. "But I'll get through it."

It did take a while, and there were messages from multiple sources, but Will eventually decompiled and decrypted everything. The first message was a satellite feed from an Asian country.

"This is like a jumbled newsreel," Will said, "skipping from one topic to the next—local news, children's shows, soap operas, you name it."

Then something caught his eye. A panicked newsperson barked out his newscast against a screen showing a mob of thousands stampeding a mosque.

"Look, Mother." He pointed.

"At what?" she asked. "It's all in Chinese."

"All except that word," he said.

"Oh, my god," she whispered.

"TIgrIS," he fretted.

There was a brief hush while Margaret considered her options.

"Okay, Will," she said, "you need to dig into this and find out exactly what the Space Council sent us. And also set up a communication link with them."

"I sent a repeating message to them before we went into cryo-freeze," he said. "It included everything we had on the planetoid and the effects on the crew. So, they knew it was coming."

"It must be ahead of us, judging by that news clip," Margaret said. "If we warned them, why didn't they do anything about it?"

Will sighed. "I'll check it's trajectory and let you know," he said. "But first, I'll make contact with the Space Council."

***

It didn't take long to reach Earth since their first message to Sys included audio files. Will aligned the transmitter dish, adjusted frequency to match the urgent message, and called for Margaret.

"I just sent a request to the Space Council," he said, "that basically says we're awake, all right, and waiting for instructions. They won't receive it at this distance for about ninety minutes, so their response will take at least three hours."

"You're sure all the technicals are right?" Margaret asked. "We can't waste too much time before we cryo-freeze again."

"I'm sure," he said. "And by the way, the urgent message was for us to contact them ASAP." Will rubbed his face to stay focused and took a deep breath. "I'm more concerned about contacting and staying in contact with them," he said. "With everything going on down there."

"Okay, we have plenty to do around here while we wait," Margaret said. "I'll go prep the freezers."

***

Recovery from cryo-freeze required lots of fluid for hours, and Will had barely sucked down eight ounces since Margaret had woken him. He pecked away at his keyboard until his eyes got sleepy, then his head dropped.

***

"This is not good!" Will grunted. He couldn't count the number of flashing lights as he struggled to slow the shuttle down to sub-sonic speed. He'd barely held the ship together on reentry, but things were worse now, and panicked voices from control didn't help.

"I can't find the runway!" he shouted. "Everything's a blur!"

More chattering came through his headset until he finally got visual on the runways and approached with estimated airspeed.

"I don't understand!" he shouted. "My airspeed...What?"

The shuttle came in too hard, blew out its landing gear, screeched down the tarmac in a trail of sparks, rolled up on one side, then finally dropped to a flat and upright position.

Will unbuckled and ran back to check on the cryo-freezers, but they were damaged with lights flashing.

"Mother! Mother!" He scrambled, pushing buttons.

Margaret and Libby lay inside the containers, both shaking with seizures. In a panic, he ran for help. At the exit door, he pulled the emergency latch, the door popped open, and unfurled an inflatable slide.

At the bottom of the slide, multitudes of red-eyed madmen ran toward him across the tarmac. They gave chase beneath the light of a comet tail that seemed to engulf them like fog. But up in the sky, one star was bright enough to cut through the mist; it was the Star of the Sun, Saturn.

Will ran as hard as he could toward the next-generation rocket assembly building, but the harder he ran, the slower he went. He finally stopped to catch his breath and noticed an arrow stuck in his leg. He reached to pull it out and stumbled to the ground. Before he knew it, the red-eyed mob pounced on him.

"Get off me! Get off me!" He panicked.

***

Margaret heard a familiar alert from the cockpit; it was the incoming message tone. She hurried up there and found Will asleep in the pilot's chair.

"Wake up, wake up." She nudged him.

"Get off me!" Will was startled out of his deep sleep and took a minute to gather himself.

"Hey, it's me," she said, clutching his face. "Calm down, calm down."

Will quickly came out of his dreamy stupor and focused on the incoming message tone, reached up, and turned off the warning flasher. He studied the monitor momentarily. "Oh, I'm sorry, Mother," he said, then studied the console.

"Hey," he said. "We have something here." Will flipped some switches and adjusted the audio.

"It's a mess down here, Margaret," a voice came through a staticky feed. Then the screen locked up to a still shot of a well-dressed man.

"Hang on," Will said. "It's just buffering. Give it a minute." He typed in a few commands.

"That's Max Barry," Margaret said. "My supervisor for the Mars training missions."

"This should do it," Will said. "Here we go."

"We've been tracking your shuttle for some time now and decided to have Sys wake you up early," Barry continued. "Commercial air travel has been grounded for months, and the entire world is under martial law. People are holding out in basements eating canned food. Economies are at a standstill, and food chains are getting stressed.

"We received everything you sent months ago regarding this object, but unfortunately, it fell on deaf political ears. That is until the tail of that damned thing erupted into view. It's almost 200 million miles long, Margaret. It's like a giant broom sweeping the inner solar system and delivering whatever radiation that moon-sized comet spews out.

"We've lost contact with all manned space missions, no communication of any kind. We've been sent back to the stone age here, Margaret. No more manned missions in the foreseeable future. We lost contact with ISS-3 before the worst hit, then it burned up on reentry. The same goes for the Mars bases and ISS – Luna, when it slammed into the Sea of Tranquility."

Margaret covered her eyes in disbelief.

"Last week, we lost contact with Gaia 1," Barry continued, "but we think there may still be survivors. You're the only ship out there, so we're transmitting a new flight path to slingshot you around Earth for a slow-down approach to the Moon, where we want you to land and stabilize that station. If you can salvage Gaia 1, it will be a boon for humanity's hopes and our future in space."

There was a noticeable disturbance nearby, glass shattering, and cries of struggle. Barry's eyes turned away from the computer monitor, then forbiddingly back. "If you fail…" he paused. "It might be centuries before we get back up there."

"Audio's cut out," Will said, studying the received file. "But a data file is coming in. He must have sent it while talking."

They received the course correction and input the data to Sys' flight control program.

"Mother, flight time to Gaia 1 is nearly 9 weeks," he said. "There's not enough food on board, so we have to hibernate. I'll set controls to wake us again once we reach lunar orbit."

"And, hopefully," Margaret said, "There's something to eat when we arrive. It's not shielded like Gaia 3."

***

Two slingshots later, the shuttle was orbiting Earth's moon, and the four-plus year trip was nearing an end. Lights on the cryo-chambers flashed, and three glass covers rolled back. In time, Margaret and Will were at the controls checking flight status while Libby tended to waking the sleeping monkeys.

"Looks like we're safely in an equatorial orbit around the moon," Will said. "I must adjust to a polar orbit and prepare for a South Pole landing."

"Radiation levels are acceptable inside here," Margaret added. "Let's roll back the shields and see what it looks like out there."

They were on the moon's dark side but moved quickly toward the terminator. When Earth popped into view, it was nighttime across the Americas and Western Europe.

"Look, Mother," he said. "I can't make out the land masses, even at night. North America, South America, and the rims of Western European countries aren't there."

"And what does that tell you?" Margaret asked.

"I'm not sure?"

"It's all dark," she said. "Stone-age dark like Barry said. North America, in particular, should light up like a Christmas tree, but it looks pre-industrial."

Will sank back in his seat with that sobering observation.

"Power grids are all down, everywhere," Margaret said. "I don't know what happened down there, but this is worse than I thought it would be."

"And when we reach Gaia 1," she said. "I only hope we're not too late."

"So, we're jumping right into another fight?" Will said.

"Gaia 1 is on the south pole of the moon," Margaret said. "And nestled down inside a crater. With any luck they've been spared the brunt of the radiation blast."

"So, you're saying this could be easy?"

"Hoping."

Chapter 28
AMUNDSEN CRATER

With their flight path and velocity corrected, the shuttle cruised low toward Amundsen crater at the moon's south pole.

"This doesn't look like Earth." Libby approached from the shuttle's rear, cradling a half-sleeping monkey.

"No." Will sighed. "It's not."

"How do you feel?" Margaret asked.

"Just fine 'till I came up here," she replied.

Will chuckled.

"Is this the moon?" Libby asked. "I mean, Earth's moon?"

"Unfortunately, yes," Margaret said. "The Space Council rerouted us to check out Gaia 1."

"Why are we going to Gaia 1?" Libby panicked.

"They lost contact with it," Will said.

"The inner solar system was affected the same way as Saturn was," Margaret said. "When that thing passed."

"Wait." Libby gathered her thoughts. "So, the same madness we saw on Titan is happening here?"

No response.

"Then Gaia 1 probably has seriously ill, red-eyed monsters on it!" she fretted.

Margaret sighed.

"Let's just don't go and say we did," Libby said. "I'm not going through that again. Gaia 1 is way bigger than Gaia 3, so there could be many more madmen to deal with."

"Just calm down," Margaret said. "Look, all spacecraft have been lost, and no one else out here can host a rescue. They're desperate on Earth, and we're the last chance to stabilize the base."

"Can't we just go back home?" Libby begged. "And feel safe for once."

Margaret regrouped. "There's not much of a home to return to right now," she said. "They need us to take care of business here while they do the same on Earth."

"But the comet's tail has cleared the planet, so we don't have to deal radiation with this time."

Libby was taking it in but needed to digest it better.

"We do a recon fly-by," Margaret continued, "And formulate a plan to enter and stabilize Gaia 1."

"We'll be at the crater in thirteen minutes," Will said, studying the console.

"Good, we make an aerial assessment," Margaret said. "And if everything looks secure, we prep for a landing."

Libby retreated back to the cryo-chambers, shaking her head.

"There's the rim of the crater, just up ahead," he said. "Have you been here before? What's the layout?"

"Three times," she replied. "It's larger and more advanced than Gaia 3. Even though older, its constant upgrades keep it on the cutting edge. There are vast storage bins of grain and seeds in the Dead Hemisphere. There's no cryo-tech there and a lot more housing. It can support 125 people, and the hangar bay is similar to Gaia 3's.

"There's a supporting campus of tin can testing labs and a controversial nuclear power plant on the opposite side of the crater. Since this facility is a spaceport, the Space Council wanted a fail-safe power system.

"High level security, too. It's essentially an international spaceport, so, as you can imagine, the place is stocked with guards and special ops personnel. Not my cup of tea."

"So, it's a combination space station and military base," Will said.

Margaret scoffed.

"Okay, here we go," he said. "Up over the rim."

When they cleared the rim of the Amundsen crater, the entire campus came into view with long shadows trailing away from structures. Gaia 1, the first off-world biosphere, dominated the horizon. Its crystal-clear glass Living Hemisphere glistened against the pitch-black heavens. And a satellite dish on a tall mast projected from inside the roof structure.

"The dish beacon isn't flashing," Margaret said. "Probably why communications are down."

"Take a wide circle around the campus."

They dropped from the crater rim and approached the campus slowly.

"See how the campus is in shadow and the lunar surface is covered with dusted ice?" Margaret said. "The crater wall naturally shields the base from most effects from solar radiation, allowing for the use of a transparent multi-pane glass dome. So, you look up at the *real* stars from Gaia 1."

They passed the nuclear power plant that looked undamaged, and the perimeter lights were still on. All other structures looked the same until they saw the biosphere.

"Mother, look," he said. "The hangar doors are open, and all shuttles are gone."

"That's not the worst," Margaret said, pointing a hundred (or so) meters from the base. "Look out there."

"Is that a wrecked shuttle?" he asked and veered toward it. Parts of a shuttle lay in a debris field with bodies strewn everywhere, some in E-suits, some not.

"Okay," Margaret said. "I think we can guess that what's going on in there is something we've already faced."

They made a full circle around the base, no light or sign of human activity was visible in the Living Hemisphere.

"How much fuel do we have?" she asked. "Can we just park in relative safety in plain view of the hangar bay and the Living to see if anyone shows up?"

"That's a great idea," Will said and dropped down for a landing.

Margaret unbuckled and went back to check on Libby.

"What are you doing back here?" she asked.

"Waking up the rest of them," Libby replied.

"Why?"

Libby handed Margaret a tiny collar.

"These little guys can be our eyes and ears," she said. "They're very sneaky and good at hiding from humans. And with these cameras on their collars, we can see what's going on before we ever go inside."

"That's the best idea I've heard yet," Margaret said.

Chapter 29
GAIA 1

Margaret patiently waited outside Gaia 1 inside the shuttle cockpit, but there was no activity. She unbuckled, left Will on watch, and went back to check progress with the cryo-work.

Libby had just finished waking the capuchin monkeys, and one hopped on her back when she knelt to check on the troop.

"They all look healthy," Margaret said, grasping at a collar. "Is this one of the cameras?"

"Yes, I wanted to get them all hooked up before checking them," Libby replied, typing in commands. "Here we go," she said.

The screen popped up with visuals from all the monkeys' collars. "OK, that's all good," she said.

Libby voiced a primate sound they were used to hearing from her, and the room exploded with capuchin chatter.

"So, they respond to your voice," Margaret complimented.

"Yes, they do," she replied. "And I think we're ready to roll with this."

"So, they're all connected to that device?"

"Give me a second," Libby said and punched away on a hand-held device. "should be good now."

"Can you send them up to Will?" Margaret smiled.

"No problem," Libby replied. "Hey, Will! Clap for the monkeys!"

Seconds later the pack of capuchin monkeys darted away and scurried up front.

"Oh, my god," Will laughed. "Hey, guys! What's up?"

Libby tossed Margaret the hand-held that displayed the view from each collar.

"OK, I'm sold," Margaret said. "Great work, Libby."

Then more commotion up front.

"Mother!" Will shouted. "Get up here!"

***

Margaret hurried to the cockpit and saw a human figure waving from the shuttle hangar.

"That's got to be a good sign," Will said.

"Bet your ass it is," Margaret followed.

Minutes later, the shuttle was docked, and the giant bay doors rolled to a close. The person at the controls waited while the hangar pressurized, watched the dust settle, and removed her helmet. Margaret and Will entered the cylindrical chamber and descended.

"Margaret!" the woman shouted. "Is that you?"

Margaret was shocked to see Elena Torres approaching.

"I almost hate to say it, given the circumstances," Elena said. "But you're a sight for sore eyes."

Margaret chuckled, relieved to see a friendly face. They embraced awkwardly in E-suit gear.

"How long has it been?" Margaret asked.

"Gaia 2, Mars," Elena said. "Four years ago."

"This is my son, Will."

He extended a hand.

"Will, we were stationed on Gaia 2 for about a year," Margaret said. "And now Elena is commander of Gaia 1."

"What's left of it," Elena said. "I must say, seeing a shuttle hovering out there with Gaia 3 markings was the last thing I ever expected."

"The Space Council rerouted us here to help stabilize the base," Margaret said. "Just how bad is it in there?"

"Let's get inside where we can take these damned E-suits off and talk," Elena said.

Elena had risen through the ranks in a much different way than Margaret. Raised a military brat, she was a West Pointer, where she'd found an interest in chemistry and biology.

After her service commitment was complete, she'd enrolled at Cal Tech and received a degree in Bio-Chemical Engineering. There she'd met John Avery and became fascinated—as Margaret had—with the study of Ecotechnics. His recommendation to the World Space Council was all it took to start Elena on her upward trajectory.

But the administration of an international spaceport was entirely different than the science-based Gaia 2 on Mars. When she'd first come through Gaia 1 enroute to Mars she'd noticed the airport-like feel to it but hadn't paid much attention. But administering such a place, where people issues took priority over technical issues, was a drastic change. Security took center stage in this facility that acted as the United Nations for the moon. And never in her wildest dreams had she ever thought she'd have to issue a public address for a lost dog.

Elena could see the light at the end of the tunnel and wanted to get back to Earth. Her resignation was all but penned when the comet came through the inner planets.

"Will, go get Libby," Margaret said. "We'll meet you on the other side of the sky bridge."

Elena and Margaret rode up an elevator to the sky bridge and talked as they walked.

"I'm sorry to hear about what happened on Titan," Elena said. "We thought we'd be protected from those effects, being at the bottom of a crater on the bottom of the moon, but no such luck. The radiation from that damn thing was hundreds of times greater than anything we get from the sun."

"We didn't realize it 'till it was too late. Most people went to see the beautiful comet daily, not knowing what was happening to them."

"I'm so sorry," Margaret said. "And the side-effects, the madness?"

"The crazies are everywhere in the Living," Elena said. "And have taken the two upper levels of the Lower Hemisphere."

"Taken?"

"It was a battle, Margaret," Elena said. "They have horrible red eyes, with black dilated pupils, like giant bug eyes. We couldn't control them, so we started using tranquilizer darts, then they came back at us with poison darts."

"Poison darts, how?"

"They're deadly, Margaret," Elena said. "I've lost four men already. They fashioned blowguns from bamboo shoots and darts tipped with curare, both growing in the Living."

"Jesus." Margaret sighed.

"At first, we tried to send the sick back to Earth," Elena said. "But it was too late already. We launched three shuttles full of affected people, lost contact with two, and one crashed over there. All in all, we lost seventy-three passengers and crew.

"There's a war raging in there, Margaret," Elena said. "I have five men on level four guarding all possible entry points to the lower decks. The Red Eyes got control of the comm center and cut off all outside communication. They're foraging for food and supplies, working toward the lower-level storage bins."

"My god." Margaret sighed, then regrouped. "How many passengers and crew are still on the base, affected and not?"

"There were 123 passengers and crew when the comet passed through the system," Elena said. "We had twenty-two crew down here."

Elena sighed. "But now we're down to eighteen." She grimaced. Her lovely dark Hispanic eyes closed and turned away. "Twenty-eight were up in the Living, and four or five fell to their deaths. Three down here went over the rails, and two were thrown off the mountain."

Elena depressed an airlock switch that swished the door open. She and Margaret crossed from the sky bridge into Gaia 1, where Margaret instinctively studied the surroundings.

"So, you're facing up to twenty-four seriously ill individuals," Margaret calculated. "We had three on Titan, and that was all I could handle."

Margaret digested the information.

"How are supplies holding out?" she asked.

"We're fine down here," Elena said. "The storage bins can feed us for years, and assuming we get control of the Living again, then we're self-sufficient."

"What about weapons?" Margaret asked.

"We have gallons of tranquilizer," Elena said. "And we cleared everything out of med-lab to keep it safe. We ration darts and use them only when necessary. We retrieve them when possible."

"Okay, then," Margaret said. "What about their access to the lower levels?"

"At first, they had a free run of the place before we knew what was going on," Elena replied. "Then, they started smashing out lights and cameras, so we disabled the elevators and posted guards at the stairways. We lost one man in a second-level ambush, a good man."

She paused.

"Darted?"

"No, taken," Elena replied. "After that, we welded all lower-level doors shut. Now our main priority is keeping them out of engineering."

"So, you can't even see what's going on up there?" Margaret asked.

"No, not in the Living or the upper levels."

A buzzer sounded, and the airlock door opened. Will and Libby stepped inside with the troop of capuchin monkeys hanging all over them.

"There's three of you!" Elena said, amazed. "And these little guys are adorable!"

Elena reached out to one that scrambled up her arm and perched on her shoulder. Margaret did the same, and after introductions with Libby, they moved on.

"We'll go up to engineering," Elena said, "and check-in with Michael."

Clanging metallic footsteps led them to a caged ladder that connected all lower levels. Margaret craned her neck and studied the framework. "So, this is it, huh?" she asked.

"Best we can do without elevators and stairs," Elena replied. "It's only five flights."

"Okay, you first," Margaret said.

As soon as Elena grabbed the sidebars, the little monkey on her shoulder hopped onto the side cage and scampered up.

"Wish I could do that." Elena scoffed.

The entire troop hopped off their hosts and did the same, and before Elena took her first step, they were all at the first level, cackling away.

"Okay, here we go." Elena chuckled.

With each new level the team reached, the monkey troop was one higher, cackling and jumping about. When Elena came to level four, an engineer stood waiting with two capuchin monkeys on his shoulders.

"Elena," Michael Keller said. "What's all this?"

"Passengers from the Gaia 3 shuttle," she said. "I think you know Margaret, and you've already met these little guys."

"You're here from the Titan base?" Michael asked.

"Rerouted," Margaret said, "is a better choice of words."

"Understood."

"This is my son, Will, and scientist, Libby Owens," Margaret said.

"My pleasure."

"Michael," Elena said. "I've brought Margaret up to speed on most of the events here. Anything new in the past hour?"

"Nothing," he replied. "Lookouts on level three check in every fifteen minutes, and engineering is still secure."

"Well, that's good to know." Elena sighed. "And now we have some seasoned veterans here, that survived Gaia 3."

"Elena," Margaret said. "Now that you've seen these little guys in action, we have a proposal, or I should say, Libby has a proposal."

"I'm all ears."

"Capuchin monkeys are very adept to change," she said. "When the chaos started on Gaia 3, they found ways to hide from the madmen who started hunting them. I figured they were all dead until I found they'd broken into the concrete mountain through vent covers. They smuggled in food and hid in the waterfall cave."

"And your point being?" Elena asked.

"They're very clever," Libby replied. "They go unnoticed, and best of all, I've attached these camera collars on them."

"Excuse me?"

"If we can get them up in the Living," Libby said, "they can be our eyes and ears."

Elena sighed. "I'm not sure how we do that, since the elevators and stairs are disabled."

"Good point," Margaret said.

"You saw them scamper up the ladder cages," Libby said. "They don't need elevators or stairs."

"So, how?"

"Have you been inside the concrete mountain?" Libby asked.

"No one has," Elena said. "No access."

"We have," Libby said. "We just followed these little guys."

"But they were already inside the Living when they found the ventilation hatches," Will said.

"True," Libby said. "But there's access from below, remember?"

"That's right." Will flashed back. "Miller used an access hatch."

"We have one, too," Michael interjected. "But we must get up to level one to do it."

"Levels two and three are solid plate floors," Elena said. "Like the Living. So, the only way down to these levels is stairs or elevators."

"That's right," Michael agreed. "But there are access panels in maintenance closets on both floors with ladders, and one goes up to the mountain floor."

"Does that mean the red eyes can drop down through these closets?" Elena asked.

"No, they can't do that," Michael replied. "I cranked them both shut from below after we disabled the elevators. And I doubt they even know about them with their failing eyesight. They're not easy to find and poorly labeled."

"But still, what if they've broken into a closet," Elena said, "and the door is wide open when we open the hatch?"

"Those are security doors," Michael said. "If they open, the boards in engineering light up."

"So, if we try this," Elena said, "and get these little guys into the underbelly of the mountain, then what?"

"I'll have to go with them," Libby said. "To lead them up to the waterfall cave where they migrate out into the Living. The collars have infrared, and I'll carry a flashlight."

"Wait," Michael said. "Can you do this?"

"On Gaia 3, there's an access ladder on the inside wall that goes up to the waterfall cave," Libby replied. "There's a platform and an access hatch to the holding pool."

Michael still looked confused.

"Believe me, we found out the hard way," Libby regretted.

"And I'll go with her," Will said.

"Wait!" Libby held up a hand.

But Will was not hearing anything of it. "Do you really want to face another insane person alone?" he asked.

"Hey," Elena cut them off. "I'm making decisions here, and I've lost too many people already."

"Elena," Margaret said, "you need recon in the Living and upper decks to know what's happening and make proper decisions."

Elena sighed and reconsidered. "I know," she replied. "Maybe you're right."

"The monkeys are our eyes and ears," Libby said. "As terrible as it makes me feel, they're the ones in danger, not me."

"Okay, then," Elena conceded. "Two of you can go, but proceed no farther than the holding pool. At the first sign of danger, you back out and lock that door behind you. Don't wait for your little monkeys to return, understood?"

"Yes," Will said, and Libby gave a reluctant nod.

"And take these with you." Elena handed them night vision goggles. "It's not easy to see up there, even in the daytime. When you turn them on, we see what you see on these monitors. Understood?"

"Yes, ma'am," Will replied.

"And grab a couple of those, too." Elena pointed to a rack of tranquilizer guns.

Chapter 30
QUEEN OF THE MOUNTAIN

Four men gathered near the maintenance door at the foot of the mountain. One man turned a key and gently opened the door. Once inside, they turned on a light and frantically searched for ropes, tie-offs, and anything to aid in a climb. They found plastic storage crates with ropes and tie-off clasps stowed inside. Andrus fished through cabinet drawers and found a pocketknife and stuffed in his coat pocket.

Then Andrus studied farm implements hanging from the wall and reached for a pitchfork.

"What's that for?" a voice whispered.

"Do you really think we'll be alone up there?" Andrus replied.

All men exchanged glances. Engineers and scientists never work well together, but in this case, there were no calculations to debate. This was about trying to save Gaia 1 and its remaining healthy crew.

"Andrus," a young engineer said, lifting a sledgehammer. "What do you think?"

"Too heavy," Andrus sighed, realizing none of these men had combat training. "Grab that axe over there instead."

"Andrus," Henry, the young engineer, said. "We're not soldiers. We don't know how to fight."

"Don't worry about that," Andrus replied and handed another man the pitchfork. "It's just a precaution."

"Besides," He said. "I'll be first to the top."

Andrus threw the climbing rope over his shoulder and studied the faces of the other three men. His years in the military trained him for situations like this, and the main thing was don't panic. Always try and have reason outweigh fear.

"Look, I know this is dangerous," he consoled. "But we work as a team. Safety in numbers, watch each other's back."

Frightened eyes didn't change their expression. Andrus took a deep breath and looked around the room.

"Hey," Andrus offered. "What about this? We can fashion these plastic crate lids into shields."

Andrus flipped open the pocketknife and carved two holes in each lid. Then he cut two lengths of rope, pulled them through the holes, and knotted each end.

"Here, try it," he said.

Two men grabbed the rope handles and held the shields in Greek warrior positions.

"Well, you look like soldiers to me!"

They all broke smiles.

Andrus bent over with his pocketknife and started cutting away at the floor rug. After cutting it in half, he cut midway slits in each, threw one over his head, and tossed the other to Henry.

Then he cut two more lengths of rope for belts and pulled his tight.

"So, now we all have some defense against their darts," he smiled.

Tension in the room faded.

"So, here's the plan," Andrus continued. "We step out of this room quietly. Circle around to the back side of the mountain and locate the inset ladder rungs. I haven't been back there for a while, but ladder rungs were cast into the concrete walls for mast access. And we have to find them in the dark."

"Two men with shields will stay at the base and guard the ladder. Then we rug men will climb up and access the dish via a bypass panel at the base of the mast."

"That panel requires a key for access," Henry said.

Andrus confidently flashed the key.

"We might encounter resistance before we get to the ladder," Andrus followed. "And Mara is likely to have guards on top of the rock."

***

It was near midnight when Andrus gently pushed open the door and stepped out onto the sandy soil. He panned in all directions for signs of anyone awake and moving, then motioned for the others to follow. He glanced up to study the mountain and the great mast that cut through the glass panels toward the southern stars.

"Remember," Andrus said. "their darts are lethal, so stay low."

The team quietly made their way through the forest underbrush to the rear of the mountain. They quickly spotted the built-in ladder rungs scaling the faux mountain. Andrus motioned to the team to crouch down and be silent. He studied the mountainside and its surroundings for signs of movement, nothing but nighttime stillness, a welcome sight.

Andrus turned his attention to the mountaintop, but again, nothing. He waited in silence for ten minutes, until a dark shadow crossed in front of the mast. He elbowed Henry and pointed up.

Once the dark shadow disappeared, they quickly moved toward the mountain's base.

"Are you ready for this?" Andrus asked. "It's gonna take both of us."

Henry nervously nodded.

They started up the cold metal rungs of the 40-meter precipice. At the halfway point, there was a sudden noise coming from the brush below. Andrus looked down to see the shield men trying to fight off half a dozen other men. Andrus turned back and moved faster, with Henry right behind.

Seconds later, the dark shadowed figure emerged, peering down at the commotion below. Fortunately, and for the moment, the noise was so distracting that he did not notice two men scaling the wall a few meters away.

At the top, Andrus grunted as he rolled onto the hard rocky surface. The dark-shadowed man turned, scowling with his eyes blood red, and charged toward Andrus. The two men clashed in full stride and crashed onto the concrete deck. A fight ensued as they rolled over and over for position. Andrus finally pulled out the pocketknife, but the madman knocked it away. He quickly wrapped both hands around Andrus's throat, pressing him against the concrete.

Andrus struggled against the man but was losing consciousness when suddenly the death grip was released. Henry had hit him on the head from behind.

Andrus gasped for breath, got to his knees, and saw the kid holding a plumber's wrench.

"I grabbed it in the maintenance room," he said.

"Good thinking," Andrus said, getting to his feet. "Let's go align that dish and get back down to communications."

He made his way over to the mast, located the panel, and unlocked it. He hurriedly studied the controls and was pleased to see the circuit panel flashing green and yellow.

"OK, I got this," Andrus said, still gasping for air. "There's no sabotage here."

He set about realignment procedures while Henry looked on.

"Go over to the ladder," Andrus said. "and make sure no one is climbing up here."

Henry went off in a flash.

Andrus labored away from memory and was making good headway.

"Hey, kid," he muffled. "How's it looking over there?"

No response as Henry ran past Andrus with a handful of rocks. Andrus did a double take but kept working away with realignment. About the time he finished aligning the dish, he heard Henry yelling and throwing rocks.

"Oh, shit," Andrus whispered, locked the panel door, and ran over to help.

"Look," he said. "The last thing we need is for people to know we're up here."

But as the words left his mouth, he looked down to see half a dozen men scaling the ladder.

"There's a big pile of rocks over there," Henry pointed.

Minutes later, they tossed rocks over the side and dropped two men to their deaths. The sound of blowing darts picked up, but they bounced helplessly off the precipice wall below.

"I'm not sure why that sound feels comforting," Andrus said. "But at least they can't get us with darts."

"We're almost out of rocks," Henry said. "Any other way down from here?"

Andrus looked around.

"Only those ventilation grills, but they're at least five meters down the side, and that would be a difficult climb if we're *not* under attack."

Henry ran for more rocks while Andrus surveyed the situation below, where a dozen more men were gathered at the base.

We're not getting out of here, Andrus thought.

Henry raced back with rocks and saw Andrus tying the climbing rope around the mast base.

"What are you doing?" he stopped to ask.

"Just go keep them occupied for a bit."

After tossing more rocks down at the faction on the ground, he heard "C'mon!" and turned to Andrus.

"I figure everyone is on the backside," Andrus said. "So, we'll go the other way."

"What?"

"We'll try for the waterfall," Andrus followed. "Even though this pumped pool up here supplies the main fall, there's another pool a few meters down for the secondary fall."

"And?"

"And that pool is pocketed inside the mountain," Andrus said as he sloshed over to the falls' edge. He clasped the rope with two hands and readied to repel. "It's a cave with an access door inside the mountain."

Andrus hopped out and down through the falls, then kicked away from the main fall and reached the pool of the secondary fall. He waded his way to the back of the artificial cave and found the metal door.

When Henry sloshed his way in to meet him, they found the door latch was jammed from the inside.

"Do you still have that plumbers wrench?" Andrus asked. "We need some leverage."

Both men grunted and pulled as hard as they could, but nothing. They took a breather and considered the predicament.

"I thought it was just after midnight," Henry said.

"It is. Why?"

"Then why is it getting so bright in here?"

They both turned to see an illuminated figure hovering above the water at the cave's entrance. As it floated toward them, the luminescence faded from an unrecognizable shape to the figure of a woman, a naked woman with dark sunglasses.

"Can't you boys find some warmer water to play in?" Mara asked.

Henry charged at her, wielding the heavy wrench. With an extended hand, Mara unleashed a thousand glowing micro-drones that shot over and seized the wrench from Henry's hand. He recoiled in disbelief, rubbing his tingling hand.

"Mara!" Andrus shouted.

Just then, Henry lunged out in anger toward her. But with another extended hand, the swarm shot at Henry, inside his ears, nose, and throat. He grasped his throat, choking as he fell into the water.

"Release him!" Andrus roared. "Mara, stop this!"

For the first time since she took power over the Living Hemisphere, Mara showed signs of regret and released the boy. Instantly, the fireflies left his body and swarmed back around Mara. At least she still had feelings for the man she once loved, maybe still loved.

Andrus had no idea she had developed the power of teleportation; such control over the drones seemed impossible, yet he could not deny what his eyes just witnessed.

He knelt down to check on Henry, who was coming around, and got him to his feet. The beautiful queen approached with redeemed confidence. She lifted her hand, and micro-drones shot over to the door. They raised the jammed latch instantly, and the door swung open.

"See how easy it can be," Mara said, placing a caressing hand behind Andrus' neck. She pulled him affectionately close and moved her other hand slowly down toward his beltline, but Andrus pushed her away.

At first, she was upset but then recoiled.

"Take the stairs then!" she shouted. Two men armed with clubs and blowguns appeared at the open door and stepped into the water. "It's a long walk down those steps to the gallows!"

Chapter 31
RECON 1

Michael Keller turned a latch control, and a floor hatch labeled 3 popped open. He peered into a dark room, except for a faint glow under a door and a green flashing light on a doorknob. He pushed open the hatch, shone a flashlight around, and climbed the ladder into the room. The small utility room was mostly empty and, best of all, undisturbed. He shone the flashlight up to the next hatch, labeled 2, and motioned for the others to follow.

The monkey troop was up and around him before Will and Libby made it through the hatch. From level 2, they reached up to a hatch labeled L that cranked open to the dark and dry interior of the Living Hemisphere mountain.

Capuchin monkeys quickly rushed past him and disappeared into the darkness. Michael instinctively rushed up to find them with Will and Libby right behind. Libby turned on her flashlight to survey the surroundings and made her faux monkey cackle sound. Seconds later, they were back at Libby's feet, climbing all over her.

Libby's ears followed the pump noise. She flashed her light in that direction and soon found a caged ladder scaling the wall.

"I'll be damned," Michael said. "I can't believe I didn't know about that ladder."

"Just like Gaia 3," she murmured. "It even has that metal platform at the top. That's where we're going."

She shone her light all around the tops of ductwork and concrete appendages, but no signs of debris of any kind, or worse, carcasses. Everything looked new, like it was first built.

"It looks safe in here," she whispered.

"How can you tell?" Michael asked.

"Nothing's trashed in here," she said. "On Gaia 3, this place was a shop of horrors."

"All right," Michael said. "I'll go back and report this to Elena. You two be careful up there."

"In the meantime, I'll leave all the hatches open and prop wood blocking against the doors, just in case."

"Okay, thanks," Libby said. "Here we go."

She walked into the darkness with the troop of monkeys in tow and Will right behind. When she reached the caged ladder, the monkey troop scrambled up to the top, landing before Libby started. She slung the dart rifle over her shoulder and started up the forty-meter climb.

They stopped for a breather at the top and whispered their next move.

"The latching mechanism is stainless steel," Will said. "No rusting or corrosion. I'll gently pull so it doesn't make any noise."

"Will, I don't think it matters. That waterfall is so loud, I can barely hear you talking."

Will rolled his eyes.

"Okay, just a second," she said. "What time of day is it here?"

"It's nighttime," Will calculated. "Around eleven PM. Why?"

"So, they're most likely asleep," she said. "And that's good. But either way, I don't want these little guys rushing out there all at once, making a ruckus that attracts attention. We should go out there first and look around."

"Makes sense," he said. "I'll go first, ready?"

He pulled, grunted, and the latch finally slipped. Then he gently pulled the hatch open to the sound of rushing water. Libby held the anxious monkeys back as Will crawled through and pulled the hatch closed behind him. He stayed low and waded over to the cave's opening on hands and knees.

The first thing that grabbed his attention was the outside view. Back on Titan, the Living had a Cerametallic roof with 24/7 skyscape displays, but this was completely different. Transparent multi-pane glass windows looking out into space gave a depth of perception of the moonscape and the crater rim of Amundsen.

Then he kept his head low, remembering Miller's arrow, and looked out over the Living Hemisphere. It was a different design than Titan, more spread out and had paved walkways throughout. It was more like a theme park than a living habitat. But then again, this base had the advantage of a nearby home planet that kept it constantly supplied.

Something else caught his attention—torches. Lots of torches surrounded the island at the base of the mountain. There was a primitive hut centrally located with a thatched roof and twenty or so people asleep nearby. Fireflies gradually drifted in from the surrounding trees and wetlands, hovering in the desert.

Will reached for his night vision goggles, and noticed a lone figure emerge from the hut. A tightly built, middle-aged female wearing nothing but dark sunglasses. She stopped momentarily as the fireflies swept in and swarmed around her, forming a golden, luminous cloud. The glowing, ghostly angel walked slowly through the sands as if watching over her sleeping flock.

She sipped from a glass while stepping over sleeping bodies. Some, awakened by her glowing presence, humbled themselves, and bowed in the sand. She continued to the line of torches, where she stopped and took a long drink.

Will refocused his view from the naked, glowing female form to the heavy wooden torches. Two of them had wooden crossbars with corpses swinging from nooses. The luminous vampiress approached the makeshift gallows, raised her glass, and sipped the drink. She focused on the dead man in front of her and reached to caress his pale blue face.

Terrified, Will rushed back to the half-open porthole, pulled himself through, and cranked it shut.

"What are you doing?" Libby implored. "Let's to go out here!"

Will struggled to catch his breath.

"Shh, we need to go," he quietly demanded. "Now! Quickly, quietly. Now, now, now!"

Libby didn't question him after seeing the look in his eyes. They descended the caged ladders, with capuchin monkeys huddled over them, and crossed the mountain floor. Will sweated and trembled the entire way. After tripping across the dark concrete floor, they reached the partially open hatch, and descended through the maintenance closets.

Michael waited at the base, helped them down and secured the hatch. He saw Will was out of breath, sweating and shaking.

"What's going on," he asked, but Will was overtaken by an adrenaline rush.

Michael escorted them to Engineering where Margaret and Elena waited.

Margaret was relieved to see them run into engineering with cackling monkeys draped all over them. But Elena didn't move, she remained seated in front of a computer monitor, shocked at what she'd seen through Will's glasses.

Margaret approached and placed a hand on her shoulder.

"Elena," she said. "Who was that? What was that?"

"Mara," Elena softly said. "My second in command. A brilliant engineer with an ego to match."

"I'm so sorry," Margaret offered.

"I never liked that arrogant bitch." Elena scoffed, then regrouped. "We need to get eyes and ears up there, now. How long before you can get the monkeys back up there?"

"I suppose any time," Libby replied. "No one was inside the mountain, and they weren't alerted to our presence."

"Okay, then…"

"Wait," Will cut in, re-grouping from his shock. "I just figured it out."

"Excuse me," Elena burst out.

"Just hold on a second," he continued. "You said Mara was a brilliant engineer, right?"

"Her specialty was robotics," Elena replied.

"At what scale?" Will asked.

"Not sure exactly—why?"

"Because I think her sunglasses," he said. "serve more than one purpose."

Elena calmed down.

"Okay, I'm listening."

"They could be some kind of enhanced reality glasses," Will said. "And the fireflies are micro-drones that communicate with the glasses. I've heard of micro-drones but only in experimental stages."

A lot of wheels started turning in that room. Elena got to her feet and paced.

"That sneaky bitch has been developing this all along," Elena hypothesized.

"What do you mean?" Margaret asked. "How long?"

"She was at Livermore for years," Elena said. "In the high-tech weapons division. She brought a cannister of those drones here to continue her work. They looked harmless, so I let them pass on her word."

She sighed, then hit the console.

"Fuck!"

"Elena," Will offered, "for all we know, Mara could be completely blind from iritis-induced glaucoma, but it's *possible* the glasses are synced to her brain, and she controls the drone swarm."

A lot of raised eyebrows.

"In fact, that can be the only explanation," he said.

Chapter 32
RECON 2

While Elena tried to digest Will's explanation of Mara's micro-drones, she was caught in the emotional anguish of seeing Andrus hanging in the gallows.

The hush in the room was too much to bear, but suddenly interrupted by a loud static noise.

"Oh, Elena?"

All heads turned.

Computer monitors in the room all displayed the same thing: Mara's beautiful face awash in a light-yellow glow.

"I see you have some new friends," she said. "A new supply of victims?"

Elena scowled at her nemesis.

"You know, I felt so sorry for poor Andrus," Mara said as the view screens changed to the pale blue face of the man on the gallows.

Elena turned away.

"Oh, it's all right, dear," Mara consoled. "I loved him, too, you know. But he couldn't see things my way. He chose death over immortality," Mara soothed while her beautiful face reappeared on the screen.

Elena raged with grief and anger. Tears streamed uncontrollably, and her voice trembled at the sight of her dead husband.

"I am going to rip your fucking heart out!" she screamed.

"Ha, ha, ha," Mara maniacally laughed. "That won't be easy, you know. I don't have a heart."

Elena slammed her fist on a kill switch, and all screens went dark. A long silence followed until Margaret broke it.

"I'm so sorry, Elena," she consoled.

Elena placed her face in her hands and wept until she couldn't cry anymore. When she finally looked up, and re-grouped, anger and revenge had replaced grief.

"Michael," She said. "Get everyone ready. This time we go after them."

Margaret turned as if to counter that order but said nothing and silently left the room.

"I'll get on it," Michael replied and headed out the door.

Only Will and Elena remained.

"Elena," Will said. "I know this might not be the right time to ask."

"Ask what?"

"Are there any capuchin monkeys on this base?"

"Excuse me?"

"You know, the-"

"I heard you," she cut him off. "We started out with quite a few, but they were getting into everything, so I shipped them back to Earth. Why?"

"That was smart," he sarcastically replied. "But the point being, if we send these little guys up to scout the Living and Mara spots them, she'll know we're up to something. Worse yet, her swarm of micro-drones might be able to track them down as targets."

"Then we all go at the same time," she replied.

***

Margaret lay on the bed in her living quarters, contemplating the situation on Gaia 1. It would take months to catalog the events on Gaia 3, let alone the battlefields of Gaia 1. She found an old bottle of bourbon in a kitchen cabinet, sniffed it, and took a swig. She started to cough but managed to keep it down. She found a glass, a cube of ice, poured a drink, and sat at the kitchen table.

An hour went by, and so did half the bottle. Her head spun on where this was all going. Would Will be safe? Could they even defeat Mara and her henchmen? What was happening on Earth? Maybe they should fly away and call it even. Then she heard a buzz at the door.

"Enter," Margaret said, and Elena stepped inside. She walked over to the table and pulled up a chair. Margaret filled her glass with bourbon and pushed it across the table.

"I've had enough," she said. "You're turn."

Elena smiled and threw it back.

"Ugh," Elena choked. "Where'd you get that stuff?"

"In the cabinet, but it's not my kitchen," Margaret smiled.

Elena stared into space.

"Do you think I'm still fit for command?" she asked.

"Because of what happened to Andrus?"

"Because of a lot of things," Elena replied. "So much has happened here since that damned comet passed through the system. We went from a thriving scientific community on the south pole of the moon to a colony of rabid apes overnight."

"I wasn't prepared to manage this. And now my husband has been murdered."

Margaret paused.

"I think you need to step back," she said. "And consider what's best for the crew and the facility."

"But we are at war, you know," Elena replied. "Against a seriously ill force of people. They're basically insane."

"Understood, but there's a base to save and many healthy people too."

"And Mara?"

"She has to be stopped," Margaret sighed. "Captured or killed, she has to be stopped."

"I'll stop her all right."

"Look at me," Margaret said and reached for her hand. "Vengeance kills you both. If you have to take her out, then take her out. But do it for the right reasons."

Elena's angry eyes were not consoled.

"Look, when Max Barry re-directed us here," Margaret said. "He said if we can't save Gaia 1, it will be a blow to all nations and a death blow to space travel for decades."

"What?"

"It's all gone, Elena," Margaret continued. "Gaia 3 was a total loss when we escaped. Barry said there are no missions left alive. The space stations orbiting Earth and the moon are gone, as are all interplanetary spacecraft and most likely Gaia 2.

"The world's hope depends on our saving this place, at whatever cost."

Elena mulled it over.

"I had no idea it was that bad," she said. "I guess I was too preoccupied with trying to survive here."

"Well, that's our reality," Margaret said. "We have to save this base."

"Then first things first," Elena said. "We cut off the snake's head."

Margaret reluctantly nodded. Elena grabbed the bottle of bourbon and left.

***

Elena was almost out of options. She'd been running for so long she lost track of time. But she could still hear the cackling cries of the evil witch not far behind. The sounds of slashing sickles and chopping axes gave notice that the witch's guards were closing in, cutting through thick underbrush.

Elena could not make out exactly where she was, but the foliage was tropical. How could a mid-west woman have been chased this far? It didn't make any sense. She finally burst out of the jungle, splashed through a wide, shallow stream, and ended up in a thick swamp of cattails, reeds, and grasses. She ducked low, but the pursuers still made chase.

The brilliant light from a passing comet illuminated the swamp, and soon she was spotted. Exhausted and terrified, she made a last-ditch effort for a nearby mountain. She crossed back through the shallow stream and found herself on an island of tall dunes near the mountain. When she cleared the first dune, she fell to her knees in exhaustion. Her pursuers were already there.

"What took you so long, Dear," a smiling Mara asked. "We thought you'd never make it to the party!"

Elena looked up to see Andrus and three others hanging from the gallows. She melted down in tears and anguish.

"This isn't real," she sobbed, face in hands. "This can't be happening."

"But it's all right," Mara soothed. "We have a seat picked out for right next to poor Andrus."

Unable to resist Mara's henchmen, they tied Elena's hands, carried her to the gallows, and placed a noose around her neck.

"Oh, that won't do, Dear, no tears," Mara mocked and wiped Elena's face. *"This is a party."*

But the sobbing did not stop.

"Oh, maybe this isn't right," Mara said, tightening the noose. *"Okay, here we go!"*

Mara maniacally laughed and kicked away the chair under Elena's feet.

***

Elena awoke screaming, her sheets soaked with sweat.

Chapter 33
THE UPPER LEVELS

Elena's mind was a steel trap, she and her men were tired of waiting this thing out, and seeing her nemesis murder Andrus was the last straw. Her men would storm a beachhead for her after seeing what Mara had done and what she had become.

"All right, we have twenty-one crew," Elena stated. "Including those from Gaia 3, a band of monkeys, and plenty of tranquilizer darts."

She called up the floor plans of levels two and three.

"We move quickly since they're still asleep up there." Elena ordered. "The first step is to take medical and communications at the same time. They're on different levels, but we can ambush them from the maintenance ladders. The first sign of anyone, and we dart them. Once we take them down, we retrieve darts and get them immobilized or strapped down in medical."

Elena pointed to the fire safety cabinet on the wall.

"Whatever you're comfortable fighting with, take it," she continued. "axes, clubs, you name it. If it comes to hand-to-hand fighting, you take them out. We spill their blood now. They've spilled enough of ours."

"Elena!" Margaret shouted.

"Not now, Margaret!"

"William," Elena continued, "your job is to keep them sedated. Even if we run out of tables, tie them up on the floor."

"Michael," she ordered, "you take one man and secure the stair shafts. Weld the doors shut if you have to."

"Gentlemen," Elena barked to the assembly. "After both levels are secured, we regroup back here and plan the assault on the Living."

***

Mara surveyed the encampment of torches and hanging corpses. She crossed the desert in her newfound form. The shining figure stepped through her cowering coven with the power of a goddess. She entered the hut, pulled back a drawn curtain, and proceeded to a bamboo altar where three translucent orbs lay in a row. She waved a hand over them, and they elevated, floated together, and stacked on one another.

She studied her hands. *That's a nice trick.*

With another wave of her hand, the orbs started to glow. A tiny orifice formed at the top of the upper sphere where firefly drones flew out and joined the swarm around Mara. She felt a new surge of power grow inside until she was interrupted.

"Mara," a voice came from behind.

She angrily turned. "I told you never to come in here!" she ordered and stormed out to confront two men.

She moved so fast the swarm could not keep up, exposing her nude body, but the hive re-formed when she confronted them. The two men coward a bit and dropped their heads. Mara's new, heightened senses alerted her to something. She flicked her fingers, and part of the swarm fanned out around the men. Mara seethed to find that each man held a knife.

The two men glanced at each other and started to lunge at Mara, but her glowing swarm throttled them. They were inside the men's ears, noses, and mouths in a split second. The two assassins clutched their throats and dropped to the ground; it was over in seconds. Then the swarm retreated from their melted brains while blood oozed from their noses and ears.

Mara furiously thrust out her arms, and more drones clouded over a mass of whimpering bodies. But no feelings of revenge or rebellion came to her mind, only fear—delicious, lovely fear.

"There, my pets," Mara soothed, stepping over them. "That's better."

Mara knelt and caressed a sobbing woman's hair.

"Now, now," Mara promised. "Everything is going to be simply fine, dear. But first, we need to get ready for Elena."

***

Michael Keller approached engineering, pushing a heavy, wheeled cart with a duffle bag on top. The smoke black cart had no markings, and many metal locking latches lined its secured lid. All eyes turned when he pushed it through the doors.

"What in the hell is this?" Elena asked.

"The stuff we thought we'd never need," Michael replied. "Most of it stored in the special ops area."

"Special ops?" Elena queried.

"Yeah, most of them died on the shuttle escorts," he said. "And as you know, two fell to their deaths fighting Red Eyes."

Michael pointed to the duffle bag. "It took a while to find them down there, tangled up in piping and steel beams in the lower decks. I salvaged all their gear, but their tasers were smashed in the fall."

"Shit." Elena sighed. "So, still no real weapons."

"No, I double checked the supply room," Michael replied. "Just in case. But I did find this."

Michael sat the duffle bag aside and flipped open the lid latches. Inside were unused tactical uniforms and armor helmets.

"Including the duffle bag, we have eight complete suits," he said.

Elena sorted through the stack of uniforms.

"We have an edge now," she said. "Good work."

***

Two teams with night vision headgear stood ready at maintenance doors on levels two and three. At Elena's command, they burst out and rushed through the dark hallways. They darted two hostiles near level three medical. Three blue eyes inside surrendered in the lab while two more took darts, running to stairways. The fallen were dragged into medical, bound, and sedated.

Level two was a different story. Communications was fortified with booby traps and guards. When Elena's forces crashed into the hallways, alarms sounded over the entire deck, and they met a hail of poison darts from waiting guards. Thick armor took the brunt of the assault, but one man fell to a shot in the neck. Elena ordered third-level troops up to level two for support.

Some Red Eyes scrambled for the exits, their forms glowing green through night vision goggles, while the rest held out in the communications center. Red Eyes hid behind computer consoles when Elena's troops unloaded a round of darts at them.

"What's going on in there?" Elena shouted.

"We've taken three," a voice returned. "Michael is welding doors down there. We have the hostiles cornered in the comm center, and we're low on darts."

"How many?" Elena asked. "How many are cornered?"

"Hard to say," the kneeling man replied, peering over a half-wall. "Maybe a half dozen. They were disabling everything when we rushed the place."

"Shit." Elena gasped. "Then take them out, now! We need that comm center. Go hand-to-hand, if you have to, but do it quickly."

The man reached for his axe, tapped his headgear, and held out the axe for the team behind him to see. Clanging sounds followed while they readied for the assault. With a snap of the fingers, they rushed inside, straight for the green glowing figures. A hail of blow-gun darts whisked through the air, but they were no match for axes, clubs, and knives. It didn't take long; all the hostiles were killed.

Minutes later, the blood-soaked squad was back in engineering with Elena. Their bloodied faces and weapons told the grim story. Margaret and Libby turned away, but Elena stayed focused.

"So, we have them?" she asked. "Both floors, right?"

Exhausted heads nodded. Elena pointed to a box on the floor.

"We collected these," she said. "More night vision goggles, knives, and retrieved darts."

"Michael's guys will reactivate the elevators once they seal the stairway doors. Then we attack the Living."

"More bloodshed?" Margaret asked.

"What else, Margaret?" Elena asked. "Does this illness eventually kill them, or do they get better?"

Margaret sighed. "On Titan, they just got worse and died."

"Look," Elena said. "We're doing the best we can. We dart them when possible. If they won't surrender, it means they've already gone mad. Now we have control of all lower levels, and we're taking the Living before it's too late. Mara has to be stopped."

"Mother," Will said, "this situation isn't much different than Avery's, and he destroyed Gaia 3. What's to stop Mara from doing the same on this base?"

"The radiation madness affects people in different ways," Margaret reasoned. "Some revert to animal instincts, like Miller did, and some have expanded egos like Avery and Mara."

"But she's developed powers," he added, "that Avery could never have imagined."

"Maybe this is the only way to salvage the base," she admitted.

"Margaret," Elena said, "you know me. I'm not a violent person. But this—what Mara has done—leaves me no choice. She has to be stopped. I must regain control of Gaia 1 before it's too late."

Margaret took a deep breath and regrouped. "Okay. What's the plan?"

Elena nodded. "I've been thinking about this. And it'll take everything we have in a surprise attack. If we ambush them, we have an excellent chance of taking them out quickly.

"We send everyone up there in two teams. We load up both elevators, and when the doors open, we come out shooting.

"I want a sniper up in the waterfall cave with plenty of darts and a repelling rope. And someone needs to grab a torch and light up that hut."

"What about Mara?" Margaret asked.

"We have to disable her," Elena said. "Or take her out."

Margaret pursed her lips but concurred.

"Hey guys, check this out," Libby added, and grabbed a pair of safety glasses from a worktable. "They really don't like me wearing safety glasses."

"Who?"

Libby placed them on her face to the sound of screeching capuchin monkeys that stole them and ran off.

"And?" Elena mocked.

"Maybe they should be part of our surprise attack," Libby said. "They don't like *anyone* wearing glasses."

"Brilliant." Elena smiled.

Chapter 34
BATTLE FOR THE LIVING

Elena assembled her two attack teams in communications.

"Okay, we're light on supplies here," she said. "So, those experienced in hand-to-hand combat grab tactical gear, knives, and clubs. The rest of you take dart rifles and anything else you can wield.

"Tactical people will be last in the elevator and first out. We go straight to the desert and take out anything that moves. The rest of you follow in support. Watch the trees, rocks, and water for anything suspicious. Take cover behind rocks once we've stabilized the area and look out for Mara's thugs. There must be some tough bastards watching her back."

Will and Margaret half-heartedly reached for dart rifles, studied their construction, and loaded spare darts while Libby tended to her capuchin monkeys. The geared-up teams headed to the elevators while the monkeys hitched rides on Libby and Will.

Margaret walked next to Elena, whose carbon-fiber tactical gear was plated with plasto-metallic armor on her chest and shoulders. She carried a small axe, a nightstick, and a Bowie knife sheathed on her back. But nothing as lethal as the warrior look in her eyes.

"All right, this should do it," Michael said when they reached the elevator. "We have power to both elevators, but when we push the *Living Hemisphere* button, air exchangers activate automatically, and Mara will know we're coming."

"Good!" Elena scoffed. "Let's do it."

Elena was last in the elevator, nodded to Michael, and fisted the button.

"Elena?" Margaret worried.

"I knew these people, Margaret." Elena's face raged, her clutched hands lifted to her chest. "I just can't let her kill more innocents."

"But—"

"That was my husband she killed, not yours."

A brief silence, then the mechanized sounds of elevator motors and cabling churned into gear. For Margaret it was the fastest ride of her life, for Elena the slowest. She fidgeted like a sprinter before the timer's gun fires.

"No lights up there. Night vision goggles on," Elena ordered. "And remember, the desert terraces are behind us, so keep low and check your positions. First, we scale the terraces and attack the desert. Dart anyone, stay close and watch our backs."

***

Elevator 2 was the first to the Living, where the airlock opened to the sound of blowguns. The team quickly scattered into the jungle and pulled their axes, but poison darts and rocks rained down from the mountaintop. Their number was halved before they knew it. The few remaining lashed out in anger toward the foot of the mountain where they met a blinding light.

***

Then Elena burst from elevator 1, and her team quickly ascended terrace after terrace until they reached the desert plateau. A field of organ pipe cactuses blocked the view, but she could make out a thatched hut and human figures.

"Okay." she motioned and whispered, "Here we go."

"I'm right behind you." Margaret aimed her dart rifle.

Elena led a charge through low brush out to the desert sands, where she tomahawked a charging Red Eye in the chest and clubbed another. The next Red Eye met a first-team axe, and yet another was tossed off the twenty-meter cliff. Tranquilizer darts dropped two more. The rest fell to their knees, surrendered, and took darts for their effort.

Elena pulled her axe from the dead man's chest and surveyed the battlefield.

"It's done, Elena," a man nearby said, breathing heavily. "We did it."

"Not yet," she said, walking. "We have to bring her out in the open."

Elena pulled a torch off a wooden post and threw it at the thatched roof. She stood in satisfaction as the hut was engulfed in flame; she hoped a burning Mara would run out in terror. Her whole team gathered around in a silent vigil, but the silence was broken.

"Elena," a soft voice echoed through the Living Hemisphere.

Elena readied her battle axe.

"Elena." She heard it again.

Elena listened but couldn't locate her; Mara's voice emanated everywhere. Then a faint light shone from behind the concrete mountain. It started at the base and lifted like a rising sun, casting shadows as it went. The light went up and up until it cleared the mountaintop, then Mara's nude form emerged from the light, holding her prize creation, the tri-orb. She smiled at her weak adversary and carefully placed it on the ground.

"Oh, pumpkin." Her voice echoed.

Elena's bloodied hands dropped their axe and reached for the bowie knife sheathed on her back. She stepped forward and snarled.

"What say we light things up a bit?" Mara chuckled and motioned toward the tri-orb. She touched the giant mast of the comm dish that extended up from the mountaintop through the glass roof, and countless fireflies from the tri-orb scaled the mast, circling as they rose. Some went straight up through the glass roof to the satellite dish, and others followed the steel framework to a band line midway up the dome. The satellite dish started to spin while the cameras and lights on the band line activated.

"Now then, even the folks back home can witness your attack on my beautiful new world," Mara taunted with a pleasured clasp of her hands while micro-drones flew in and formed to her body from neck to toe. No longer a dark shape inside a glowing cloud, Mara studied her newfound golden aura in goddess fashion and modeled the new look as if she were born with it.

Elena's troops, including Margaret, moved to her side in support.

"Oh, and it won't be as easy as you may have hoped," Mara grimaced.

Below her from the waterfall cave, one of Mara's men kicked the sniper's body over the falls. It crashed into the rocks below and floated out into the river. Then a half dozen of Mara's men tossed out ropes and repelled down the mountainside.

Mara clutched her hands and burst into a crazed laugh. Then she lifted her arms, and fireflies from the tri-orb swarmed out to form an umbrella shape beneath her feet, lifted her, and made a slow descent to the desert floor. The firefly swarm reconfigured into an egg shape with Mara at its center. She stepped onto the sand and paused to watch the body in the river float away.

"And your warriors from the other elevator," Mara delighted, "met the same fate."

"We need a diversion," Elena whispered to Margaret. "Or this bitch might shoot lightning bolts at us."

Margaret searched for anything, any idea. Then her eyes caught something. Will and Libby had sneaked ahead during the skirmish and were near the edge of the tropical forest behind Mara.

"Keep her occupied," Margaret whispered. "I have an idea."

Elena maintained focus on Mara's ghostly image.

"That may be true, Mara," Elena shouted. "But it's going to take more than sorcery to stop me."

Elena turned, motioned with her knife, and the remaining men followed her back down the terraces. Margaret took advantage by moving behind the burning hut and crawling to the other end of the plateau, where she climbed the cliff. She had to circle back through wetlands and cross the moat but eventually made it to the tropical forest.

Elena kept an eye on Mara while she and her team hopped off the last terrace, crossed the river, and hiked through high dunes. At less than fifty meters apart, the simple battlefield was assembled: Mara stood at the mountain's base, wreathed in firefly drones, with five red-eyed madmen at her guard. Elena faced her from atop a five-meter dune with six troops in front of her.

"Oh, sweetie," Mara said. "Do you really want it to end like this?"

"It is going to end, Mara," Elena promised. "But not the way you want."

As the game of high-stake bantering rolled out, Libby, Will, and Margaret crawled to the edge of the tropical forest draped in capuchin monkeys. They were behind Mara and facing Elena, but Mara's sunglasses were still easy to spot. Margaret stood and waved her arms at Elena, then pointed at the little monkey on her shoulder. When she made a fist, Elena knew it was time.

"Remember when I said I would rip your fucking heart out?" Elena growled.

"I thought that was just a joke, dear," Mara taunted.

But with a guttural cry, Elena stormed down the dune, followed by her troops wielding weapons and charging full stride. Mara's red-eyed guard readied for the assault, but their impaired vision forced them to wait for the attack. Mara saw they were outnumbered, she panicked, and lifted skyward.

Libby released the capuchin monkeys, and they went for Mara quickly, but she was off the ground before they got there.

The attack was brutal. Elena slung her Bowie knife from five meters and struck a Red Eye in the neck. Her troops did the same and took down two more before engaging hand-to-hand. With only two of Mara's men remaining, the work was finished quickly.

Elena saw Mara elevate and scrambled for repelling ropes hanging from the mountain, but the monkeys beat her to it and were up the ropes in a flash. Margaret stepped out of the underbrush, following Will and Libby, with dart rifles ready.

Before Mara knew it, two of the obsessed capuchins were on her, reaching for her sunglasses. She twisted, screamed, scratched at them, and tossed one away through the field of fireflies. The last monkey pulled the sunglasses from her face, and the field of firefly drones instantly dispersed and scattered. They streamed away from Mara and the dome framework toward the tall mast.

Mara screamed as she fell through the dissipating swarm and hit the ground hard. She was dazed by the impact and partially blinded. She struggled to her feet and called for her guards, but none responded.

Her vision partially restored itself as hundreds of guardian fireflies huddled back over her eyes. These pre-programmed drones interfaced with her eyes, even without the sunglasses, as the bare-skinned beauty took on an entirely new persona with gleaming golden eyes. She clenched her fists and readied for anything.

But Elena, running full speed, launched in the air, double fisting her Bowie knife, and thrust it through Mara's chest. Mara fell back to the ground, gasping for air. Her golden eyes faded as fireflies whisked away like glitter in the wind, revealing her red eyes. The micro-drones flew like dominos in a chain up the mountain and joined the other returning fireflies.

Margaret approached as Elena knelt next to Mara.

Mara's head moved slightly. "I'm so sorry, kitten," she regretted as if the veil of insanity had lifted. "Elena, is that you?" Mara sobbed. "What did I do? What did I do?"

Elena covered her face and wept. Deep down, this was not what she really wanted. So much loss, so much pain—what she'd done did not seem like a victory.

Elena's guards and Margaret's team gathered around her. Will took in the carnage on the battlefield. As quick as the battle was, he was not prepared to see all the bloody bodies scattered in the sand. He'd thought violence and destruction were left behind on Titan, that he was prepared for things to come, but this was too much. Adrenaline shock set in, and he shook uncontrollably. Libby grabbed him and hugged him long and hard.

Margaret knelt and put her arms around Elena to console her. "It's over," she said. "It's finally over."

EPILOGUE

Will and Margaret sat at her desk with morning coffee.

"As you might already know," she said. "I'm very proud of you."

"For what, exactly?" he replied. "My great discovery turned out to be one of the most catastrophic events in human history."

Will was caught up in trying to make sense of all that had happened on Titan and the moon. He felt the grief of losing friends, old and new, and suffered emotionally from fighting for his life, and the lives of others. What started off as the great science experiment turned into a nightmare.

Margaret reflected. "Consider this," she pointed out. "If I had not brought you on this mission, that planetoid would not have been discovered until it was too late. The oxygen problem on Gaia 3 would have never been resolved. *You* piloted us from Saturn to Earth, and on this base, you figured out Mara's secret."

Will considered her perspective.

"You may not have added this up yet," Margaret said. "But in my book, you saved my life many times over."

"I don't know about that." Will blushed.

"In fact, you're not only the son I love," she said. "You're also my hero."

Will hugged her. "I love you mom."

***

Margaret continued with her summary log.

"It's been nearly two weeks since the battle for the Living Hemisphere," she said. "And regaining contact with the Space Council. Their questions just keep rolling in."

"Max Barry must be the happiest man on Earth. He's planning a mission later this year with dignitaries from multiple countries to show strength and resilience. He wants the world to see that Gaia 1 and our colonization of the moon is as strong as ever."

"Also, he's going to decorate Elena and me before the entire solar system. I'm not sure I agree, but who am I to Argue with Max."

She took another sip of coffee. "Elena's team has made amazing progress getting this station back online. After bagging and tagging bodies, they restarted the deep ice O2 converters and pumped oxygen into the Living to replace all consumed by torches and fire.

"Will set up shop in engineering, testing the tri-orb he found stacked on the mountaintop. The firefly drones were huddled inside it like bees in a hive. Mara put on quite a spectacular display, and he's determined to uncover its secrets. Libby found where the capuchin monkeys had hidden Mara's sunglasses, so now Will is even more excited.

"Today, we make the final step in putting this whole thing behind us." Margaret sighed. "There is a burial ceremony outside in the lunar soil. It took time, but the guys dug graves for all those from Gaia 1 and the wrecked shuttle. The cemetery is laid out with temporary markers fashioned from bamboo.

"I suppose, in time, I can put all this in its place," she said. "But for now, it just haunts me."

She took a deep breath and turned off the recorder.

"It haunts me." She stared into space.

***

The ceremony was brief, with a few Gaians in E-suits gathered before a makeshift cemetery at the center of Amundsen crater. A crescent Earth looked down from the crater's rim where Gaia 1 stood firm; it had survived the battles that threatened its existence.

Elena delivered a heartfelt speech, then dropped to her knees, grieving for her lost comrades and loved ones. Will's eyes remained fixed on the long shadows from bamboo grave markers and the loss they embodied.

He had survived the most painful and tragic experience of his life. But even in this sad moment, there was great consolation in knowing that Margaret and Libby were with him. He took a long, healthy breath and thought of things to come when something caught his eye that made him smile.

He saw three supply shuttles cruise in low, just off the hook of the crescent Earth.

ACKNOWLEDGEMENT

While authoring this book, I have drawn on the work of the Biosphere 2 project in Tucson, Arizona, its book Biosphere 2: The Human Experiment, and its concepts of off-world habitats. However, this is a work of fiction, and interpretations herein are entirely my own, including factual errors.

COMING SOON:

WESTERN LIGHTS

A new sci-fi novel from C.P. Schaefer.

Be the first to know when
Western Lights releases!

Join the mailing list at cpschaefer.com

Please enjoy your exclusive preview
of Western Lights on the next page.

Prologue:
The First Incident

National Petroleum Reserve, AK
In the near future

"What exactly is this?" the co-pilot asked. He held the mouthpiece tight in hand to get above the roar of the plane's engine. "Nothing natural can register these readings. Have you ever seen this before?"

He turned to the pilot, who was still dumbfounded, gazing at the arctic skyline in front of them. Whatever it was, they were close to it, and it seemed to come out of nowhere. The Aurora appeared to be on fire, ignited by something. The usual slow, silent watercolor appearance had lightning overlays with bursts of new color. The pilot instinctively pulled down and away from the atmospheric disturbance. The lights reached downward, fingerlike, toward the ground with crackling light rippling along their lengths.

They were only a mile or two from the strange phenomenon when the pilot brought the plane into a circular pattern around the cyclone shape forming before them.

"I can honestly say," the pilot said, "I've never seen anything like this before. Here, use my phone to take video."

Then, as quickly as it came, the phenomenon disappeared. Without a sound, without a flash, as if a light switch turned off. The Aurora was back to normal, as were the readings on the compass and magnetometer, but a significant, circular impression remained on the ground with dis-colored vegetation.

"There's a good spot." He pointed. "That small lake over there."

"We're landing?" the co-pilot asked, afraid, still shaking from what he had just seen.

"Don't worry," Ethan grinned. "I do this all the time."